TRIAL AND RETRIBUTION V

Detective Inspector Pat North and Detective Superintendent Michael Walker are back, and this time they face their biggest challenge yet . . . A derelict house is being demolished when workmen find the remains of a young girl. Walker is far from happy at being assigned the seventeen-year-old murder case, especially as North's career is really taking off. However, things soon hot up when the murder team unearth more skeletons and Walker suddenly finds himself in charge of one of the biggest investigations in recent years. But when a secret has been buried for seventeen years, the path to justice is more tortuous than ever. Can Walker and his team expose the truth behind one family and their shadowy past? Meanwhile, North is struggling to keep it together at work after her recent miscarriage and with an old flame back on the scene emotions are running high . . .

TRIAL AND RETRIBUTION V

Lynda LaPlante

WINDSOR
PARAGON

First published 2001
by
Macmillan
This Large Print edition published 2004
by
BBC Audiobooks Ltd
by arrangement with
Macmillan
an imprint of Pan Macmillan Ltd

ISBN 0 7540 8726 3   (Windsor Hardcover)
ISBN 0 7540 9386 7   (Paragon Softcover)

British Library Cataloguing in Publication Data available

Printed and bound in Great Britain by
Antony Rowe Ltd., Chippenham, Wiltshire

This book is dedicated to Liz Thorburn,
the chief executive of La Plante Productions.
Lis is also one of my dearest and most trusted
friends,
whose loyalty and dedication to the company
makes her a very special lady.

ACKNOWLEDGEMENTS

Trial and Retribution V has been very honoured to welcome back the talents of its leading artists, whose friendship and performances I value immensely: David Hayman, Kate Buffery, Dorian Lough, Paul Kynman, and to the guest stars: Maggie McCarthy, Liz Smith, Sean Chapman, Simon Callow, Inday Ba, James Simmons, David Fleeshman, Dermot Crowley and all those whose professionalism and dedication have made it such a special series to work on.

Special thanks to our wonderful team of advisors: Jackie Malton, Dr Liz Wilson at the Forensic Science Service and Dr Ian Hill at Guy's Hospital.

A very important thanks must go to the wonderful David Martin-Sperry, who is a fund of stories as well as being our awesome legal mind. He has also become a dear friend.

A very special thanks to the brilliant talent of our director Aisling Walsh, whose innovation and expertise made the very first *Trial and Retribution* such a landmark. Aisling took my idea for the split screen and adapted it to the programme with a fluidity and artistry that still keeps me in awe. Aisling worked alongside Ian Sutherland, who has edited *Trial and Retribution III, IV*, and *V*. Together they have proved to me that the lengthy edit sessions required for the split screen have been, without doubt, worthwhile. Along with George Mallen, our wonderful assistant editor, they have made a remarkable team and are proof that pressurized work need not lead to flared tempers and arguments. I sincerely thank them for their dedication and desire to always get it right.

Thanks, too, to the very talented and dedicated crew, led by the calm and steady hand of executive producer Peter Richardson, who has been so much a part of the success of the series. Special thanks to Simon Kossoff the director of photography and Bill Bryce the production designer. My sincere thanks must also go to Joanna Eatwell our costume designer, who is a major link in the team. Joanna's artistry and dedication to the script and to her actors have made her not only a special person to me but to all the actors she meets, as her input is not only artistic but really enhances the characters. We are so lucky to have formed such a strong team over the years of making the series of *Trial and Retribution*.

A big thank you to my wonderful sister, Gill Titchmarsh, who casts all my productions with great skill, and also to Susie Tullett and all at JAC for their dedication and support.

Thanks to Jonathan Channon and the team at EMI, to Mark Jordan for all the incredibly creative work he's done, and of course to Evelyn Glennie and Greg Malcangi for their inspired and imaginative soundtrack.

Further thanks must be directed to my PA George Weatherill who, between handling the party lists, somehow manages to keep my life running on an even keel.

It is a very special thanks I give to the LPP team: chief executive Liz Thorburn, head of development Nikki Smith and script editors Kerry Appleyard and Kate Fletcher. The team work long hours, and are always encouraging not only to each other but to me. The LPP team probably eat more birthday cakes and drink more champagne in our office ritual celebrations than anyone I know, but are worth every crumb and fizz; they are all very special to me.

I also wish to thank Nick Elliot and Jenny Reeks who have been so much a part of the success of La Plante Productions. They remain supportive of us and are a constant encouragement along with David Liddement of the Network Centre.

Thanks to my literary agent Gill Coleridge and to Imogen Taylor my editor at Pan Macmillan who publish all my novels. Also a very special thanks to Philippa McEwan, who sits with me during all those down-the-line radio interviews and never looks bored.

I would also like to say thank you to Stephen Ross, Andrew Bennet-Smith, George Brook, Julie Phelps and all at Ross Bennet-Smith, but especially Stephen, who is not only one of my closest friends but also my racing companion.

The other racing companion who must be thanked is also my agent, Duncan Heath. I also say a big thank you to the lovely Sue Rodgers. I am so lucky that my agents are also my friends, who make both my working and leisure time worthwhile.

There is also someone else to whom I would like to say a very big thank you and that is Mark Devereux, whose constant support and guidance, along with that of members of his team at Olswang, Julia Palca, Nigel McCory and Linda Francis, has been so important to the success of LPP.

In the pressurized world of producing, writing and building up the La Plante company, many people have been so supportive and I would like to take this opportunity to say a very big thank you to all at The Nine Network, Australia, especially to John Stephens and Geraldine Easter.

I would like to thank sincerely the following for all their generosity and assistance during the research and making of *Trial and Retribution V*: Master McKenzie CB QC from the Court of Appeal, Jungian analyst Ann Casement from the UK Council for Psychotherapy, Richard Neave from the University of Manchester's Unit of Art in Medicine, crime scene coordinator Callum Sutherland, pathologist Peter Dean, Emily Hands from the Department of Health, Roy Webster, Matthew Tucker and the team at the Prison Service Press Office, John Towers, Lionel Rawl and Frank Hartles from the University of Wales College of Medicine, Adrian Pardoe-Blackridge and Fran Smart, Gillian Dines from the Forensic Science Service and Alison Wood from the National Childbirth Trust.

Last, but by no means least, I would like to thank the very talented writer Robin Blake for his care and skill in adapting the film of *Trial and Retribution* for the page. He is an exceptionally dedicated writer, of so much talent, and he is a joy to work alongside.

CHAPTER 1

SATURDAY, 23 SEPTEMBER

When the wreckers came, with their diggers, demolition balls, sledgehammers and skips, the houses of Hallerton Road had stood boarded and unloved for half a decade. In its time, this place had had its measure of dignity, even a touch of class: a row of villas standing squarely on their own small patches of North London ground. Each of their gothic-inspired porches was approached by a short gravel drive, shaded by lavender and laurel. The rear gardens had enough grass for a game of miniature croquet or carpet bowls, and inside there was all the space to make the family of a middle-ranking civil servant or bank official comfortable, and perhaps even happy.

But in the course of a century the road had suffered a long fall from grace. One house was taken out by a bomb in World War II. Several were divided into flats and let out, becoming increasingly dilapidated. Others remained in single occupancy but, more and more, it was pensioners, the widowed and poor families with too many children who lived in them. Penny-pinching and neglect led to dereliction and squatting. The houses grew so unsafe and unsavoury as to attract the attentions of the Borough Council's Health and Safety Committee. A Demolition Order was the inevitable consequence. Hallerton Road, for the sins of its inhabitants, had been condemned to death.

The demolition men, beginning their work at

number 34, did not at first think this particular property offered an unusual challenge. These were practical men who truly liked to get their hands dirty. Methodically, but with considerable zest, they stripped out the interior, smashing windows, ripping out doors and hacking down old plaster walls to lay bare the studwork. Dennis, the ganger, had been in this job twenty years and enjoyed efficient demolition almost as much as he liked a bet on the horses. Harry and Nick were a pair of larky types. They followed Chelsea Football Club with the kind of devotion some people reserve for religion. But what they relished about this job was the destruction, the licensed mayhem. And with Dennis's gruff Yorkshire ways to take the piss out of, the young men found it a happy, carefree site.

But Harry's girlfriend Sheena had come up a few days ago to collect him and it was she who spoiled it. She said the old house gave her a bad feeling and, to be honest, she wished Harry didn't have to work there.

'I don't know what it is exactly,' she said, standing in the blitzed kitchen. 'Not a smell but like a smell—a nasty aura. And, with me, first impressions are never wrong. The council done the right thing condemning this place because it ain't healthy, that's all I'm saying.'

'Don't talk rubbish, girl,' Harry told her. But she'd had a shiver in her voice that he could not deny. All week he'd felt a growing sense of unease towards the house. On Wednesday, in a cavity of the wall, he had found a stash of discarded syringes. Yesterday he noticed a few words of graffiti, scratched on the wall under the stairs in jagged writing: CAN'T YOU HEAR THE VOICES?

2

Harry tried not to let it get to him. The addicts' needles and the paranoid message would have been down to the squatters. It was obvious that none of them had stayed long enough to make a go of the house, which was a filthy, stinking dump of dog mess downstairs, and pigeon shit above. Sheena was right. Demolition was the best thing that could happen to the place.

'Harry, you coming down?' shouted Dennis 'Tea's up, mate.'

Harry was upstairs turning a section of banister rail over in his grimy hands, weighing its possible resale value. Few items of architectural salvage had survived the years of squatting so there were few opportunities to make some beer money. He clumped down the stairs in his mud-caked boots, showing Dennis the banister.

'I reckon we can use this. Nice. Hand turned, not machined.'

Dennis took the banister and examined it critically. With a stumpy fingernail he scraped off a flake of paint to reveal the wood underneath.

'Yeah. Good piece of wood this, mahogany. Strip the paint off and it'll polish up nice.'

They walked through the kitchen and out the back door into the wreck of the garden.

'We found a panel once,' Dennis reminisced. 'Hand carved that was. Got—how much did we get for that, Nick?'

'Thirty quid,' said Nick, joining the others outside. A stone patio had covered most of the garden, but the digger working on it for the last half hour had been smashing and rooting up the slabs with its great beak-like shovel, before scooping them into a skip.

'Eh, Steve! You coming down?' called Dennis to the taciturn digger operator. Steve left off his assault on the patio, silenced his engine and climbed from the cab.

Dennis settled himself with a sigh into a decayed armchair, which he had dragged out of the house. Soon he was sipping a mug of sweet tea with the *Racing Post* spread across his knee.

'Right, are we on for a flutter this afternoon?' he said. 'I fancy Bound For Pleasure in the two fifteen at Plumpton.'

'Where's Plumpton?' asked Harry.

'Down in East Sussex. And I got a good tip at Thirsk an' all.'

'Where's Thirsk?'

'*York*shire,' said Dennis acidly. 'God, you need a nag dribbling a football to get you interested! Right, a fiver each and we can do a treble.'

He fished a pencil stub, and a mud-smeared piece of paper from his overall pocket and began transcribing the selections. At the same time Harry was having trouble unscrewing the top of his flask. Suddenly the plastic cap flew off and bounced to the ground. In a second Nick had pounced on it, controlling it with his feet and shaped for a goal-scoring shot while Harry leapt up and attempted a tackle.

Dennis was musing over a third horse, weighing an experienced old chaser against a young gelding just out of novice class. Looking into the middle distance his eye caught a small clump of rust-coloured fur, protruding from the soil near the blade of the mechanical digger. He nodded at it and looked around for Steve.

'What's that you dug up, Steve? Looks like a

4

dead cat. See it? By the edge of the blade.'

Harry and Nick glanced up from their scuffle as Dennis heaved himself from his chair and sauntered towards the digger for a closer look.

He tapped the tuft of fur with the toe of his boot. It was attached to some object half embedded in the mud.

'It's not a cat. Don't know what it is.'

Watching him, Harry felt a chill, inexplicable shudder run through him.

'Kick it over, then!' he said. 'Let's have a look.'

Dennis knocked at the thing with his toecap. The soil around it fell away and it rolled sideways. Suddenly they all recognized what it was. Though caked in filth and partly decayed, there was no possibility of a mistake. They looked at the object they had unearthed for a long few seconds, then glanced at each other slack-jawed. It was a human skull, to which a shock of bright, carrot-coloured hair still adhered.

*   *   *

'Mike, we've got a body in a garden in North London, edge of Kilburn. Fancy it?'

The Commander's voice, heard over Detective Superintendent Michael Walker's mobile phone, sounded urbane as ever. He might have been inviting Walker for a drink. Not that his 'Fancy it?' implied any choice in the matter for Walker. He was being assigned.

'What's it look like?' Walker replied. 'Recent?'

'Hardly. It's a skeleton. Probably female. Could have been in the ground for years. Anyway, let me know the score when you've been up there. And do

5

follow procedure, Mike, OK?'

Walker sighed and shook his head. Since migrating south as a sergeant from his home-town force in Glasgow in the early 1980s, he had served the Metropolitan Police with a dedication that was nothing if not single-minded, though some said it was bloody-minded as well. For the last decade he had been with the elite pool of officers investigating London's murders and other major crimes—a unit nowadays known as the Serious Crimes Group (SCG). Walker had made mistakes over the years and he was anything but biddable. He had been particularly contemptuous of what he called the procedure-driven, management-speak type of policing, built around performance models and operational parameters, that had been gaining momentum over the last few years. Yet he'd always had a higher than average clear-up rate and the top brass had put up with his bolshiness. But now Walker was wondering if the Met was growing tired of him at last. A really tasty case had not come his way for months, and this one was hardly promising. It was probably a Victorian body, with no living relatives, no living enemies and no chance of ever finding out what happened.

The local police had been first on the scene, in response to Dennis the demolition ganger's panicky call. A chain of further messages linked the garden at 34 Hallerton Road all the way to a floor high up in New Scotland Yard, from where, besides Walker's appointment as Senior Investigating Officer—SIO—and the assembly of his team, scene-of-crime officers—SOCOs—were despatched and the pathology unit was alerted. Driven by his friend and long-time colleague

Detective Sergeant Dave Satchell, Walker got to the scene shortly after midday. Several police cars were already parked in the driveway. Rubber-booted men and women in white disposable overalls were coming and going: pathologists, forensic examiners and local officers. Walker and Satchell, too, put on the regulation protective suits before passing through the house and into the garden.

The grave was being treated exactly like a find in an archaeological dig. The soil, around where the skull had been disturbed, was meticulously turned over with spatulas and spoons, then sifted and removed. Any small objects—stones, bones, fragments of crockery—were brushed clean, labelled, photographed and packed into evidence bags before being boxed up. Dr John Foster, the Home Office pathologist, was already in attendance, primarily interested in organic remains but also wanting soil samples. A video camera operator recorded every procedure and every find.

Most of the skeleton was lying exposed now in a shallow pit of excavated earth. It had been buried no more than a foot down. Walker watched the operation for a few minutes then took Foster aside.

'Tell me it's a monkey, from London Zoo,' he pleaded, 'preferably pre-war. Then I can wrap this and get straight back to what I'm paid for—catching the bad guys who walk the streets.'

Foster shook his head in his familiar, deliberate way.

'Oh, there's no question of a monkey, Mr Walker. It's all too human, I'm afraid. I'm having the whole thing bagged up now to be taken down to my place for proper post-mortem examination.'

7

Walker looked around, beyond the boundaries of the garden. Neighbouring gardens stretched for some distance on each side.

'All right, then. Maybe this is a medieval graveyard everybody forgot. Maybe this is a plague victim.'

Foster shook his head.

'No dice, I'm afraid. It's old, but not nearly as old as that. We've found a scrap of material that could be the remains of a dress or shirt. And another thing: there's something in the soil around this corpse which looks like quicklime. You know what that might mean, don't you?'

Walker nodded. It was the first indication that he might be occupied with this case for some time. He clapped Foster lightly on the shoulder.

'Well, thanks, Professor. I'll see you at the mortuary. I've got to go off and round up a posse.'

He beckoned Satchell. Just as the two were leaving, there was a cry from the officer crouching at one end of the shallow, oval pit. He was easing the remains of a woman's shoe out of the earth around the skeletal foot.

*   *   *

Walker's first task was to move with his team into one of the dedicated Incident Rooms, in a building specially equipped to service the investigation of serious crimes in the North London area. By late afternoon a first group of officers had arrived for a preliminary briefing. Walker strolled in, taking a hasty look around. He had worked with most of them before, but one of the Investigating Officers, and a key figure, Detective Inspector Jeff bloody

Batchley, was a far from welcome addition. Last he'd heard the guy was in the sticks in Kent.

'I saw you were on this,' Walker said, striding right up to the offending presence. He did not remove his hands from his pockets.

Batchley, tall and muscular, seemed unruffled by Walker's ill-concealed hostility. He, too, stood with his hands in his pockets.

'Yes,' he said, nodding. 'Moved from Cobham. Applied to the crime directorate and got the SCG.'

'Spare us the CV,' said Walker, cutting him short. 'You remember Dave Satchell?'

Walker inclined his head towards the Detective Sergeant, who acknowledged Batchley with a nod and a smile. Walker shoved his hands deeper into his pockets and began pacing around the room.

'Right, listen up. The Home Office pathologist found some kind of garden lime doused all over the remains, could be a bungled attempt to destroy the evidence, which is why we're all gathered here. And, as a little warning, this will be a very long and laborious investigation so if any of you bright sparks are thinking of jumping ship you can think again . . .'

He jabbed a thumb into his chest.

'Because if I'm on it, you're all on it.'

Walker looked around at each face.

'OK. The skeleton is currently being assembled in the mortuary. She is female, with well-preserved dark brown hair, dyed red. The other evidence found, in the form of bits of material and the victim's shoes, are being analysed at the labs. Now our first priority'—he pointed at Detective Constable Doug Collins—'and I'm afraid it's yours, Doug, is a complete history of that house. All

9

previous occupants need to be traced. Good luck. There are two important questions: who is the skeleton, and how long has she been buried?'

Walker drew breath and glanced at Batchley.

'What does our Investigating Officer have to say for himself?'

Batchley blinked. He gathered his thoughts.

'Erm, well, firstly, Gov, we need to make a preliminary assessment . . . study scene forensics, begin a witness search, victim inquiries, identify suspects and see if we can figure out any possible motives.'

Walker smiled thinly.

'Eh, you have been reading the manual, Batchley! All right, since you're so on the ball, I'm putting you in charge of the crime scene. Now, another priority is to establish when the patio was laid.'

Batchley broke in.

'Yeah, judging by what the builders have told us, the stones hadn't been disturbed before the diggers moved in. So we can reasonably assume the victim was buried before the patio was laid.'

Walker glanced at Satchell with raised eyebrows. Then he turned back to the room and clapped his hands to close the briefing.

'OK. That's all, thank you, I will see you all in the morning.'

'You off home, then?' Batchley enquired.

Walker, who was already making for the door, turned sharply.

'Yes, if that's all right with you.'

Batchley hesitated, then said, 'Give Pat my regards. How is she?'

Walker did not move, still staring Batchley in the

10

eyes.

'Why?'

'Er, no reason. Just haven't seen her for a while. Wondered how she was, that's all.'

Walker paused for a moment as if reviewing possible replies. He settled for, 'She's fine.'

And he turned on his heel and headed out. Satchell caught Batchley's sigh of exasperation. He offered a word of conciliation.

'Nice to see you again, Jeff. You still playing rugby for the Met?'

'Yeah, we're getting together a team, there's a tournament later in the—'

'Satch!'

It was Walker's voice from the corridor.

Satchell shrugged.

'I'll catch you later, yeah?'

With the door safely closed behind them, Batchley sighed again and looked around at his colleagues.

'That went well, don't you think?'

*   *   *

As Walker sat at the kitchen bar, forking food voraciously into his mouth, Detective Inspector Pat North was at the table chewing her pencil. She was going through the typescript of her lecture for the umpteenth time. 'Imaginative Crime-Scene Management', she'd called it, and she knew its delivery on Monday would be a substantial career moment for her.

North had been pregnant with Mike Walker's child when the Metropolitan Police had singled her out for promotion on a fast-track Home Office

11

scheme. But, after a fall down the stairs of the apartment she shared with Walker, she had miscarried. Returning to duty in the knowledge she could probably never conceive again, she had put aside grief and thrown herself into the work of assisting in 'cold case' reviews and other SCG investigations. Currently she was attached to a 'scoping' team, reviewing managerial strategies, and had been invited to distil her thoughts in an address to a conference to be held in Manchester. The hall would be stuffed with senior officers from all over the country—a fantastic chance to impress, to get her face known.

Work, setting promotion goals and slogging towards them, was the only way she could relieve her feelings. Sleep was elusive. Her love for Walker was awkward and always on tenterhooks. A miscarriage wasn't illness, exactly. But she had never felt quite the same since it happened, never quite well. She did love Walker, that at least wasn't in doubt. But the insidious question that came in the night was just as pressing. Did he love her? And, even more desperate, like a sinister whisper in her head, was the other question: did she really love herself?

'I tell you, I am getting the dross thrown my way.'

North jolted back to the present. It was another Saturday night, like the last and the one before that. She had spent it at home while Walker was at the pub. Coming in late, and hungry, he was nevertheless anxious to tell her about his day and the skeleton in Hallerton Road.

'We've no idea how long the skeleton's been there—could be a hundred years for all we know!'

North laughed.

'Except not many Victorians wore slingbacks. There's more pasta if you want it.'

Walker stabbed the last pieces of food on his plate and pitched them into his mouth.

'Thanks. Unless . . . is there any of that apple thingy left?'

She laughed.

'You and your pies! It's in the fridge.'

He pounced on the fridge door, yanked it open and bent to peer inside.

'And you'll never guess what.'

He reached for a bowl containing the pie and drew it out.

'Batchley's on this one too, he's been moved from Cobham! Just my luck!'

He placed the apple pie on the counter. But, shutting the fridge door, he spotted something else inside.

'Custard too!'

He brought out a jug and showed it to North.

'Will this heat up? I hate it cold.'

'Course it will. So, Jeff's on it, is he?'

'Yeah. Like I said, I'm getting all the dross.'

North looked up.

'Hey! You always have to get a dig in about him.'

Now he was searching through the cupboards. She watched him as he noisily extracted a saucepan.

'Batchley's the one that's going to be digging. I've put him in charge of the site.'

Walker now had the saucepan in one hand and the jug of custard in the other. He sighted carefully and began to tip the custard jug towards the saucepan.

'Mike, what are you doing?'

'Heating up the custard.'

'Well, why don't you just pour the custard on top of the pie and stick the whole lot in the microwave?'

Walker put down the saucepan.

'Right.'

He poured the custard over the pie, put it in the microwave oven and studied the control.

'How long do you reckon? Five minutes?'

'No, no! Far too long.'

It was time to intervene. She crossed to the microwave and set the timer while he stepped back with his hands in the air.

'All right, all right. I'll just leave the technology to you.'

As the microwave whirred, she returned to the table, suddenly feeling a knot of tension at the top of her spine. She rubbed the back of her neck and, looking up, Walker noticed for the first time how pale she was.

'You OK?'

'Yeah, just been a long day. I've been going round in circles with the wording of this lecture.'

'Sounds riveting. Rather you than me.'

'Don't knock it, Mike! Some of the strategies I'm working on at the moment could make a big difference.'

'I'm not saying they won't, but you can't tell me you get the same buzz from this as you did from getting criminals off the streets.'

'No. But at least I feel like I'm moving things forward.'

'So when are you giving this lecture, then?'

'Monday. I'm off up to Manchester.'

'What? Tomorrow?'

'Yes, for the conference. I did tell you. It's just you never listen to a word I say. I'm going to finish packing.'

She tidied the pile of papers and headed for the stairs. The microwave pinged and Walker punched the door open. He reached for the bowl containing his slice of pie.

'Yeow! Shit!'

The bowl was searingly hot and he burnt his fingers.

CHAPTER 2

SUNDAY, 24 SEPTEMBER

Walker knew that the progress of the Hallerton Road inquiry would hinge on how long the victim had been in the ground. He had asked for a preliminary report from Foster today, never mind that it was Sunday: it was vital to get this fact established as soon as possible. The more recently the body was buried, the more urgent—not to mention exciting—his work would become. On the other hand, the longer ago it was, the colder grew the trail and proportionally smaller the chance for a quick breakthrough. As a policeman, Walker had always known his own best assets were explosive energy and inspiration, rather than the patient application of method. He was more of a sprinter than a marathon man.

When he breezed into the Incident Room at nine in the morning, the search for the history of 34 Hallerton Road was already on. The room was buzzing with talk, and bleeping with phones and computer terminals. The Land Register had been accessed and legal documents searched. Computerized lists of registered electors, Social Security claimants, tax-payers and missing persons were now being combed for the house's owners and residents.

'Good morning, everybody,' called Walker above the noise. 'Cracked it yet, have we?'

Doug Collins sat back in his chair and yawned, scratching the back of his head.

16

'It's going to be a pain in the neck, Gov. The house has been a squat for the past five years, DSS before that, and way before that, a bed and breakfast!'

This was not good news. Walker closed his eyes.

'Shit, Doug! It must have a list of residents as long as my arm!'

'Oh, longer than that,' said Collins. 'Tracing traffic through the place from the time it was DSS alone's going to take weeks.'

Walker shook his head slowly.

'We've *got* weeks,' he said sadly.

'Gov, it's for you!'

Detective Constable Lisa West was holding up a telephone. It was Satchell, from the mortuary.

'Gov, they're piecing the skeleton together,' he said. 'You want to come and have a look?'

'OK, Satch, I'm on my way.'

*   *   *

Pat North's best friend Vivien Watkins, still a Detective Constable since their time together in Divisional CID, was driving tomorrow's increasingly nervous lecturer to Heathrow. North sat in the passenger seat with her overnight bag on her lap. By travelling up a day in advance she was taking no chances over her appearance at the conference.

'So,' said Watkins brightly, 'when are you back?'

'Day after tomorrow.'

'Well, rather you than me.'

North clicked her tongue audibly.

'I *do* wish people would stop saying that.'

Watkins laughed.

17

'Sorry! I only meant I'd never have the nerve to stand up and give a lecture in front of so many people.'

North did not reply and Watkins could gauge the tension in her friend. The two women had been drawn together by mutual sympathy and the similarity of their experiences. Watkins lived with a man who was not in the force. But, like North, she desperately wanted children and she had also suffered the agony of miscarriage.

'You OK?' she asked after a few moments.

'Yeah, just tired. I've not been sleeping well.'

'Sounds familiar, I suffered the same after my miscarriage. Have you tried St John's Wort?'

'What?' North gave a puzzled laugh. 'What wort?'

'St John's Wort. It's a herbal remedy. Makes you feel more positive. Really helped me.'

North wrinkled her nose.

'No offence but I'm not really into all that homoeopathic stuff. Vodka and tonic does the same for me.'

They had pulled up at the setting-down area of Terminal One. North unslung her seatbelt and got out.

'Thanks for the lift, Viv.'

Watkins gave her a wave.

'Any time.'

North shut the car door and began to walk away. Watkins lowered the passenger window and called after her.

'Pat! I know you don't like people fussing, but look after yourself, hey?'

'I will. Stop fussing!'

18

The bones of the skeleton had been laid out, in correct anatomical order, on a table at the mortuary. Gowned in green overalls, Walker and Satchell stood looking over them with Dr Foster, while an assistant diligently counted the bones of one foot.

'I can confirm the gender already suggested by the shoes,' Foster was saying.

'Not a cross-dresser, then?' remarked Satchell.

'No. She's female and five foot eight.'

'How long has she been dead?' asked Walker.

Foster shrugged.

'Who knows? But she's got quite a complete set of teeth. At this stage I can't tell you whether there are any bones missing or broken. We can't see any marks on the skeleton. But we have been able to estimate her age. She's young—somewhere between sixteen and nineteen.'

'You can't give me any idea what year she died?'

'Well, we should be able to get a broad idea but there'll be nothing concrete—except for the piece she was found under.'

Foster looked down fondly at the skeleton.

'Interesting thing, you know. In the 10 Rillington Place murders, the period of time one victim had been buried was determined by the length of a tree root which was found growing through her vertebrae. Fascinating.'

Walker looked at Satchell. The things these pathologists found fascinating.

'Anyway,' Foster went on. 'My guess is she's been there longer than a decade.'

'Great!' growled Walker, hammering the side of

19

the table with his fist and shaking the bones, to the considerable alarm of Foster's assistant. 'I said this case was going to be a bastard!'

'Yes,' said Foster, looking severely at Walker over the rim of his glasses. 'You're going to be heavily reliant on forensics for this one, aren't you, Detective Superintendent?'

*   *   *

PC Lisa West was visiting Dr Sudah Malik at the Metropolitan Laboratory of the Forensic Science Service. The Service had been established since the mid-1930s and had always been a world leader in forensic criminology. Nowadays it employed hundreds of scientists working on more than 28,000 cases every year, and aimed to produce neither suspicions nor hearsay, but solid facts. It was only on such facts that a case could be built without fear of refutation in a court of law. Dr Malik, a specialist in inorganic and material forensic science, had begun a series of tests on the garden soil from 34 Hallerton Road, as well as the patio stones, the shoes and the scrap of material that had been found with the body.

She told West she had already confirmed the presence of an unusual concentration of garden lime in the soil sample—more of the stuff, certainly, than a gardener would be wise to use. The clothing material presented a more difficult problem. Clothes found with a decomposed and unidentified corpse were always of crucial significance: the only link between the skeleton and the living person.

The first step in the identification was to

establish which composite dyes had been used in its manufacture. As much of the sample as possible was to be kept intact, exactly as it had been found. The piece cut off for testing was carefully washed, the residues from the washing being retained for further analysis. A single strand of the cleaned fibre was then placed in a tiny test tube with a small amount of solvent, which was heated in a hot sand bath. The solution was then dotted onto a silicon gel plate, which was dipped in more solvent until it ran down to form a line of about two centimetres, which was blow-dried. The different component colour dyes used in the compound could be seen to have separated and the compound itself could then, perhaps, be tracked down.

Dr Malik showed West the material she had been working on.

'This could have been a skirt, or a dress . . . anything really, it's just fragments. But thankfully it's synthetic which will help us with the date. And it's a rather unusual pattern. One of our contacts at the dye houses might remember it.'

West followed the scientist across to another bench, where she recognized the black shoes, slingbacked and high-heeled, that had been found with the body at Hallerton Road.

'These are the shoes,' said Malik, picking one up. 'Apparently one was still on her left foot, and the second was close by.'

She peered at the sole, close to the base of the heel.

'Size six,' she pronounced. 'Thirty-nine if you want to be continental. They're probably a cheap High Street shoe, British made. Not Gucci, by any stretch of the imagination.'

21

'Nothing else on the shoes?' asked West. 'No prints or DNA?'

'Well, you'd normally expect some prints but according to the fingerprint officer there was nothing usable in this case, I'm afraid. Just smudges. We're seeing if there's any DNA, of course, but you know that takes time.'

'I'll tell Mr Walker,' said West, knowing the Governor would be disappointed that she had so little to tell. 'What's the next move?'

'That's up to Mr Walker. Apart from the DNA we'll continue looking at these dyes and also at scrapings we've taken from the soles of the shoes. We're also looking at the composition of the patio slabs to see if we can get a fix on when they were manufactured. Should have something on that tomorrow. But Mr Walker will probably want to trace the dress material first. It's all in here.'

She handed the officer a slim file.

'The details of the dyes.'

*   *   *

That night, coming back late to the deserted flat, Walker called North at her hotel.

'What are you doing?' he asked.

'Revising the lecture yet again, would you believe? I can't tell if it's any good.'

'It is,' he said. 'Take my word for it.'

She laughed.

'How can I? You haven't read the bloody thing. Did you find some food at home?'

'Yeah, no problem. You know me. Beans on toast hits the spot. You been out for dinner with some handsome local gigolo?'

'No, I decided against that. So I ordered a Caesar salad twenty minutes ago from room service. It still hasn't come and I'm starving. But never mind about me, what's your day been like?'

'Hallerton Road, all day. And it'll be the same tomorrow and for weeks or months unless I get lucky. How the hell am I going to find out who this girl was? All I've got is a pair of shoes and a scrap of material which may be from her dress.'

As they talked on North realized, in this far from sumptuous hotel room, that there was one thing about her domestic life with Walker that she'd come to depend on. It was those moments when they were together in the evening, and he told her about his day. And his voice on the phone, doing exactly that, was so intimate now, so obviously meant just for her. Despite the geographical distance between them she felt, if possible, closer to him here than at home. When she hung up she was sad. She quashed the feeling by putting an angry call through to room service.

CHAPTER 3

MONDAY, 25 SEPTEMBER

A few minutes after ten the next morning, North was listening to herself being introduced to the audience in a Manchester University lecture hall. Three hundred senior investigative officers, technical specialists, forensic scientists and pathologists heard her described by an assistant chief constable as 'one of a new generation of officers, with a refreshing approach to policing for the twenty-first century'. To the sound of scattered applause she approached the microphone.

She began with a question.

'Why continually worry whether we are doing the right things at a murder crime scene? On the face of it a clear-up rate of better than 90 per cent is much superior to our performance in all other crime categories. The trouble is that, as far as the public are concerned, solving nine out of ten murders is never going to be good enough. We are expected to clear up all murders—without fail. And it is the unsolved murders that have the highest press profile. That is the measure of the daunting task we face in this area. For many officers, it is science, and in particular DNA profiling, that is the key to this. But forensic science is only a tool. What matters is how well we understand its use.'

The audience was paying close attention as, rapidly, she ran through some of the newest techniques for extracting DNA evidence from even the most unpromising surfaces at the crime scene.

24

But these developments presented the police with a challenge, she warned. Rather than being satisfied with the obvious bloodstain or discarded cigarette end, investigating officers must think their way more laterally around the crime scene. There are always many less prominent items on the scene that may have been touched by the perpetrator.

'Never think that the surface you are testing is unreceptive to DNA,' she advised. 'Believe it or not, results have been obtained from a maggot before now.'

The audience laughed lightly but quietened down as North continued. New techniques and technologies could create as many problems as they solved. No individual police officer could possibly grasp the whole range of procedures and detection aids now available, so that effective communication between the officers on the ground and the forensic experts was crucial.

'In this room,' she said, 'are some of the most experienced officers in the country, sitting next to expert advisors from many of the fields that we are discussing—it would be a tragedy if you all walked away from here without having made new contacts. None of us can afford to think that we know everything there is to know about a murder. We have to work together to understand. So let's bring the real experts into our investigations. We can learn from them direct. Get your footprint specialist to talk to your DNA expert and they will come up with conclusions together that they would never have reached alone: very quickly they could map the history of a villain's movements. Let's start this process now. Talk to each other. Make use of each other. Make this new technology work for us, not against us. That's all I've got to say, so let's hear from you . . .'

*　　*　　*

'An email came through from Forensics about the patio slabs,' Satchell told Walker. They were donning their paper suits and wellingtons at Hallerton Road, where Walker had gone to check on Batchley's progress. 'Thomson followed it up and got a result. Those patio stones were only made between 1979 and 1984. So the patio was most probably laid during that time or soon after.'

'Have we tracked down the owners of the house at the time?'

'Not yet. We know it was owned by a Mr and Mrs Philip Norton but we've yet to trace them.'

'Shouldn't be difficult.'

'They may not be alive, though. Or they're lying gaga in an old folks' home, oblivious to the difference between right and left.'

Walker pulled a face.

'Or right and wrong. Don't go there, Satch. We need a bit of luck on this.'

'By the way, Pat's still away, isn't she? Like to come over for a bite to eat tonight? Catrina's having a go at Creole chicken.'

Walker waved his hand apologetically.

'If you don't mind, I'll give it a miss, Satch. Her moussaka gave me the runs for a week.'

The garden, as Walker and Satchell entered it, was in a terrible state. The strong pervasive smell was of drains. What had been a small grave pit had become a large hole in the ground, half filled with brown water. Around the edge Batchley's team

26

were getting themselves muddy and miserable.

'How goes it, Cobham?' called Walker cheerily as he strode into the search area. It did him a power of good to see Batchley knee-deep in it.

'We're searching around the area she was buried in,' said the harassed Crime Scene Manager. 'But we haven't found anything else yet.'

'You mean she *wasn't* lying on a newspaper with the date intact?' asked Walker in mock surprise.

Batchley winced. Whatever he did or said, Walker would have it in for him.

'No, Gov. Afraid not. But the whole search is going to take longer than we thought. We've got a sewer pipe burst. We're up to our eyes in shit.'

Walker surveyed the scene with a satisfied smile.

'So I see.'

Leaving twenty minutes later, Satchell nudged Walker.

'Good job I failed that DI assessment.'

'What?' asked Walker incredulously. He knew Dave Satchell had been seriously choked by the setback. But Satchell chuckled.

'I get the overtime and that schmuck's up to his eyes in doo-doo and not a penny extra!'

*   *   *

'Yes, in the back row?'

North's questioner was a grey-haired uniformed man.

'You say that DNA tests can be carried out on fingerprints. Wouldn't fingerprint dusting contaminate these tests?'

'Well, as I said earlier, I'm not a forensic scientist, but I believe that it's not so much the dusting that can damage the fingerprints but the cleanliness of the dusting brush itself.'

'So how can this be avoided?'

'Well, in an ideal world, I suppose we'd all be using disposable brushes, but discussions are still in progress about the cost of that. Next?'

She pointed to another uniform, who wanted to know how these techniques might assist in victim identification. North thought of Walker, with his anonymous skeleton. DNA was no use to him.

She told the conference that, for identification purposes, DNA was still no better than a fingerprint was, if you didn't have a database of the DNA profiles covering the whole population with which to compare it. That of course raised massive political and civil liberties issues. At the same time, as knowledge of the human genome was refined, things were bound to change: colour of hair, eyes, skin, ethnic background, even the body shape would in theory be discernible from a DNA sample, one day. But not yet.

*   *   *

Walker and the Incident Room had convened for their evening debriefing. It had not been a bad day, with progress made on all fronts. A whiteboard on the wall displayed a time-line on which secure dates connected with Hallerton Road were recorded. The tenure of the Norton family with their bed and breakfast (from the 1970s up to about 1984) and the laying of the patio stones (between 1979 and 1984) were looking the most significant at the moment. But now they were able to feed in some more information about the piece

28

of material, as DC Lisa West was explaining to the room.

'We sent an illustration of the tartan to retail manufacturers who were operational in the late seventies and early eighties. A catalogue company gave us a swatch from a dress they made, which we tested against the blue dye, and it's definitely the same one.'

Walker looked pained.

'A catalogue company? There must have been thousands of them made.'

West shook her head.

'Actually no. Surprisingly, only five hundred dresses were made using that particular dye.'

'So when *were* they produced?'

West strode to the time-line chart with a black marker pen. She crossed through the years 1979 and 1980.

'That was in August 1981. Which means we can chop this time-line down.'

She turned back to her desk and picked up a garishly coloured booklet and flashed it in the air for them all to see.

'They had back copies of all their catalogues so we've been able to get hold of a picture of the dress.'

Walker was delighted.

'Good work, Laura!' he beamed.

'It's Lisa, Gov. Lisa West.'

Walker almost did a double-take when he heard the name. West was an unfortunate enough surname, considering the nature of this case. He took the catalogue.

'What page?'

'It's page sixty-two,' she said.

It was a tartan frock of an unremarkable type, though even to Walker's untutored eye the garment looked, like all the others on the page, seriously out of style with its shoulder pads, low neckline and nipped-in waist. He studied it. When he was twenty-five he'd gone out with girls dressed like that.

'What about her shoes? Any joy there?'

This time it was Doug Collins who knew all the answers.

'The manufacturer, Fletcher-Smith Shoes, went out of business years ago. Unfortunately, they had outlets all over England and sold thousands of the same style shoe. They were first manufactured in 1980, before our dress, so they don't help us narrow down our dates.'

Walker looked from face to face.

'OK. Anyone got anything else? What about you, Satch?'

'Yes,' said the Detective Sergeant. 'I've finally managed to trace the Nortons who ran the B&B at number 34. They now run a retirement home in Kingston, Surrey.'

As a phone rang, and was quickly answered by Collins, Walker was rubbing his hands briskly. Things were looking better and better.

'Well, we'll have this wrapped up faster than a dog out of a trap. First thing tomorrow we take a trip to Kingston.'

There was a buzz of talk as the team began gathering up their papers.

'Gov!'

It was Collins's voice cutting through the noise. They all looked. He was holding out the phone.

'They've found another one.'

'Another what?' asked Walker, but he already knew.

'Another skeleton.'

*   *   *

Walker and Satchell were back at Hallerton Road within half an hour. Both men were excited. A second body made the case much more interesting, much more high-profile. One skeleton meant a few paragraphs in the local rag. Two were national news.

They found that the second grave was several feet further away from the house than the first. Arc lights were being set up to compensate for the gathering dusk as Walker looked down at the crouching Batchley, who was slowly uncovering a grinning, blackened skull still half sunk into the earth. Hair, which seemed to be long and blonde, was clogged with mud.

'What's that on the top of the head?' demanded Walker as Batchley jumped aside to give him a view.

'Some kind of hairband,' said Batchley. 'But have a look at this.'

He was pointing just below the jawbone. Protruding from the mud was a section of what looked like a leather belt, for attached to the end of it was a metallic buckle. Bizarrely, the buckle was in the form of a skeletal hand.

'It's been wrapped around the neck.'

'Right,' said Walker. 'Get it photographed and send copies to the press. That'll get them on our side. They're bound to get excited now we have more than one body.'

31

'Yes,' said Satchell. 'We're moving into serial-killer territory. Not to mention the similarities to you-know-who.'

*   *   *

The conference had closed and the delegates were mixing convivially, exchanging comments. North was feeling tired but satisfied with her day's work when a diffident, middle-aged, professorial type of man approached her.

'Inspector North?'

'Yes.'

'I attended your lecture and I must say it was very interesting.'

She smiled.

'Thanks.'

The man cleared his throat. He obviously had more to say.

'I am a specialist in cranio-facial identification— the guy who builds clay heads . . . ?'

'Oh, yes, of course! Angus Taylor, here at the university, right? I'm *very* pleased to meet you.'

They shook hands.

'Me too,' he said. 'I, er, just wanted to pick up on a point you made at the end about witness identification. You suggested that once genetic e-fitting becomes feasible, techniques such as I have been employing will become obsolete.'

Oh God, thought North. *He's worried about his job.*

'Well,' she said hesitantly. 'I *have* been led to believe that genetic e-fitting is the way forward, yes.'

Taylor coughed nervously a second time.

32

'Yes, but we're already combining the new approach with my more traditional methods and getting some great results. Look, my lab's just a couple of floors up. Care to see?'

She nodded and he showed her the way, talking as they walked.

'The last one I had, a body was found chopped up, wrapped up in plastic sheeting in a railway station locker, so decomposed we couldn't tell how he died.'

'No fingerprints or DNA?'

'No matches on the DNA and the killer was careful to remove the hands. It was a nasty mess.'

Angus Taylor was warming to his theme.

'Hadn't a clue how long he'd been dead, but I was able to make up a life-size model of his head which we used at a press conference.'

'And?'

'Loads of calls from the public. Turns out he was some nasty gangland character.'

Taylor's laboratory was small and, for the beginning of the twenty-first century, strangely devoid of computers and imaging devices. Instead there were bones, plaster casts, wax and plastic models arrayed on shelving that reached to the ceiling. North asked Taylor how he set about his task.

'You take a cast from the skull, right?'

'Oh yes. I never work on the original.'

'And then you build up the skin . . . how?'

'I tell you what, let's take old Gloria here as our model.'

Taylor reached down a plaster-cast model of a skull, with short pegs protruding from a dozen or more places around its surface. He placed it on the

33

desk in front of them.

'We drill small holes into the cast at carefully measured intervals and then pegs of various lengths are placed into these holes to indicate the soft tissue thickness.'

'And you use clay to build up the face?'

'That's right.'

He turned the model skull appreciatively: a man who loved his work.

'Once the basic muscle groups are developed, we can pad it out by putting on the fatty areas, the cheeks, chin, etc. before applying thin clay layers in strips, to act as the skin.'

'So how do you know how to build up the features of the face?'

'Well, the shape of the face, nose and lips can be done pretty accurately, but the rest—ears, hairline, etc.—have been pretty much guesswork up to now.'

'And that's where genetics will eventually come in?'

'Exactly! Once they've identified which genes correspond to which physical characteristics, we'll be able to be much more accurate. But until then, I'm always careful to say to the police that my heads are "similar to". But it's pretty useful to stimulate recognition, if a detective only has a bag of decomposed remains.'

Suddenly, she had a flash of Walker on the phone to her hotel room last night.

'How much does this cost?' she asked.

'About a thousand pounds which, when you have sweet FA to go on, isn't bad!'

North pondered the clay head.

'And how long does it take?'

'Only a few days, and in my mind worth every

penny.'

North nodded. In the case she was thinking of, that would be right. She turned her sweetest smile on him.

'Er, how busy are you at the moment?'

'I'm always busy. Have you got something for me?'

'I *might* have.'

CHAPTER 4

TUESDAY, 26 SEPTEMBER

'How was the Coronation chicken?'

'Creole. Burnt.'

Satchell had collected Walker and was driving up the A3 to Kingston. Walker's eyes were closed, his head slumped back on the rest. He was tired as hell. It had been a restless night, his dreams visited by mud-encrusted skulls and metal skeletal hands.

'So where's Pat gone to exactly?' enquired Satchell.

Walker roused himself.

'She's gone up to Manchester to some conference.'

Satchell raised his eyebrows.

'Playing with the big boys now, eh?'

'Hardly *playing*, Satch. She's been giving a lecture.'

'What on?'

Walker shook his head wearily.

'Oh, I don't know. Crime-scene management, pooling resources, something like that. Course, if you really want to hang onto a case, you can't pool your resources with anyone.' He coughed. 'Right. What have we got on the Nortons this bright and breezy morning?'

'OK,' said Satchell. 'The husband, Philip, died in '83. It's just Mrs Norton and her daughter, Kathleen.'

Walker yawned and rubbed his eyes.

'And they were running a bed and breakfast at

number 34 seventeen years ago? Correct?'

'Yes, ran it from 1976 until 1984.'

'Right.'

Walker leaned back and closed his eyes again.

'Just give me a nudge when we get there, will you?'

*   *   *

At the Norton Retirement Home for Select Residents, Kathleen Norton was ponderously preparing dinner. Of course, all four of the select residents would have been in the dining room since half twelve, their feet under the table, their serviettes tucked under their chins, waiting for her. They had nothing better to do, even though they knew she never served until one o'clock. And they'd pass the time maundering on about the old days, and the times there was such a thing as standards. Or they told interminable anecdotes—of questionable accuracy—about the war.

In her more fanciful moments she tried to think of it as 'lunch', which she felt was better class. But she could never kid herself for long. This was dinner. It was what the residents called it and what it actually was: the home's main meal of the day. Today it was pea soup followed by sausages, onions, carrots, mash and a thick brown gravy. The residents were very particular about their gravy. Kathleen stirred the almost viscous liquid with a wooden spoon. She knew her face would be red above the steam. She was sweating, her feet felt mushy with tiredness and her varicose vein throbbed. But this was her place. It was duty. 'Offer it up,' the priest told her, when she complained

37

about her lot in the confessional. 'There are millions of poor souls worse off.'

At ten to one the doorbell rang. Probably the grocery order. Kathleen listened for a moment and heard her mother Dorothy attending to it. Then she went on stirring.

*   *   *

To Walker and Satchell, the Norton Home, established in a large Victorian house, had all the appearance of a well-run establishment. The drainpipes and window frames had recently been painted and the doorstep was clearly scrubbed regularly. Tubs of flowers and hanging baskets surrounded the large front door.

'They're obviously at home,' said Walker, inhaling the smell of cooking as he rang the bell a second time.

'Someone's coming,' said Satchell.

Slowly, the door opened. An elderly woman wearing a severe but well-cut black dress peered out.

'Are you the delivery? It's to go round the back . . . to the back door.'

Walker held out his warrant card.

'No. I'm Detective Superintendent Walker and this is Detective Sergeant Satchell. I'd like to speak to a Mrs Norton, please.'

The woman looked puzzled rather than alarmed. She said, 'I'm Mrs Norton. How can I help?'

'Do you mind if we come in?'

Mrs Norton hesitated.

'I'm afraid it's dinner time . . . It's rather inconvenient right now.'

38

'That's all right,' Walker told her cheerily. 'We can wait.'

She let them into a large, ill-lit hall with a wooden staircase equipped with a chairlift. There were several rooms off it. From one they could hear a murmur of voices while from the back of the house came the clatter of dishes.

'You'd better come through to the office. The residents are in the dining room.'

Dorothy Norton led the two policemen through a set of glazed double doors into a kind of annexe with its own hallway and then through another, panelled, door into the office.

'All these doors! Fire regulations, you know. We've got far more doors than we've got rooms. Please, sit down.'

The room was furnished practically with a desk and a filing cabinet. A garish picture of the Sacred Heart of Jesus, with spiky golden haloes surrounding the heart itself, hung on the wall. Walker remembered one just like it in the head teacher's office of his primary school, back in Glasgow. He sat down beneath it.

'Mrs Norton,' he began, 'we're here regarding a property you used to own, 34 Hallerton Road, Kilburn.'

'Hallerton Road . . . that takes me back! Would you like a cup of tea?'

Walker shook his head.

'No, I'd just like to ask you some questions. You see, two skeletons have been uncovered in the back garden of number 34.'

This time she was taken aback. But it took a few moments for the facts to sink in. Walker waited while they did.

'Well . . . Well, I never. Two skeletons? But that's terrible. God rest their souls. In the *garden*?'

She looked from Walker to Satchell, and back again.

'Of course,' she went on, 'I'd heard it'd got very run-down after we left. But we've not lived there for years.'

'Well, we were wondering,' asked Satchell, 'do you recall when the patio at Hallerton Road was laid?'

Dorothy Norton considered.

'The patio? My husband did all the handiwork.'

Satchell and Walker exchanged looks. Walker asked, 'Your husband laid it?'

'Yes.'

'Do you recall when?'

'I'll have to ask Kathleen, my daughter, but Philip died in 1983 and I always said it was laying those heavy stones that killed him.'

'So the patio was completed just before he died?'

Dorothy nodded.

'Kathleen will remember the exact date. Shall I get her?'

Walker held up his hand.

'Not just yet.'

'How many rooms did you let to guests, Mrs Norton?' asked Satchell.

'Five. But Philip, my husband, was planning to convert the cellar also.'

'What sort of guests stayed with you?'

'They were mostly travelling salesmen, but we did have a few regulars over the years . . . Oh, Kathleen!'

A red-faced, considerably obese woman in her

mid-forties had come in. Dorothy indicated Walker and Satchell.

'These men are police officers . . . my daughter . . . They've found some skeletons in the back garden at Hallerton Road, Kathleen. *Two!* Two skeletons.'

'*Skeletons?*'

Walker watched Kathleen Norton intently, to see how she would absorb the news. She did so more readily than her mother. And, perhaps because she understood the possible implications more quickly, there was an element of shock in her reaction that her mother had not shown. This was quite an intelligent woman, Walker decided.

'Kathleen,' probed Walker, 'can we ask you a few questions?'

'Er . . . Yes . . . I'm sorry, that's dreadful . . . What did you want to know?'

'Can you remember when the back garden was paved over?'

'Yes, it would have been, ah, around July 1983. Yes, it was, yes. Isn't that right, Mother?'

Walker nodded his approval.

'You've got a very good memory.'

'Not really,' Kathleen replied, stiffly rejecting Walker's patronizing tone. 'My father *died* that September.'

Dorothy bubbled up with incongruous enthusiasm.

'I *said* it was around that time. He'd been ill for years, but he insisted on doing all the conversions and decorating himself.'

Kathleen gave her mother a disapproving look.

'Mother, I don't think the police officers want to know about that. I only remember because that's

41

when he'd started having heart trouble, and lifting those paving stones . . .'

But Dorothy was getting interested now. She knocked her daughter lightly on the arm.

'What about that boy? The one that helped your father?'

Kathleen nodded.

'We had a guest at the time and he helped my father with the patio.'

'Do you remember his name?' asked Walker.

Kathleen looked up at the ceiling.

'Let me think . . .'

'It was Graham!' exclaimed Dorothy. 'Graham Richards.'

Walker noticed the look Kathleen gave her mother. She did not like being interrupted or pre-empted.

'So how long did he stay with you?' asked Satchell.

Dorothy fluttered her hands as she thought back.

'Oh, it must have been a good . . .'

She appealed once again to her daughter.

'About a year, don't you think, Kathleen?'

Kathleen assented by briefly closing her eyes.

'Something like that.'

'Why did he stay that long?' Walker wanted to know.

Dorothy shrugged.

'He'd had some problems with his business, gone bankrupt, that was why he stayed with us. He couldn't get a proper job so he couldn't afford to get a place of his own. Couldn't even afford to pay us half the time, which was why he did jobs around the house.'

42

'What else do you remember about him?'

Suddenly Kathleen took charge of the conversation.

'Well,' she broke in, 'he'd be, what? About mid-twenties. We didn't see much of him, unless he was helping Dad, isn't that right, Mother? Now look, I've got to get on with the—'

'Do you know where we can contact him now?'

Kathleen shook her head: a definite no.

'I'm sorry. We didn't keep in touch.'

'And did you have many female guests staying around that time?'

He looked from the mother to the daughter and back to the mother. It was Dorothy who answered.

'One or two. But like I said, it was mostly businessmen.'

'Did any of your guests ever bring back girlfriends?'

'Girlfriends?' said Kathleen in a startled voice. 'No, not to my knowledge. Mother wouldn't allow it.'

'Oh no,' put in her mother. 'I *wouldn't* allow it!'

*   *   *

Everyone in the Incident Room had had a long day. So far there had been very little in the press about Hallerton Road, partly because Walker was biding his time, waiting until press disclosure of his discoveries would be more of a help than a hindrance to the investigation. But media pressure was growing and, with it, political pressure. The Commander had twice been called by the Home Office asking about developments.

Walker carried on running the inquiry in his own

way, unruffled by the Commander's requests for haste. No one wanted a quick result more than Walker, but he was no magician. He couldn't produce a suspect like a rabbit out of a hat.

'OK,' he asked, looking around the team at the start of their evening briefing, 'who goes first?'

It was Doug Collins.

'We've just got back from the National Missing Persons Helpline, Gov. It's heartbreaking, so many people missing for so many years, and their families never give up hope.'

Walker didn't want to hear this.

'Can we cut the hearts and flowers? What have you got?'

'Well, they've given us loads more information than police records could. We've got a list of names of girls who are of the right age, height and shoe size who were missing between 1981 and 1983, our top and bottom end dates. We're attempting to trace their dental records so they can be cross-referenced with the teeth of the skeletons.'

PC West had been given the job of collating information about the new, second victim.

'Victim two had white porcelain fillings,' she told the meeting, 'which were only introduced in the early eighties. They weren't that common over here then, so it's likely she had them done privately, or abroad.'

She turned over a page and showed a photograph of the shoes, which were found, as the first victim's, on or close to the body.

'Her shoes were made by a French company in early 1983, and they also have branches in England, so we're checking to see if they were imported.'

Walker grunted.

44

'French shoes, foreign teeth . . . Sounds like we need to get on to Interpol. What about the hairband?'

'Unfortunately they were ten-a-penny so that's not much help.'

'And the leather belt?'

Batchley, the belt's discoverer, felt proprietorial towards that particular piece of evidence. He said, 'Belt has a distinctive silver buckle in the shape of a skeleton's hand, which is quite bizarre. Should be easily recognizable. That belt was more than likely used to strangle the victim. She had this much round her neck . . .'

He held his fingers ten inches apart.

'No more than four inches in diameter.'

'Have you briefed the DPA, Satch?'

Satchell had a contact of his own down at the Met's press office, the Directorate of Public Affairs, and had been given the job of liaising with them on Walker's behalf.

'Yes,' he said. 'They're issuing a picture of the belt tomorrow but holding back the fact that it was found round the victim's neck.'

Walker's cellphone sounded.

'OK,' he said, fumbling for the phone. 'We need to make tracing Graham Richards a priority. If he helped lay the patio he might know something.' He had the mobile in his hand now. He checked the caller number showing on the display.

'We also need to extend the search to include the cellar of the house. Batchley—get onto it. Apparently Mr Norton had been doing work down there as well.'

He thumbed the power switch of the phone and held it to his ear. It was his wife.

45

'Lynn, look, I can't talk now. I'm at work.'

He hunched his shoulders and headed into a corner of the room.

'Yes, I *do* need to speak to you, because I want to see the kids at the weekend. But . . . oh, just hang on, will you? Yes, Batchley?'

The Crime Scene Manager was agitated.

'The demolition company won't be happy. They're chomping at the bit to finish the job. In fact, I wouldn't be surprised if we also run into problems with digging up the cellar. The house is pretty unstable as it is. I'll have to confirm it's safe before I send the team in.'

Walker's eyes narrowed as he listened, unimpressed.

'Well, I'm sure you can sort it out . . . Is that it, then? Nothing else?'

He looked around. The team shrugged, shaking their heads.

'OK, let's call it a day,' said Walker, 'and get those actions moving first thing tomorrow.'

He put the phone back to his ear.

'Lynn, the thing is I—Lynn? . . . She's bloody hung up!'

Those who had previously worked with Walker had long experience of these frequent fractured conversations with his estranged wife. Lisa West had not. She frowned.

'Dave?' she whispered. 'What's that all about?'

'Don't ask.'

*   *   *

Walker found North, just back from Manchester, unpacking her overnight bag in the bedroom.

46

'God, what a day!' was the first thing he said. 'I've schlepped up and down the A3 and I'm sure it won't be the last time. Did you know we've got another one?'

North was dumping worn underwear into the laundry basket.

'What—another body?'

'Yes. This one with a belt wrapped around its neck. Hey, I'm starving. What have we got to eat?'

He thumped out and down the stairs to rummage through the fridge. North stood still for a moment, leaning on her dressing table, examining her face in the mirror.

'So, how have you been, Pat?' she whispered. 'Good, thanks for asking. The lecture went well, thanks.'

CHAPTER 5

WEDNESDAY, 27 SEPTEMBER

Secretly, Walker enjoyed appearing on television. Not that he thought much of the media, but he considered plain clothes policemen—doing their work in mostly unsung obscurity—ought to be foisted on the viewing public from time to time, just to remind the world that they existed. In this case, as he wrote his appeal, he knew that skeletons, and quasi-archaeological forensic digs, were exactly the type of stuff that got the public going. In such cases, a well-judged TV appeal could be sensationally effective.

He waited, sitting between Satchell and a DPA press officer, as the press and cameramen assembled. The green light came on and the press officer introduced him and Satchell. Walker then cleared his throat, glanced at his notes and began.

'Good morning, ladies and gentlemen. You will all be aware that we have been digging in a garden in North London after demolition operations revealed a body buried there a number of years ago. So, here are the details as far as we know them. We have, to date, discovered two female skeletons in the garden of number 34 Hallerton Road, Kilburn. Victim one was between sixteen and nineteen, and victim two was between nineteen and twenty-one when she died. Both were buried between 1981 and 1983. We are appealing for anyone who stayed at the house during the time it was a bed and breakfast to come forward.'

Passing down a corridor at New Scotland Yard, carrying a file that the Assistant Commissioner wanted to see, Pat North heard Walker's voice coming from an open door and saw a television was on. She paused to watch.

'We are also appealing for anyone who may have information about these murders, or who thinks they may know the victims, to contact the Incident Room on the freephone number. All calls are strictly confidential. We are also trying to trace the owner of this distinctive leather belt.'

North drew closer to the screen as Walker dramatically held up two photographs, one showing the whole belt, the other a close-up of the buckle. She saw the look on his face and thought, with a smile: *Pure showmanship.*

The picture editors of all the national papers received email copies of the belt photographs simultaneously. But only one of them was in a position to print it straight away. The second edition of the *Evening Standard* hit the street with the sinister skeletal clasp dominating the front page. The news vendors' hoardings shouted the message: *VITAL CLUE TO SKELETON MURDERS.*

*   *   *

Graham Richards had been holding meetings all morning, organizing a tender for a complicated job he wanted his building firm to win. Now the meetings were done and he thought he might just catch the four-fifteen train home from Marylebone station. Crossing the street he saw a taxi with its yellow light shining. It stopped and he climbed in.

49

The driver had a folded evening paper on the dash, with the close-up shot of the distinctive belt clasp fully visible, even from the passenger back seat. Richards leaned forward and tapped on the glass.

'Can I have a look at your paper?'

The driver reached for the paper and handed it back over his shoulder. Unfurling it, Richards stared at the picture intently. Then he turned to the story which he read through twice, with intense concentration.

THURSDAY, 28 SEPTEMBER, MORNING

At seven forty-five, North drifted down the stairs to find Walker eating breakfast and reading a selection of papers at the breakfast bar.

'Great coverage! The belt's on every front page.'

He tapped the copy on top of his pile of papers and shoved back his chair.

'Batchley's late, I'm going to have to get the tube. Got a meeting with the Commander.'

'Problems with the case?' she asked lightly.

'No. He just wants the bodies identified as quickly as possible.'

He yanked his coat down from a hook in the hall and rammed his arms into the sleeves.

'Oh yes,' she said suddenly. 'I meant to ask. Have you thought about building clay heads?'

Walker frowned. Was he getting the good word on how to conduct an investigation? He suppressed the urge to voice the thought and said only, 'The best way to ID a skeleton is by looking at its teeth. Besides, I'm stretching my budget as it is.'

50

'Well, putting a set of gnashers on the front page isn't going to help much, is it?' She smiled wanly. 'It was only a suggestion.'

He nodded and looked at his watch.

'Yeah well, thanks but no thanks. Right, I'm not hanging about any longer. When Batchley eventually decides to show his face, tell him I'll be with the boss and to pick me up from there. I've got to go.'

He circled her waist with his arm and gave her a fleeting kiss.

'See you later.'

*   *   *

Batchley's car drew up seconds after Walker had turned the corner on his way to the Underground station.

'Hi,' he said to North at the door. 'I've come to collect Mike.'

She felt she might be blushing.

'You just missed him.'

Batchley clenched his fist.

'Shit! I got jammed up at the Hammersmith roundabout, it's gridlocked and—'

'Hey!' North interrupted. 'Long time no see.'

It had been. She'd first met Batchley three years ago and they'd got within a few dates of becoming an item. Then came Walker and Batchley had faded quickly out of her life, only to live on as a kind of bogeyman in Walker's mind, as if Batchley was only waiting to pounce and spirit North away from him. She had not seen him since he'd gone off to join the Kent force, but she'd always liked his unassuming manner and broad shoulders.

51

Batchley was embarrassed. Standing on her doorstep, he'd been acting as if he and North didn't know each other at all.

'Sorry, sorry,' he said, leaning forward and kissing her cheek. 'How are you? Er . . . I was going to drop you a line, you know about . . . I was really sorry, Pat.'

It was kind of him, she thought, to remember the miscarriage, even though he probably hadn't been going to drop her a line.

'Thanks,' she said.

North hesitated, then offered impulsively, 'Do you want a coffee?'

He thought, then shook his head.

'Better not, you know how he is. I'll get it in the ear all day.'

North guffawed.

'Tell me about it. He's in a bad mood already. He said to tell you he's with the boss so you've got a minute, come on.'

She drew him in and led the way into the living room.

'Coffee's on. What do you want, black or white?'

He followed her into the flat.

'Black, thanks.'

Batchley closed the door behind him.

'If he was in a bad mood this early in the day, it doesn't bode well for me. He gets the needle in whenever he can as it is. He's got me out on that site, mud up to my armpits, and he's loving it.'

His long face was comical and touching. She laughed.

'He'll never forgive you for us going out together. But you're not the only one he's stroppy with. I make a simple suggestion about the case

52

and he gets all uptight, as if I am treading on his toes.'

'Why? What did you suggest?'

She poured the coffee.

'I simply said that as you haven't ID'd either of the victims yet, he should make heads up from the skulls.'

Batchley clearly didn't follow her.

'There's a specialist,' she continued, 'who makes clay heads from skulls. Based up in Manchester.'

'Bit old hat now, though, isn't it?'

North shook her head vehemently.

'Not at all, there's no other method which competes and they've made some major advances; once the head's made you can photograph it, scan it into a computer, digitize and colour it.'

Batchley smiled.

'Sounds perfect for us.'

'You'd think so, wouldn't you?'

She proffered his cup and he took it.

'Thanks.'

He sipped.

'Well, he's always been a prickly sod.'

He sipped again.

'You've got a different haircut.'

She stopped to consider.

'I suppose I have . . . since I last saw you.'

He nodded and smiled.

'It suits you.'

'Thanks. Just a bit longer that's all.'

Now they both sipped.

'How's work?' he asked.

'Good, thanks. Not quite what I'm used to but I'm getting there. How are things with you?'

'Well, Mike certainly keeps me on my toes. Or

on my hands and knees more like. It's more interesting than Cobham anyway.'

'What about social life?' she asked.

Now it was Batchley's turn to blush, just a little.

'Pretty good too, thanks. I've been seeing this air hostess.'

He moved his hand slightly in the air.

'Nothing serious, but she's a nice girl and her jetting round the world gives us both plenty of breathing space.'

Suddenly she felt again that knot of tension in her neck. She sat down, shut her eyes and rubbed the place.

'You OK, Pat?' he asked.

She looked at him.

'Yeah, just a bit knotted up. Must have slept funny.'

All concern, Batchley came round the kitchen counter and stood beside her.

'I tell you what you need—a good massage.'

Now he was behind her with his thumbs gouging into her shoulder blades.

'Oh, that's lovely,' she exclaimed.

'There's this excellent guy at my gym, twenty pounds for half an hour, but he really does wonders. Sorted out a couple of sporting injuries for me.'

He ceased his kneading for a moment, took out his wallet and extracted a card. He gave it to her.

'Here. Give him a call.'

She looked at the card as he resumed his manipulations.

'Thanks. I might just do that. Hey, you're good at this. Oh yes, you're on it now. Can you feel that knot?'

                    *   *   *

Walker's meeting with the Commander was brief. He'd been asked to summarize what steps were being taking to identify the two bodies from Hallerton Road. He said they were steadily checking missing girls' dental records against the remains found, but had the feeling this move failed to impress his senior officer. *North was right*, he thought. In the whole field of murder investigation, there was probably nothing less sexy than dental records. The Commander had been more enthusiastic when Walker mentioned Interpol. That organization always made for good copy.

Walker was buoyed up again by finding the Incident Room buzzing with response calls from the previous day's press conference. Most of the information was about missing girls, from parents and relatives still keeping a flame alive for their loved ones, and came through by phone, fax and email. A few scraps of information from people who had used the guesthouse were added to the various charts and lists displayed on the Incident Room noticeboards. Everything was being collated by Collins.

He came over as soon as he spotted Walker.

'We have several more possible names for victim one that need checking out, Gov.'

He shuffled through the files he was carrying.

'Julie Bowling, Stella O'Kane, Hayley Baron, Jessica Jameson, Kerry Willis . . . all missing around the right time and all about the right age and height.'

He handed over the bundle of files.

'Great,' said Walker. Without ado he passed the files to PC West.

'Lisa, can you get on to these leads?'

'No problem, Gov.'

He pointed to a desk where the catalogue that West had extracted from the mail-order clothing company was lying.

'Don't forget your catalogue! Dave, any news from Interpol?'

'They've sent back a stack of missing persons' dental charts similar to our girls'. The forensic dentist is sifting through them for a match.'

'We might not need it at the rate these phones are ringing.'

Looking down the room his eyes narrowed as Batchley came in. He was talking to Collins about clay heads. Where had Walker heard mention of that recently?

'Cobham!' he shouted. 'Where the hell were you this morning?'

Batchley reddened.

'Sorry. Traffic.'

'Any news from the quagmire?'

'Well, our structural engineer has finally confirmed that we can't go ahead with the house search, not at the moment. It's unsafe.'

'Christ! So what does that mean for us?'

'More expense and delays. If you still want it checked, we've got to buttress the walls, prop up the ceilings . . .'

Walker ground his teeth.

'Well, I've got no other choice, have I? You'd better give your guy the green light and tell him to get a move on with the, er, buttressing.'

'Right you are.'

56

As he moved away, Satchell was waving and calling for Walker.

'Gov! Gov! You might want to take this call.'

Walker frowned.

'If it's the Commander, tell him I'm up to my arse in parsley.'

Satchell shook his head slowly.

'No. It's a Graham Richards.'

Walker blinked and snatched the phone.

'This is Detective Superintendent Walker, Mr Richards. How can I help you?'

The voice that answered was firm and confident.

'It's regarding the belt, Mr Walker. I'm not sure, but I think it's mine—or should I say, it was once?'

*   *   *

West was working her way through the files Walker had given her, calling the numbers of those who had phoned with information. She had quickly eliminated Julie Bowling and Stella O'Kane on grounds of hair colour. Hayley Baron's mother was a muddle about dates. It turned out her daughter was last seen in 1985, almost certainly too late for her to be one of the skeletons. Jessica Jameson had eventually turned up alive in Florida.

But Kerry Willis was another matter. Reported missing from a care home in South London in 1983, she fitted all the criteria so far known, though there was no photograph of her and nothing to link her with Hallerton Road. On the other hand, Mrs Florence Cartwright had worked in the care home all through the intervening years, and must have known Kerry. An interview was essential.

The place was a pleasant surprise. Light and

airy, it operated on the basis of friendliness, good order and positive thinking.

'Come into my office,' said Flo Cartwright. 'I've found some envelopes full of photos taken here at various times. Maybe we can find Kerry.'

But they couldn't. After shuffling through every print, Mrs Cartwright shoved the photographs back into their envelope with a sigh.

'I thought I might have a picture of her, but I don't seem to. I'd only just started working here, it was a long time ago. But I do remember her, her mother had just died—of a drugs overdose, I think.'

West handed across a colour copy of the page from the clothing catalogue.

'Do you ever recall seeing Kerry in a dress like this one?'

Mrs Cartwright took the sheet of paper and studied the dress which West indicated. She smiled.

'Yes, yes, I do. This dress caused no end of trouble. It was really expensive, you see, but she just had to have it. She sent off for it from a mail-order catalogue and couldn't pay for it, of course.'

'What did Kerry look like?'

'Well, pretty attractive really. She had lovely long dark hair but went and dyed it. Typical teenager.'

West felt a rush of excitement. She leaned forward.

'What colour did she dye it?'

'Red. A shocking red.'

West sat back in her chair and exhaled. She had not known she was holding her breath.

'Is there anything else you remember?'

Mrs Cartwright shook her head.

'Not really.'

'What was Kerry like as a person?'

This time the answer was thoughtful.

'She was a troublemaker, to be honest, and a compulsive liar. You never knew where you were with her. And she was always running away, but usually drifted back after a couple of days.'

'What was different about the last time she went missing?'

'Well, we had an idea she had a drug problem. We'd found syringes in her room, but she denied all knowledge, blamed one of the other girls. I'm sorry I can't be more helpful.'

West stood up.

'No, you've been a great help.'

Mrs Cartwright handed back the catalogue page, tapping the picture of the dress she had identified.

'But Kerry definitely wore that dress.'

CHAPTER 6

THURSDAY, 28
SEPTEMBER, AFTERNOON

Graham Richards had done well for himself. His place was a big detached house, standing prosperously in a suburb that bordered the countryside to the north-west of London. A new Jaguar stood in the driveway. Satchell whistled as he turned into the gate and swept up to the front door.

'Bet this cost a bob or two.'

Walker looked around, noticing the almost fanatical standard of maintenance in the landscaped area between the house and the road. Hedges and bushes had been trimmed. The grass looked sleek, the ornaments scrubbed, the tarmac black.

'Yeah, it's a bit of a step up from Hallerton Road.'

The front door opened before they even reached it and there was Richards himself, a tall, handsome man in a well-cut, charcoal business suit, seeming to fill his doorway. Walker sprang up the steps towards him.

'Mr Richards, Mr Graham Richards?'

'Yes, hello.'

Richards extended his hand and they shook. Walker classified the handshake as firm, confident.

'I'm Detective Superintendent Walker. This is Detective Sergeant Satchell.'

Satchell, too, put Richards through the

60

handshake test. He sensed a trace of sweat in the man's palm.

'Come on in.'

The interior showed taste as well as money, but not too much of either. There were children's toys scattered across the wood-tiled floor of the hall.

'Toys!' remarked Richards, scooping up a furry bunny and a toy car. 'Kids! My wife is on the school run collecting them.'

'We'll get this over and done with as soon as possible, Mr Richards,' Walker said reassuringly as he settled himself on the sofa.

* * *

Still insomniac and tense as ever, North had decided to take herself in hand. This afternoon she had made appointments with her GP, to get some sleeping pills, and with the masseur at Batchley's gym, to pummel and smooth away the tension.

'You've been through one hell of an ordeal, Pat,' Dr Andrews said after taking her blood pressure.

North shook her head emphatically.

'This had got *nothing* to do with losing the baby—if that's what you're trying to say. I feel fine! But I'm busy at work and I can't sleep. I just need some sleeping pills.'

Dr Andrews sat at his desk with his prescription pad in front of him, pen in hand. Yet he hesitated before rapidly filling out the prescription.

'Here, I'm writing you this but, ultimately, I don't think sleeping pills are the answer.'

He signed the form with a flourish, tore it off the pad and placed it on the desk in front of her. Then he opened a desk drawer and took out a card.

61

'We have a counsellor I can refer you to, and I think it would be useful for you to pay her a visit.'

North laughed.

'I'm not depressed! And I don't need some bloody shrink telling me this is all down to a tricky childhood.'

Dr Andrews held the counsellor's card out.

'Here's the card, Pat. I strongly recommend it. Sometimes it's difficult to sort your own feelings out after such an ordeal and depression is very confusing, but it's nothing to be ashamed of.'

Reluctantly she took the card. She saw the name: Sylvia Newberg. She dropped it into her bag, with no intention whatsoever of using it.

*   *   *

Graham Richards studied the close-up picture of the belt buckle in the shape of a skeletal hand. He was nodding slowly.

'Yes, I had one identical to that and it definitely went missing when I was at Hallerton Road.'

He handed the picture back to Walker.

'A skeleton's hand doesn't look like your style, Mr Richards.'

Walker was observing Richards with close attention, not just his replies but his mannerisms, the movements of his eyes.

'It isn't now,' Richards replied. 'But back then it was. I was into bikes and leather in those days. Look.'

He indicated a photograph on the table. It was silver-framed and showed him as a proud young Hell's Angel astride an old Triumph.

'And why did you live at the B&B for so long?'

62

Walker asked.

'Well, you see my father had left me a few thousand and I went into business with a pal. But it was a disaster, went belly up.'

'In the building trade?'

'No, actually it was importing stuff from India. That's where I got the belt. It was the tail end of the seventies and I was just a kid. Anyway, we went bankrupt. I lost the flat I had. In fact, I lost everything. And that was why I went to stay at the Nortons' place. Philip Norton said that if I helped out round the house I could pay less rent.'

'What sort of work did you do?'

'Well, it was a bit of a nightmare, actually. One minute he'd be doing the bathroom, then he'd move to converting the dining room into a bedroom, then he was going to do the same with the cellar. He was always looking for ways to squeeze more guests in.'

'What about the patio?' put in Satchell. 'Did you help with that?'

'Yeah. Philip was quite frail, so I had to do all the lifting and carrying of the slabs. It was a real problem because there was no back entrance to the garden and they had to be carried through the house. Mrs Norton did her nut, she was very house-proud, place was immaculate. Their daughter used to be forever cleaning.'

'Did Mr Norton prepare the ground to lay the stones?'

'Yes I think so. It was all prepared before I was there.'

'How long did it take to lay the patio?'

Richards shrugged, trying to remember.

'A few months.'

63

Satchell frowned.

'Seems a long time to lay a few paving slabs.'

'Yeah, it was. I think we got held up midway . . .
He'd not ordered enough stones or something.'

'Which end did you start on first?' asked Walker.

Richards cocked his head to the side.

'How do you mean?'

'Well, from the back of the house outward or
from the back of the garden towards the house?'

Richards nodded.

'Oh, I see. From the back of the house out,
finishing at the end of the garden.'

'And you were living there when the patio was
completed?'

'Yes.'

'Did you notice if the ground had been disturbed
at any time?'

Richards shook his head.

'No, Mr Norton always did the preparation. I
was just there to do the heavy lifting really. I told
him he should have had a compressor to level off
the soil. I'll tell you one thing, that patio was about
the only job Philip Norton ever completed.'

'What else do you remember about Mr Norton?'

'Well, he was very friendly. Had a bad heart, or
so he said. Liked his Scotch. Mind you, you didn't
want to be around him when he'd had a few.'

'Why not?'

'Well, he had quite a temper on him. Don't get
me wrong, I'm not saying he was the murdering
type, just he could get a bit out of hand when he
was three sheets to the wind.'

'Do you know if he ever had affairs?'

Richards laughed, a sudden jerky sound.

'Well, he was a wily old sod, always trying his

64

luck with ladies down the pub, but I'm not sure he was ever successful.'

'So he never took anyone back to the house?'

'Not that I saw. Mrs Norton ran a *very* tight ship.'

'What about his daughter, Kathleen?'

Richards picked at a loose thread on his sleeve.

'Well, she was . . . a bit of a lump, actually. Like I said, she did most of the work around the house for the guests, cooking and cleaning. They treated her like a skivvy. She and her mother used to have some screaming matches. They were kind of odd together, like they were vying for the old man's attention, and he certainly played them off against each other.'

He looked up and his glance again met Walker's steady, appraising eyes.

*   *   *

Walker was deep in thought as Satchell drove them back through tortuous traffic. After ten minutes the Detective Sergeant broke the silence.

'Don't you think it's odd that he never asked where the belt was found?'

The question surprised Walker.

'You think he knew?'

Satchell nodded judiciously.

'Hmm. Possibly.'

'But then why did he come forward?'

'Well, that's obvious. He's playing a double game to deflect suspicion off himself.'

Walker reminded himself of the personal (and very preliminary) conclusion he himself had reached about Richards.

'Maybe . . . but there's more to it than that, I'm

65

sure.'

Satchell shook his head darkly.

'I'd say he was trying to put Philip Norton in the frame.'

'Well, there was obviously something odd about the family.'

He lapsed into silence for another mile, then said, 'We need to build up a better picture of what went on in that house.'

Walker said nothing more until they had crossed Putney Bridge and, less than a mile from his home, he saw they were passing his favourite oriental restaurant.

'You fancy a Chinese, Satch?'

Satchell shook his head. He was seeing Catrina later.

'Some of us have homes to go to.'

'Oh, yeah, of course . . .'

Walker was staring straight ahead gloomily. Satchell, who knew his boss's ways as well as anyone, sensed the man's reluctance to go home.

'Is everything all right?' he asked cautiously. 'Between you and Pat, I mean.'

'I'm just hungry, Satch!' Walker snapped. 'I don't know about you, but I didn't get any lunch. Look, just drop me here. I'll get myself a carry-out.'

*　　　*　　　*

North lay face down on the padded bench as Batchley's masseur gave her a final rub-down. She had submitted to the full treatment, her flesh being pummelled, gouged, moulded and stretched. The man was an absolute expert. His fingers had persistently searched out every knotted muscle,

66

every taut ligament, and forced them into blissful relaxation. At the end of it she felt crisp and clean, like a shirt skilfully ironed. She was, for the time being, a woman renewed.

She left the massage room and, heading towards the reception area, made her way through the gymnasium and saw a sweating, tracksuited Batchley, with a towel wrapped around his neck, pounding out the miles on a treadmill. He spotted her and waved.

'You came in, then.'

'Yes.'

North suddenly felt a rush of warmth for Batchley as he flipped off the motor, skipped from the still-moving conveyor belt and jogged over to her.

'What d'you think?' he panted. 'Good, isn't he?'

'Well, I certainly feel a lot more relaxed than when I came in.'

'And you *look* more relaxed.'

In the awkward pause that followed they smiled at each other. Batchley removed the towel and rubbed the sweat from his face. Then North made a move to go.

'Well, I'll leave you to it. Thanks for the contact.'

'Actually I'm all done,' said Batchley, now towelling his hair. 'Have you got time for a drink?'

North glanced round at all the gym clients, red-faced, sweating, punishing themselves.

'Doesn't that defeat the object somewhat?'

Batchley shook his head.

'Not at all. Reward for hard work, I always think.'

She hesitated for the fleetest moment then nodded her head delightedly.

'Well then, I think I definitely deserve one, after all the hard work I've been doing.'

He rubbed his hands.

'OK. Well, there's a nice bar five or six doors from here. Turn left and you can't miss it. I'll get dressed and see you in there—mine's a pint of Stella.'

When Batchley joined her she was sitting with her own half-finished vodka and tonic and his pristine pint of lager.

'Excellent! Boy do I need this.'

He picked up the glass, put it to his mouth and she watched a third of the pint disappear at one visit.

'They didn't have Stella, so I got you Carling.'

Batchley smacked his lips and put down his beer.

'Perfect! Thanks.'

He nodded at her glass.

'Don't tell me you're on mineral water.'

She lifted her glass.

'Of course—teetotal me! Just kidding. Vodka and tonic. Cheers.'

She and Batchley clinked glasses.

'Cheers,' he said, drinking again, not quite as deeply. 'I tell you, working with your other half is enough to drive any man to drink.'

'You should try living with him.'

'Thanks, but no thanks. Anyway, *you* can't be seeing much of him at the moment.'

'Tell me about it. We both knew it wasn't going to be easy, but up to now we've really made it work.'

'And now?'

North gave a wan smile.

'Oh, we'll be fine. Just hit a rough patch, that's

68

all.'

Suddenly there were tears in her eyes and Batchley put a hand tentatively on her arm.

'Pat . . . you OK?'

She shook her head and sniffed decisively.

'Sorry, I'm fine, really I am. Just don't be nice to me or I'll start blubbing.'

She lifted her bag to her knee and rooted around inside for a tissue. Full of concern, Batchley put down his pint and moved around the table to sit next to her.

'Come on. This is *me* you're talking to.'

He tried to put his arm around her but she pulled away.

'Please don't. I've just been a bit emotional since . . . I'm sorry.'

'It's OK, no need to apologize.'

She smiled.

'I know. Listen, don't mention this to Mike, will you?'

Batchley made a surprised face.

'As if I would!'

'I just feel like I'm in this dark tunnel and I can't see my way out.'

She sniffed again, then laughed suddenly. The line sounded like something out of a melodrama.

'Oh God, just listen to me. I really have to snap out of this. You know what I thought I'd do?'

'Leave him?'

'No. Don't be silly. I was at the doctor's reading some magazine and they had this questionnaire: "Is Your Love Life Going Nowhere?" Yes! "Has the Spark Gone Out of Your Relationship?" Yes! So the suggestions were the usual clichés like surprise him in sexy underwear . . . or *no* underwear.'

She laughed, beginning to relax.

'But one suggestion was . . .'

'Leave him?'

'No, no. It was to take up a new hobby together, go to the gym or . . . have tango lessons.'

'*Tango* lessons?'

'Yes. Apparently the tango is a dance of love, desire and passion. Now, I ask you, can you imagine what Mike would say if I suggested it? "Tango lessons, you say? Have you been drinking, Pat?"'

'Well,' said Batchley sagely, 'you know what they say: it takes two to tango.'

Several vodkas and lagers later—after they had been round the conversational houses on the Hallerton Road case, her lecture in Manchester and the usefulness of clay heads—Batchley and North stumbled out into the rain.

'Hey, Pat,' said Batchley with a lopsided grin. 'Don't forget about the tango.'

He seized her hand and waist, spinning her round on the wet pavement.

'And—*one!*'

And they were tangoing along the pavement in the rain, laughing and not caring about the curious looks of passers-by.

*   *   *

An hour later North, her head still buzzing from the vodkas, stood in the small spare bedroom which since June had been known as Baby's Room. In all that time it had not changed. Soft toys sat around in expectant silence. The wallpaper was still in place, its teddy-bear pattern for ever askew where Walker's paper-hanging skills had been most severely tested. The barred cot stood opposite the door, crowned by a mobile of plastic policemen that would have turned in the air a foot above their baby daughter's head. A selection of Mothercare garments, from bootees to Babygro, lay in the brightly painted chest of drawers. So did a selection of non-tip drinking cups, easy-grip spoons and plastic bowls that could be fixed in place by rubber suction. On the chest's top was a nappy-changing mat. North sighed.

She fetched a large cardboard box and heaped into it the changing mat, garments, toys and plastic crockery. She unhooked the brightly coloured curtains, unpinned the nursery-rhyme posters and unscrewed the clamp that fixed the mobile to the cot. All this stuff was as good as new, but it was just clutter now. A charity shop was the best place for it.

When she came downstairs with her box of refuse, Walker was sitting in the lounge scanning papers from a document file. In front of him on the coffee table lay a stack of these files, alongside the remains of fish and chips in their greasy newspaper wrapping. He looked up from his reading and nodded at the box.

'Where are you taking those?'

'Oxfam.'

She put the box down and, drawing a wisp of hair away from her face, stood in front of him, her hands on her hips.

'Are you going to paint the nursery or shall I make a start on it?'

Walker could be astonishingly self-contained, and had cultivated a lifelong disdain for emotion.

But even he could appreciate that when a woman who wants children is forced to abandon the idea, that's a fairly serious moment. He reached out to catch her hand but she denied him, stepping smartly away. Walker lay back on the sofa.

'If it's *really* what you want then I promise I'll get round to it. I've just been up to my eyes lately.'

North swept up his chip paper, compressed it into a ball, walked into the kitchen area and opened the bin.

'You seem to promise a lot recently and not get around to it, Mike.'

Walker knew just what she was referring to.

'Come on, sweetheart, that's unfair. The lawyers are moving on the divorce papers. It's just Lynn, she keeps messing me around.'

'Well, isn't it time you sorted it out?'

'I've asked if I can have the kids every other weekend and she's refusing.'

'Why on earth don't you discuss things with me? Surely if we go round and talk to her . . .'

Walker quickly shook his head.

'You've not met her. She's incapable of talking rationally.'

'Well, I think we should, and the sooner the better.'

She pitched the ball of paper into the refuse. Returning to the sitting room, she picked up the box of baby things and strode out into the hall to put it in readiness beside the front door. Walker did not move.

'Can't talk to you either, these days,' he mumbled.

'What was that?' she called from the other side of the door.

He felt in his pockets for a cigarette.
'Oh, nothing,' he said.

CHAPTER 7

FRIDAY, 29 SEPTEMBER

Ronald Hargreaves was an octogenarian who could still enjoy a couple of pints of mild ale in the Gun and Duck at lunchtime. This was one of the few pubs in the area, if not the only one, in which you could still get mild, hand-pulled from the pump. It was all lager these days. Even bitter, as he'd known it in his youth, was an endangered species. He thought that was a crying shame, but what did it matter what he thought? He'd fought in Italy, worked all his life for the Electricity Board, lived to see his great-grandchildren born. But now, it was all he could do to get out to the pub and the launderette. His days were in the past.

The world belonged to the young, like the chap at the bar just now in the sharp suit. The chap who'd been talking to the landlord, Jack Wooley. The chap who was now pursuing Ronald and his dog, Prince, as they left the pub to wend a slow way back to their sheltered accommodation.

'Excuse me . . . Mr Hargreaves, isn't it?'

Ronald stopped in his tracks and turned deliberately towards the young man jogging towards him. He peered suspiciously at the police warrant card in the young man's hand.

'Yes?'

'I'm Detective Constable Doug Collins. I've been talking to your friend, Mr Wooley. He said you knew a Philip Norton.'

Ronald snorted.

'Never trust a word the bugger says!'
Collins hesitated.
'Mr Norton?'
'No, Jack Wooley.'
Collins was taken aback.
'So you *didn't* know Philip Norton?'
Ronald's baggy and bloodshot eyes narrowed.
'Oh yes.'
Collins, though bewildered, persisted.
'What was he like?'
Ronald looked down at Prince as if to consult him.
'Nice enough,' he said slowly and, after a pause, added, 'but his missus was a nightmare. Real troublemaker.'
This was clear enough to Collins.
'Did he tell you that?'
Again Ronald considered, then shook his head.
'Not in so many words, but we all knew about the police being called out.'
'What? To their house?'
'Yes. I mean, Philip could get a bit punchy, but he'd never have knocked her around.'
He clenched his fist and showed it to the policeman.
'I would've! She had him working dawn till dusk. He was always knackered.'

*   *   *

Collins managed to get back to the Incident Room and write up his report in time for Walker's afternoon briefing. First to speak was a triumphant Lisa West with news of the latest development.
'We have a match, guys! According to dental
75

records, victim number one is definitely Kerry Willis. And our care worker was probably right about the drugs, the latest pathologist's report says there was periodontal disease present in her teeth.'

Walker, who was studying his shoes, looked up questioningly. West nodded to reinforce the point.

'Apparently this indicates someone who neglects their mouth and it is very common in heroin addicts. He suggested she got the disease in her late teens.'

Walker frowned.

'Good God. She's been dead nearly twenty years!'

'What about the residents of number 34?' put in Batchley. 'Do we know if any of them had a drug habit?'

It seemed like a cue for Collins to enter the evidence of Ronald Hargreaves.

'I don't know about drugs,' he said, 'but one of Philip Norton's drinking buddies mentioned the police being called to the house. Seemed to think Mrs Norton was a troublemaker.'

He handed Walker his report on the Hargreaves interview as Satchell raised a finger.

'But Graham Richards said it was Mr Norton who had a temper. He even implied he could have had affairs.'

'Perhaps the girls could have been seduced by him?' suggested Batchley.

West pulled a face.

'Not a nice thought, a sixty-year-old bloke picking up teenagers.'

'Stranger things have happened,' said Batchley with an air of wisdom.

Walker had skimmed Collins's notes. He tapped

the paper where it lay on the desk in front of him.

'What about our Dorothy, then?' he asked. 'Any *skeletons* in her cupboard?'

He looked at Satchell for an answer. The Detective Sergeant showed a sheaf of reports stapled together: the inquiries into the Norton family background.

'Well, this is what we've got from calls coming in: our Dotty Norton was middle class, well-educated but never worked, until they moved to London in the seventies and opened the B&B. Regular churchgoer, very strait-laced but well-respected in the community.'

This was in agreement with Walker's own surmise as much as with his hopes. He had never fancied having to build a case of murder against an eighty-year-old woman.

'Good,' he said. 'Anything on the daughter?'

Satchell continued.

'She ran the B&B with her mother until her father died. Then she moved to Kingston with the mother to set up this retirement home. She currently spends three nights a week at a local community centre for the elderly—arranging bingo sessions.'

'Quite the do-gooder,' exclaimed Walker. 'Right. We need to link Kerry Willis to that house. Have we got a photograph of her yet?'

'Only her teeth!' West remarked.

Walker grimaced.

'Satch?'

'Well, we might have a name,' said Satchell, 'but we still don't know how she got murdered and ended up at number 34. We don't even know what she looked like.'

'Yes, and what about victim two?' This was from Batchley. 'We've got next to nothing on her at all.'

Walker was extracting a business card from his wallet. The name printed on it was Angus Taylor's.

'Thank you, Batchley.'

He handed the card to Doug Collins.

'Here, get on to this guy. We need to move this case on, so I'm going to get those clay heads built.'

*   *   *

At the Norton Retirement Home, the television news was on in the proprietors' private quarters. Kathleen was automatically knitting a cardigan while paying close attention to the story now being reported about the goings-on at her former home, and the two bodies that had been found there. An attractive young reporter was standing in the road at the front of the house, speaking straight to camera.

'Police yesterday revealed,' she was saying, 'that the first of the two skeletons found here at number 34 Hallerton Road . . .'

Terrible state the place is in, thought Kathleen, looking the building up and down. Once it had looked so respectable.

'. . . has been identified as Kerry Willis, a young runaway, who was sixteen years old when she went missing in 1982. Police are appealing for any family or friends of the victim to come forward. The second female skeleton discovered is yet to be identified, but both are said to have been killed in or around 1983.'

Kathleen heard the shuffle of elderly feet approaching the door of the room and used the

78

handset to switch off the programme. No sense in worrying Mother unduly. As the door creaked open, Kathleen continued impassively knitting the cardigan.

'They've got a name for one of the . . .' Dorothy paused, wondering what to call the phenomenon. 'Them they found in the garden. Kerry Willis. It was on the news.'

Kathleen frowned in concentration as her needles busily clicked.

'So will we be probably.'

She stood up abruptly and faced Dorothy.

'Stand closer and let me measure this sleeve against your arm. Hold it straight, Mother!'

Dorothy wore a resigned look as she hung out her arm.

'Why would they want *us* on the news?' she asked wearily.

Kathleen smoothed the unfinished sleeve down on her mother's arm.

'Well, we were living there. Someone in the house must have known something.'

Dorothy did not comment.

'One of those wretched men in grey suits, I shouldn't wonder,' went on Kathleen. 'It makes me sick to think about it.'

She tugged the sleeve to stretch it.

'There. Another few inches and that's the sleeve finished. Do you like this colour? It's ash mauve.'

'But none of the guests went *near* the back garden,' pointed out Dorothy.

Kathleen nodded and her voice darkened a shade.

'You're right. It was Father who spent most of his time in the garden. Why did you have to tell

79

them he did all the renovations? He was claiming for that back injury, remember? All those benefits ... What if they want to reclaim them?'

Dorothy closed her eyes for a moment and lowered her arm.

'He's dead, Kathleen. How can they know if he was sick or not?'

'He laid the patio, Mother, and that's where the bodies were found. From now on just don't speak to anyone, or make sure I'm with you when you do.'

At this Dorothy bristled suddenly.

'I am perfectly capable of answering their questions and anyway, I don't like what you're implying.'

'I'm not implying anything, I'm just warning you, that's all. They'll come and ask us more questions and we should be prepared.'

Her mother moved her lips silently for a moment, then said, 'Your father had nothing to do with those women. He would never—'

'Would never what, Mother? *You* may have been able to forgive him for all the nights he didn't come home till the Lord knows when, in fact you could forgive everything that bully did, but I—'

Suddenly Dorothy flushed. The impertinence!

'Your father *loved* me.'

Kathleen softened instantly.

'Yes I know he did. I'm only looking out for our interests. Here, put your arm out again.'

With a sigh Dorothy lifted her arm once more and Kathleen laid the knitting along it.

'And I *don't* like the colour,' Dorothy stated.

Kathleen nodded.

'That's all right. This isn't for you, it's for Cybil.

80

Did you know she'd had a stroke?'

She shook her head compassionately.

'Eighty years old, and she's got no one to look after her. You don't realize how lucky you are!'

*   *   *

Thirty-four Hallerton Road was national news now and the media had been keeping the place under siege more or less round the clock, eagerly monitoring events as the focus of the search shifted from the garden to anything that might be concealed in the fabric of the house. Today a knot of journalists and photographers quickly gathered round Walker and Satchell, as they arrived in late afternoon, after receiving a call from Batchley.

'The structural engineer's given us the go-ahead to begin work on the cellar,' Batchley had said. 'And, Gov, there's something down there I think you should see.'

'Is the building safe?'

'They reckon so. We've got the place held up with scaffolding.'

'Well, don't let it fall down till I get there,' commented Walker drily.

The press were overexcited at the arrival of the Senior Investigative Officer. They were hungry for a new development, a fresh sensation. Walker fended off their questions by the simple expedient of not talking to them. When he and Satchell reached the controlled area of the site, and began putting on the regulation white overalls, he looked back at them. He knew how useful the media could be, but there was something primitive, or at least insatiable, about them that he could never get used

81

to. The police could be basic enough, God knows. But journalists at a crime scene were like a pack of alligators. And behind them, pressing close to the tape cordon, there was a drifting assortment of members of the public, craning to glean whatever information they could.

'Look at them,' said Walker jerking his thumb. 'We'll be selling tickets soon.'

'Yeah,' said Satchell. 'Apparently the neighbours are charging for garden space so they can get a good view over the wall.'

Walker grunted in disgust.

'Sick little sideline.'

'And the school caretaker across the road found photographers on the school roof yesterday—bloody near threw them off it.'

At this moment Batchley appeared and led them through the house and down to the cellar.

'Sorry to drag you out,' Batchley was saying. 'But I thought you should be here for this.'

The cellar was dank and dirty but bright as day. An array of arc lamps, powered by a throaty mobile generator up in the garden, thrust their light into the darkest corners. Police officers in hard hats—men from Batchley's team—were systematically chipping plaster from the walls.

'We've uncovered what we think is an old coal hole,' Batchley explained. 'There's a chute from outside that's been bricked up and this end was hidden behind plasterboard.'

The plasterboard, once removed, revealed an iron hatch with thickly rusted hinges and bolts. One of his men was trying to prise it open with a crowbar but without success. He stood back, panting, and looked to Batchley.

'I can't shift it, Gov.'

'Let me have a try.'

Walker waved Batchley forward.

'Come on, rugby prop, let's see you in action.'

Batchley gripped the crowbar in his large hands and drove it into the small nick that had been made at a point between the edge of the door and the cavity. He yanked with all his might, once, twice, his whole considerable body weight bearing down on the lever. With his third pull there came the explosive sound of cracking concrete and the door catapulted open. A shower of dust and rubble fell from the ceiling directly onto Batchley's head.

Walker stepped past the spluttering Detective Inspector and up to the dark aperture. He stooped, shone his torch and pushed his head into the hole. He saw that it was the lower end of a conventional coal chute, narrowing slightly as it descended, perhaps three feet wide at the bottom. He directed the torch beam downward. The foot of the chute was a square space choked with black dust and draped with filthy cobwebs. Some object, or objects, had been deposited there. He reached out and poked it with a finger. It felt like a sack.

'Something's stuffed in here,' he called back.

He pulled at the sacking, which began to come away in tufts. Further rapid exploration revealed that it was a covering, not a container, and he quickly yanked it out of the way. He shone the torch again.

'Oh, God!'

The blackened skeleton was curled up on its side, knees beneath its chin, foetus-style. A pair of shoes was stuffed beside it, and they were a woman's.

CHAPTER 8

THURSDAY, 5 OCTOBER

The Commander had greeted the news that a third skeleton had been found in Kilburn with all his usual appearance of calm. The weekend media, on the other hand, had been verging on hysteria. Their main theme, which ran on every front page and every news bulletin, was the prospect of another horror like that of several years ago at 25 Cromwell Road, the Gloucester home of the serial killers Frederick and Rosemary West. There, bodies had also been recovered from both the garden and the cellar. In the light of this similarity, the Commander had called Walker over for an early Monday morning meeting at the Yard in order to warn, in his mild, urbane way, about the complications it was going to create.

'Mike, I've known you do some pretty wacky things, but I've never known you to panic, which is one reason I'm glad you're leading this case.'

Walker was not sure he cared for the word 'wacky', but he said, 'Thank you, sir.'

'But never forget that the media are literally insatiable and very tricky and *you've* got to handle them somehow, because they'll be interested in you and everything you do. You ready for that?'

Walker shrugged.

'I've done it before. All murders are meat and drink to the press.'

'Yes and, as we all know, if you don't feed them they turn savage. But this is already different from your bog-standard murder, Mike. More intense. More sensational. Remember the Wests.'

Walker shook his head impatiently.

'We're not in West territory yet, sir, and hopefully never will be. We've only found three bodies.'

'Well, the public think that's rather a lot. Make sure you talk every day to the DPA. They're the experts. And a lot of them are former hacks so they've been on the other side of the fence. Use that experience. And apart from anything else, if you get on the wrong side of them . . .'

As he seemed to be searching for an appropriate phrase, Walker supplied one.

'They'll let me get shafted, sir?'

The Commander smiled thinly.

'You said that, Mike, not me. They're professionals, but even professionals have their limits, you know. So save the abrasiveness for your murderer, will you? The DPA's there to help.'

Christ! Walker thought as he left the Commander's office. So the Director of Public Affairs had complained that he wasn't keeping them in touch with developments. As if he didn't have enough to think about already.

That interview had been three days ago, and in the meantime Walker's workload had piled up remorselessly. He had been in the Incident Room daily from seven in the morning until midnight. The weekend had not existed for him. Free time was a distant memory. He was up to his eyes in organizing stress counselling for his officers, writing two press releases per day, lobbying for an increase in his budgets, rostering overtime, chivvying for extra equipment and staff, handling

85

complaints from Hallerton Road residents, talking to the pathologist, liaising with the Borough Council and the coroner, soothing the developers and reading every note and report generated by the inquiry, a mountain of paper that was already well past the thousand-page mark.

In one way, the discovery of a third body had forced the inquiry back on itself, to start again from scratch. The new remains needed to be recovered and examined by the pathologist. The place of concealment and everything in it, including the cobwebs, had to be scientifically examined. The missing person files needed to be searched again. And there was yet another pair of shoes to be traced back to their origins. At the same time, the new find gave extra impetus to the team's efforts, to add to what they had already achieved. More than anything they needed evidence to connect the three females with each other, and all of them with Hallerton Road.

Identification was the key and Walker was now pinning his hopes on the work not just of Angus Taylor, but of the computer imagers. Photographs of the skulls had been scanned and were being worked up on screen into digital images of the women's faces as they may have looked. The variables of eye, hair and skin colour, hairstyle, and the shape of ear and nose were all taken into account. Meanwhile Taylor was working fast, his sculptures informed by the computerized experiments, but also by his own intuition and experience.

'Skull conformation suggests that victim number three was probably black, or Asian,' Taylor told Walker on the phone after his first day of work.

'We're trying out various options on the computer, then I'll plump for one when I make the clay head.'

'Will they look as if they're for real?' Walker wanted to know. 'I don't want to feel a prat if I put them on telly.'

Taylor reassured him.

'They'll look real all right, Mr Walker. They give me bad dreams sometimes.'

Now the finished heads had arrived and Walker, wanting to be alone when he unpacked them, had the three boxes moved into an office separate from the Incident Room. He closed the door and turned to the boxes in a row on the table. Carefully he lifted the flaps on the first of them. Layers of bubble wrap shrouded the contents. He removed it, then lifted out the head itself, which was supposedly that of Kerry Willis. It was an unnerving object, fully coloured and complete with mascara, eyeshadow and lipstick. Madame Tussaud could not have done it better. He put it down on the table, stood back and contemplated.

*　　　*　　　*

Perhaps the suggestion had been implanted by Taylor, but that night Walker dreamed of the heads. In his dream he arrived at Hallerton Road, and there he saw all three of them, loosely impaled on a row of spikes mounted in the wall beside the door of the murder house. He looked up at them, startled, curious, but oddly not frightened. Their eyes stared. Their matted hair shifted in the cold breeze. And the blood dripping from their gashed and gaping necks smacked the ground in front of his feet. A stronger gust of wind whirled around the heads and caught them. Suddenly they seemed alive, turning and nodding. He could swear the lips of one of them moved.

'Witchcraft, you know,' said a smooth voice behind him. He recognized the tones of the Commander.

'Did you say witchcraft, sir? But there *are* no witches, as far as I'm aware.'

'Yes, there are. Look.'

Walker turned to look, but the Commander was not there. Instead he was confronted by the wrinkled features of Dorothy Norton, standing immediately behind him, and wearing a strangely exaggerated female version of the Commander's uniform.

'Mark my words!' she enunciated darkly, pointing a bony finger up at the spiked heads. 'Public execution. That's what they can expect when we catch them.'

He stared at her. And then, like the pages of a newspaper lifted away by fire, he watched the skin peeling in layers from her face until all that was left was the skull, set only with a pair of bulbous staring eyes. In sudden panic he pushed at her.

'Get away! Get away!'

As he woke up he realized his hands in the dream had connected with nothing but bones under the phoney Commander's uniform.

When Walker yelled out in his sleep he woke North. He himself rolled onto his back and went back to sleep but she did not. She looked at him. His dream, whatever it was, had left him and he was snoozing peacefully. She smiled and rolled back into her own sleeping position. But, after a few moments, he started snoring. *Christ!* she thought. The least romantic thing about sharing a bed. She endured it for five minutes, then looked at the alarm clock: three a.m. She jabbed at him with her elbow.

'Stop snoring!'

Walker grunted and turned away from her on his side, not waking. North straightened her pillow, then smoothed the quilt over herself and closed her eyes. She tried to relax, but her thoughts were racing. She sighed, opened her eyes again and stared hard at the ceiling. The thoughts still buzzed in her head like trapped flies. Ten minutes later, with sleep no nearer, she eased back the sheet and slid out of bed.

She wandered in her nightdress into the lounge, yawning. Some of Walker's case notes were on the table. For once he had been home last night by nine, intending to work during the evening. He had fallen asleep on the sofa instead, leaving the files all but untouched. She sat down on the spot where he had slept and read the label on the topmost file: KERRY WILLIS. She reached out and flicked it open. There was a full-colour photograph of a clay head, with dyed red hair, a retroussé nose and clear, youthful features.

North smiled bitterly. Taylor's artistry was marvellous, but why hadn't Walker told her he'd had the clay head made? It had been her suggestion. Taylor was her contact. And he hadn't even *told* her!

Tears welled into her eyes. Communication between them was at a very low ebb if he couldn't bring himself to tell her he'd actually adopted one of her ideas. She got up to fetch a tissue in the kitchen. The rest of the night stretched ahead as she caught the sound of his renewed snores drifting down the stairs. She flipped the kettle on.

CHAPTER 9

FRIDAY, 6 OCTOBER

When Walker visited the three heads first thing in the morning he found they had lost none of their spooky quality. His dream had transformed them into items of gothic horror, but now it was time to give them a more mundane role. Time to see if any of the main players in the Hallerton Road drama could identify them.

Graham Richards had agreed to come in before nine, saying he had important meetings all morning. He was smartly suited and groomed and carried an attaché case, the image of a confident and successful businessman. Yet he was visibly shaken by the sight of the three beady-eyed female heads lined up so surreally for his inspection.

'This is so freaky.'

Walker nodded.

'Good-looking girls, weren't they?'

'So it would seem.'

'So, do you recognize any of them?'

Richards walked up and down the row, bending to look more closely. The first head was of a brown-eyed girl who looked about sixteen, with the kind of gaudy red hair that could only be dyed. The second was blonde, blue-eyed and looked a trifle older while the third was black, with Afro hair and a proud, almost haughty, expression. Richards gave each of them his undivided attention for ten or fifteen seconds then stood back, shaking his head.

'No, no I don't think I do.'

Walker let another half a minute elapse while Richards studied each face once more, this time attending to the profiles, stooping sideways to get the angle.

'I need you to be certain, Mr Richards,' Walker told him. 'You did not know these women?'

Richards straightened his back again. It was impossible to tell what he might be thinking.

'No, I'm sure,' he said soberly. 'I have never seen them before.'

Walker sighed.

'OK,' he said. 'Thank you for coming in, Mr Richards.'

'No problem.'

Walker nodded to Collins who had been hovering in the doorway.

'If you'd like to come with me, Mr Richards?' he asked.

Richards followed Collins out, sidestepping Satchell who had just appeared.

'No go?' asked Satchell when Richards was out of earshot.

'No. Any problem with the prints?'

Forensics had found a thumbprint on the belt buckle and Walker had asked for Richards to be fingerprinted, something which at this stage could only be done with Richards's consent.

'He agreed immediately,' said Satchell. 'He'll do it before he leaves.'

* * *

North had taken the morning off and caught the tube to the Angel, Islington. Walking through the Camden Passage antiques market, she headed east into an area of pleasant, middle-class residences. She had Sylvia Newberg's card in her hand.

It was a basement flat, the steps and area alive with colourful pot plants and climbing shrubs. She caught a glimpse of a woman through the window, busy repotting a geranium. The figure moved towards the door in response to North's ring. A few moments later the door opened.

'Mrs Newberg?'

'Yes,' said the woman. 'But it's Sylvia. And you're Pat?'

Sylvia Newberg was a smart, attractive woman in her late forties. She led North through to a cheerful sitting room with a view through French windows of the lovingly tended garden, and sat her down in a comfortable armchair. North knew perfectly well that Sylvia was not a shrink, but for some reason she had envisaged lying on a psychiatrist's couch.

She sat but did not subside fully into the chair, but perched on it with arms folded. Sylvia took the armchair opposite and settled herself comfortably.

'Perhaps you'd like to start by telling me why you've come to see me.'

'To be honest with you, now I'm here I don't know. I really don't want to waste your time, there must be a lot of people worse off than me, it's just that . . .'

This was horrible. It cut sharply against the grain. All North's life she had tried to handle her own problems and hated the thought of bending other people's ears with them. Now she was being expected to do just that. She cleared her throat, looked down at the carpet and tried to begin.

'Well, I went to the doctor because I haven't

93

been sleeping and he prescribed me some sleeping pills, just mild ones, I think, because they haven't helped me.'

She glanced up at Sylvia, who was looking steadily at her but saying nothing.

'So, as I said on the phone, he referred me to you because he wouldn't give me any more sleeping tablets.'

There was a silence as Sylvia waited expectantly. North looked down again. Between them was a low table on which stood a box of tissues. She searched for something more to say but her mind was blank. After a lengthy pause, Sylvia smiled.

'How are you feeling about being here?'

'Uncomfortable . . . I've never talked to anyone like this before, not that I've said anything yet but . . . I mean, I don't really know what I'm supposed to say to you.'

She again met Sylvia's gaze. The woman's eyes seemed neither interested nor bored, just endlessly patient. North shrugged helplessly.

'So what do you want me to say?

'I know it's difficult, but you can trust me. Anything you say to me in this room is completely confidential.'

There was another unbearable silence.

'People often find it difficult to talk,' said Sylvia soothingly. 'But I'm here to help you, and I can only do that if you talk to me.'

North was aware that her face was set in a bewildered half smile but she could not get rid of it. She shut her eyes. Get on with it!

'OK, well, basically, the problem is I'm still not sleeping. I get really tired and I've even been a bit weepy, low in energy. I don't feel positive about

94

anything and it's just not like me. I'm usually very positive.'

At this, Sylvia visibly brightened.

'OK, let's take a look at why you're not feeling positive about anything at the moment.'

'Well, the doctor went on about depression, but no . . .'

She shook her head.

'I'm really not that kind of person. I just want to stop feeling so low. I guess I just need some advice.'

'I'm afraid it's not that simple, Pat. I don't give advice.'

North frowned. She didn't get this at all.

'What do you mean, you don't give advice? What *do* you do, then?'

'I'm not here to solve your problems; I try and teach you to do that for yourself, through reflection.'

They sat for a further moment in silence. Reflection? North felt suddenly angry. She'd been led up the garden path. She was far too busy for reflection, for God's sake!

'Look,' she said, standing up. 'I don't think I can do this. I'm sorry, there's no point in me being here. I shouldn't have come. It's a waste of everyone's time.'

Sylvia also stood up, assenting wordlessly. She guided North back to the door.

'No point in pushing it, Pat. Maybe you'll feel differently in a day or two. Give me a ring.'

North nodded abruptly and retreated down the steps. Afterwards she felt ashamed of her rudeness. But she had not been able to help it.

When Kathleen Norton saw the three clay heads, she gasped. It was an immediate and involuntary acknowledgement of their uncanny realism.

'Miss Norton, please take your time,' urged Walker, 'and really look at their faces. See if you can recall any of them visiting Hallerton Road at any time.'

Kathleen walked slowly and heavily towards the first head and stared at it. Walker closely watched the body language, the expression, but Kathleen gave little away.

'No, I'm sorry. I don't recognize them at all.'

'They don't look in any way familiar to you?'

Kathleen considered and then dismissed the idea.

'No,' she stated firmly. 'No, they don't. I'm so sorry.'

'The first girl was called Kerry Willis,' Walker pressed. 'Does the name ring any bells?'

'Kerry Willis? It's a common-sounding name but I'm sure I don't recognize it.'

'What about our third individual?'

Walker pointed to the black-skinned head before moving to a computer terminal which stood on a desk opposite. He tapped in a command.

'We know she was not white, but we don't know any more about her ethnicity than that. Here are some possibilities.'

There were three digitally imaged variations on the appearance of the third victim on the screen. The first was a girl of Chinese appearance, the second was Indian and the third African. Kathleen gave the pictures a brief glance. She shook her

96

head.

'No. I don't recognize any of them.'

Had that response come a shade too quick? Or had Walker imagined it?

'We'll get a car to take you back to Kingston, then.'

'Thank you. I'm sorry, Superintendent, but I've never seen them before. Could you ask the driver to drop me off at the supermarket?'

Walker said goodbye and, looking down, leaned on the table on which the clay heads were displayed. Perhaps they were no good. How could Angus Taylor tell these girls weren't grotesquely fat or had broken noses, harelips, stuck-out ears? How did he know they didn't wear thick glasses?

'Gov, this is Mrs Cartwright.'

He turned to greet a woman he did not recognize, being escorted in by Lisa West.

'She identified the dress worn by Kerry Willis,' explained West.

'Ah yes, the care home. How do you do, Mrs Cartwright.'

Mrs Cartwright did not reply but seeing the three heads she immediately stepped towards the red-haired one.

'Oh yes,' she said in sudden recognition.

'Mrs Cartwright, do you recognize any of these women?' asked Walker.

She bent to inspect the head more closely, then looked at the other two.

'Yes. Yes, I do. Isn't this amazing? They're so lifelike.'

'Which one do you recognize, Mrs Cartwright?'

She pointed to the spiky red hair.

'This one is definitely Kerry Willis. She dyed her

97

hair just that colour.'

She touched the hair almost tenderly, then ran a finger lightly down the nose.

'Oh and there's something else now I've seen her...'

She pointed to the left cheek.

'She had a birthmark on that cheek. It would be about the size of a fifty-pence piece. She was very self-conscious of it, used to cover it with make-up.'

'What colour birthmark? Like one of those wine-stain marks?'

'No—more a pale muddy-brown colour. Nothing too terrible.'

'So for you, this is definitely Kerry Willis?'

Mrs Cartwright dropped her chin affirmatively.

'Yes definitely. That's her.'

Walker felt a load drop from his mind. It *did* work!

'Thank you very much for coming in, Mrs Cartwright,' he said as sincerely as anything he'd said all week. They shook hands and he nodded to West to conduct her out.

Walker turned back to the head of Kerry Willis. So she had a birthmark. She dyed her hair red. She was sixteen years old. And she disappeared off the face of the earth for seventeen years.

'What went on?' he asked in a whisper. 'What happened to you?'

*   *   *

Weighed down with bulging Tesco bags, Kathleen Norton lumbered past the door of the private sitting room and into the kitchen. From the accents reaching her ears through the closed door, she knew that Mother was watching some terrible Australian soap opera.

She dumped the bags on the kitchen table, noting the platter of half-eaten sandwiches that lay there, the bread stale and curling at the edges. With a deep sigh she turned her eyes towards the sink, in which dirty utensils, cake tins and mixing bowls were heaped unwashed. Mother had been baking for the residents' tea, one of the few things she deigned to do in the kitchen these days.

'I gave them the sandwiches you left,' said Dorothy, appearing in the kitchen doorway. 'For dinner. But they didn't like it.'

Kathleen was dipping into the shopping bag, bringing out a large plastic bottle of Coca-Cola and several tins of chopped tomatoes, tuna and baked beans.

'You've been gone a long time,' Dorothy went on.

Still Kathleen said nothing. She opened a cupboard and with massive deliberation stacked the tins inside.

'Everything all right, is it?' asked her mother.

Kathleen swung round and pointed at the machine beneath the draining board.

'You see that? It's a dishwashing machine. What have you piled everything up in the sink for?'

'It was full,' stated Dorothy. 'And did you hear what I said to you?'

Kathleen let out a long, dreary sigh and busied herself again.

'Yes, they didn't like the sandwiches.'

'So everything's all right, is it? I was worried.'

From another bag, Kathleen extracted a paper sack containing ten kilos of potatoes. This she

99

dumped by the sink, then rooted in a drawer and brought out a large stainless steel carving knife. She turned a venomous look towards her mother.

If looks could kill, thought Dorothy. She turned and retreated nervously back through the door.

'I was worried, that's all,' she said, disappearing once more into the sitting room, from which Australian voices could still be heard.

Left alone, Kathleen used the knife to stab a hole in the potato sack. She fished for a potato but lost heart as soon as she'd got it out. She put the knife on the table and the potato beside it. Grabbing the Coke, she twisted off the cap and applied it straight to her lips, sucking at the sweet effervescence greedily, mouthful after mouthful, until she had to stop for air.

Kathleen put the bottle down and, without removing her coat, trundled a chair out from under the table and plumped herself down. She planted her elbows, shut her eyes and breathed in deeply through the nose. When she at last opened her eyes she realized her mother's cake was right in front of her, a plump, cream-filled sponge from which just a couple of slices had been taken. Kathleen felt for the carving knife and automatically cut a forty-five-degree wedge. She raised it for a moment in front of her eyes then stuffed the whole slice into her mouth. Little cat-like mews emerged from it, muffled by the huge plug of sponge cake which she was working to reduce with her jaws.

Within two minutes, Kathleen had mopped up the last crumbs of the sponge. Had she then looked in a mirror—something she did as rarely as possible—she would have seen her cheeks and chin smeared with her mother's sweet whipped cream and jam, and her own salty tears.

101

CHAPTER 10

SATURDAY, 7 OCTOBER, AFTERNOON

Dorothy Norton had made so many difficulties over Walker's request for her to come in and look at Angus Taylor's clay heads that he scrapped the idea. He decided instead to go to Kingston himself, taking with him the e-fit images. So he and Satchell once again made the crawling car journey through Wandsworth and headed up Shooter's Hill to Richmond on the A3. By mid-afternoon they were standing on the step of the Norton Retirement Home, where it took a long couple of minutes for their ring to be answered. At last they heard a security chain sliding into place and the door opened a crack. They saw Dorothy Norton's eye, spying them cautiously.

'Afternoon, Mrs Norton, it's Detective Superintendent Walker.'

Dorothy closed the door, disengaged the chain and opened up again. She looked flustered.

'Oh, hello. I'm afraid this is a bad time. Kathleen's not here. You'll have to come back. She won't be too long.'

'Actually, it's you we wanted to talk to,' Satchell said, stepping past her into the hall.

'Thank you,' said Walker, following the Detective Sergeant.

'Oh, I see, well . . . you'd better come this way.'

She led them through to her sitting room, adjoining the office which Walker had previously seen. This room was spotlessly tidy, and the

102

paintwork gleamed. Everything had been thoroughly dusted and polished—the brass carriage clock and silver-framed family photographs, the television set, the coal scuttle in which stood a potted fern, the window panes and glazed bookcase doors. The work, Walker was sure, of poor, lumpish, martyred Kathleen Norton. The room's décor had a strongly Catholic theme. Several religious pictures decorated the walls and on the mantelpiece stood a Madonna statuette and a plastic bottle labelled GENUINE LOURDES WATER. A sheet giving times of Mass and confession lay on the top of the television set.

'Now, Mrs Norton,' said Walker, after briskly refusing a cup of tea and sitting down on the sofa. 'We've made some computerized images based on the remains found at Hallerton Road. Would you mind looking very carefully and telling us if you ever saw anyone like them at the house?'

From his briefcase, Satchell produced about a dozen colour printouts of young female faces, each with variant noses and hairstyles, some fuller of face and others thinner. He passed these across and Dorothy leafed through them, studying each picture before finally shaking her head. She handed them back.

'No, I'm sorry. I never saw any of them.'

'We've interviewed Graham Richards,' said Walker. 'Tell me what you can remember of him.'

Dorothy narrowed her eyes in thought.

'Richards?'

'Yes. Did you like him?'

'I didn't know him very well, to be honest.'

'But he lived in your home for, what? Nine months?'

She shook her head.

'Oh, that means nothing. Kathleen cleaned their rooms, changed their sheets, made breakfast. Not me.'

There was a bump from somewhere within the house. Walker looked up. The sitting-room door was ajar.

'Did he have a lot of girlfriends?' he went on smoothly.

'I don't know,' Dorothy told him. 'He certainly never brought them to the house. I wouldn't allow it.'

'Mrs Norton, someone brought those women to your house whilst you were living there. I am sorry to have to ask you this again, but did your husband ever entertain women friends?'

Dorothy's voice had been subdued but now she raised it.

'He wouldn't have dared, for one. And for two, if I'd have found out he'd have been out the door.'

'And it was your idea to have the garden made into a patio?'

'Yes it was, because Philip never got the lawnmower out. The lawn was full of weeds and rubbish.'

'And you let Graham Richards pay less rent for helping your husband, didn't you?'

Walker heard a floorboard creak outside the door. Again, he glanced up. For a moment, his eyes met those of Kathleen Norton, steadily watching him through the half-open door. He immediately looked back at Dorothy.

'I didn't approve,' she was saying, 'but Philip needed him.'

'Yes, we're aware of that. But for someone

104

unable to work and claiming sickness benefits, he certainly seemed fit enough to carry out extensive renovations on the property.'

'But he *wasn't*! That's why he needed Graham's help.'

Walker moved to another subject.

'We understand the police were called out to your house on two different occasions.'

Outside the door a floorboard creaked faintly once again. But this time, when Walker looked, Kathleen was not there.

'I don't know anything about that,' Dorothy was saying.

Walker lowered his voice, almost confidentially.

'Was your husband ever physically abusive towards you?'

This time Dorothy looked shocked.

'Never! Philip was a good husband and a wonderful father. There was nothing he couldn't turn his hand to, but he *never* turned it on me. The idea!'

Walker and Satchell left it there. As they made their way out through the fire doors they heard bumps and bangs emanating from the kitchen. Kathleen was unpacking more shopping.

'So, do you think she was covering up for the husband?' asked Satchell a few minutes later, as they made their way back to the car.

Walker was frowning. Dorothy Norton puzzled him.

'I'm not sure, but she certainly wants us to think that they were one big happy family.'

*   *   *

North was running full pelt on a treadmill at Batchley's gym when Batchley himself came up to her. He watched her for a moment with a broad smile on his face.

'Very impressive!'

North was laughing as she slowed her treadmill down to walking pace.

'Hi, Jeff. Thought I'd join you on your health kick. Supposed to be a good way of focusing body and mind, isn't it?'

'It works for me.'

Still strolling along with the treadmill, she became serious. She needed to say something about the drinks they had had, and the tango practice.

'Listen, I wanted to thank you again for the other night. It's not often I get a chance to talk things through with someone who actually listens.'

'Are you and Mike still having problems?'

She stopped the treadmill and pushed strands of damp hair away from her face.

'Oh I don't know. He says he still loves me and all that. And he was so great when I lost the baby. But we just haven't talked about it since. It's not easy.'

'How's the insomnia?'

'Oh, the same. I'm hoping if I tire myself out here it might help.'

She leaned towards him, resting her arms on the console at the head of the treadmill.

'Anyway, that's enough about me. How's things with you?'

'Pressure's building. Still up to my armpits in mud and no closer to ID'ing two of our girls, even *with* your clay heads. I only left there twenty minutes ago.'

North shook her head sympathetically.

'You came straight here? You're mad.'

Batchley shook his head vigorously.

'No, this is my sanity, my escape. I often come here on my lunchbreak.'

She sighed.

'Makes you wonder, doesn't it?' she said. 'Here's me feeling sorry for myself because I'm a bit out of whack. But can you imagine disappearing without anyone missing you?'

Batchley nodded.

'Yes. But thousands do.'

He looked at his watch.

'Hey, I'm almost due back for a briefing. How about a drink later? I shall probably get off at eight.'

Immediately she wanted to. In fact, she wanted more.

'Why not a bite to eat?' she said, attempting to sound casual. 'Mike won't be home till late . . . Can you get off earlier?'

She had the distinct feeling of dread, of going for broke. But Batchley's honest blue eyes sparkled.

'I reckon I can. And there's a brilliant little place not too far from here, Café Casablanca. Know it?'

'Seen it. Never eaten there. Eight thirty sound all right?'

When he'd left her, she set the belt of the running machine moving again. Suddenly she laughed aloud. Was this corny or was it corny? An assignation with an old flame in a restaurant called Café Casablanca? She was still laughing as the moving belt picked up speed. Later she would slip

107

down to Covent Garden and pick up something nice to wear for her date. Bogey and Bergman were riding again.

*   *   *

The DPA had scheduled a press conference, to be fronted by Walker, in half an hour. He was to pass on a few of the latest developments and show the world Angus Taylor's likenesses of Hallerton Road's three victims. As always on these occasions he was excited, even hyper. And he wanted the briefing to be just that: brief.

'Several fingerprints have turned up on the belt buckle,' he told the team, waving a file of notes from the Forensic Service. 'Some of them are definitely those of Graham Richards and all the rest are probably his. But there is one thumbprint on there that definitely does *not* belong to Richards. And I want you to know it's the clearest print of them all.'

He began pacing up and down.

'There have been no new leads on the identities of the second and third girls. We've tied none of them in with Hallerton Road or with anyone connected with it. We don't even know for sure how they died.'

Batchley raised his finger.

'Well, strangulation is the likely cause of death for victim two, Gov.'

'*Likely*, yes. But the pathologist couldn't even make a guess about the others. So now, think. Garden lime was found with all three bodies, but why are only two buried under the patio and one is in the coal chute?'

108

West piped up.

'Perhaps victim three was killed first, before the ground was prepared for the patio.'

'Or after the patio was finished,' said Batchley.

Walker nodded.

'Well, someone took their opportunity during those renovations. And Mr Norton was a sick man!'

'Norton could have been faking his illness,' suggested Satchell. 'He was fit enough to do all the work around the house, maybe he was fit enough to stuff the last girl into that coal chute.'

Walker didn't like it.

'What's his motivation?'

'Maybe he and Richards were in it together. Say they were into prostitutes, slipping them into the house when Mrs Norton was in bed . . .'

Walker nodded. He was feeling slightly warmer towards the idea.

'It's a possibility.'

Now it was Collins's turn to pick up the idea and run with it.

'Then Mrs Norton found out and killed them to keep them quiet.'

Walker snorted.

'She would have to be the *very* jealous type.'

'It could have been any one of the other guests,' said Batchley.

Walker shook his index finger in the air.

'No. I really don't think so. The bodies were buried at different stages of the renovations. The killings had to have taken place over a period of time, a few weeks at least. Only Richards stayed long enough.'

Satchell sniggered.

'Perhaps Kathleen was running a lesbian knitting

109

circle and they were her spurned lovers!'

'For all we know,' added Collins, 'it could be the Phantom Raspberry Blower of Kentish Town.'

There was a round of guffaws but Walker was not laughing. He glared round the room and pointed at the line-up of clay heads on the table beside him.

'Hey, guys, look at them. Look at *them*. This is no joke.'

*   *   *

North got home and slung the boutique bag onto the sofa. God, she'd forgotten how she loved to shop. She opened the bag and picked out a floaty and elegant silk scarf, which she draped and smoothed around her neck, admiring it in the mirror. Good, she still liked it. It was far from typical of what she normally wore but she felt a change was demanded. Next came a cashmere top and a beautifully cut satin skirt that set off her long legs.

She left her purchases and switched on the television news on her way to put the kettle on in the kitchen. Walker's afternoon press conference was the second story to come up.

She saw that he was flanked at the table by Satchell, Batchley and a man from the DPA. An array of microphones reared up in front of him. At various points the camera switched angles to take in a view of the three model heads, which were displayed on a side table. She brought her mug of tea close to the screen to see them better.

'Victim one,' Walker was saying, 'has been identified as Kerry Willis, aged sixteen years when she disappeared from Rackham House children's home, Peckham, in 1982. If anybody knew Kerry Willis will they please call the Incident Room on the freephone number. The other two victims remain unidentified. A white woman in her late teens, height five foot eight, and a teenage girl of ethnic origin, height five foot one.'

He held up two of the e-fit images.

'The digitized pictures taken from our model heads show what we believe these women may have looked like prior to their deaths. If anyone recognizes them please contact the Incident Room.'

A young crime correspondent in the front rank of chairs raised his hand.

'Is the house to be demolished?'

'Until all tests have been completed, it will remain a crime scene.'

Walker pointed to another questioner.

'Yes?'

But the same reporter had a supplementary question.

'Do you have any suspects?' he demanded.

North could see Walker was not enchanted with this line of attack but he kept his voice level.

'We are currently following several lines of inquiry and will of course keep you informed of any arrests we make in connection with this case. Yes?'

He pointed to another reporter.

'How were the victims killed?'

Walker's tone suggested regret at the need for a certain discretion.

'At this stage I am unable to give details, sorry.'

'Do you think there are more bodies buried? Another Fred West, perhaps?'

It was the young man in the front row again. Walker regarded him steadily.

'We are continuing a thorough and systematic search of number 34 and will keep you informed of any further discoveries.'

'Had the victims been mutilated?' a third hack wanted to know.

Walker shook his head.

'It doesn't appear so. The skeletons were all intact.'

A reporter whom Walker recognized from one of the national tabloids raised a pencil.

'Mr Walker, do you have any reason to suspect sexual assault in these cases?'

'No, we don't. And none to suggest that there wasn't such an assault.'

'And have you traced the owner of the belt you found?'

'We have a lead on that, yes, but I can't go into details at the moment.'

He pointed to the back of the room.

'Yes—you, sir.'

'Do you expect to make an arrest soon?'

Walker eyed the questioner with beady discouragement.

'I never expect anything. I keep an open mind. And meanwhile I assure you we are pursuing every viable line of inquiry.'

The bulletin moved on to the next story and North switched off. She reflected that Walker conducted a news conference in the same way as he ran his life: by giving as little away as possible. She looked at her watch. There was plenty of time for a good long soak before she went out.

At the Norton Retirement Home Kathleen, too, had watched the news with keen interest. Now she was sitting by Hubert, her oldest resident, who had complained of feeling ill at dinner and was quite unable to eat. He sat hunched in his wheelchair like a pathetic, shrunken husk of a man.

'I've brought you a bowl of soup,' she was cooing. 'Now I know you might not be hungry but you need to keep your strength up.'

She tucked a serviette into Hubert's collar and very carefully filled the spoon. She lifted it to his mouth.

'This is full of vitamins and it's nice and hot, just as you like it.'

Sip by sip, Hubert obediently took his nourishment, while Kathleen thought about the policeman she had been watching so intently on the television screen a few minutes earlier. He had been in this house twice but she did not think they'd seen the last of him yet. He was hardly the type to be trifled with or easily deflected. She felt in her bones that he would not rest until he had nosed out the truth, however bitter it might turn out to be. A cold shudder ran down her spine then, but she mastered it and was able to deliver a last spoonful into Hubert's mouth with her usual steady hand. Then she gently wiped his lips and gave his head a loving stroke.

'*Good* boy,' she murmured. 'We're playing bingo tonight. I'll be your partner, if you like.'

*   *   *

To North's alarm, Walker was not as late home as she had expected. When he pushed through the front door, carrying a particularly fat bundle of files, she was steam-ironing a few unwanted creases out of her new skirt. Freshly bathed, she was beginning to feel a pleasant buzz of anticipation about the evening ahead. Walker kissed her lightly as the iron hissed and puffed out steam.

'You going out?' he asked.

'Yes,' she said, improvising rapidly. 'I'm seeing Viv. You'll have the whole place to yourself.'

He dumped the files into an armchair.

'Good. I've got a ton of paperwork to get through.'

'There's a frozen pizza if you want it.'

He looked across to her.

'Look,' he said, 'when I said "good", I didn't mean—'

She laughed.

'I know what you didn't mean, Mike.'

'That's OK, then. I need a drink.'

Half an hour later she had gone, dressed in the new finery. Walker, with his sleeves rolled up and a second whisky at his elbow, was already cutting swathes through the files when the phone rang. He snatched it up.

'Walker.'

'Hi, Mike. It's Vivien.'

'Oh! Hello, Vivien. She's already left so she'll be with you shortly.'

'What do you mean, be with me? You mean she's coming over? She never said anything to me about it. And I'm going out in a minute.'

Walker tried to remember exactly what North had said. He was *sure* she said she was meeting Viv.

114

He shrugged.

'Maybe I misheard. Anyway, did you want her? Is it urgent?'

'No, no. Not particularly. But Mike, is Pat all right?'

'What do you mean?'

'Well, I've been worried about her. She hasn't been herself lately.'

Walker thought for a moment.

'Why, has she said something to you?'

'No, look, it might be nothing. I shouldn't have mentioned it. Just tell her I called.'

'Will do. Bye now.'

He put the telephone down. He must have misheard through the puffing of the iron. Perhaps she said 'Liz'. He was sure she must have at least one friend called Liz.

He shrugged and went back to his files and his whisky.

CHAPTER 11

MONDAY, 9 OCTOBER

On the Sunday evening, after the press conference, Walker appeared on *Crime Night*. The programme attracted a huge audience with its appeals for the public's help in solving difficult police cases. The Hallerton Road skeletons had not been among the night's specially featured items. These were invariably structured around a filmed reconstruction of the crime and, as yet, too little was known about what had gone on at Hallerton Road to allow for that. So Walker was limited to a short interview during which he again displayed Angus Taylor's heads.

The viewing audience were impressed.

'We've had over three hundred calls from people claiming to recognize our girls from the model heads,' reported Doug Collins at the briefing the following day. 'We've already filtered them into high, medium and low priority, so now it's just a case of ploughing through them.'

Lisa West had been one of the ploughing team.

'I think I might have something,' she announced. 'A Greta Bertrum called in. Says she thinks victim two is an old friend of hers: a German girl called Ingrid Kestler. She's scanned in a photograph of Ingrid and emailed it to us. Here, take a look.'

She crossed to a PC, tapped in a command and Greta Bertrum's snapshot appeared. Walker and the team crowded round. Somebody whistled.

Another murmured, 'Bring on the dancing girls!'

The screen showed a fuzzy image of two bare-breasted girls wearing only G-strings. Both were blondes. Behind them, in the shadows, sat a ring of men, all of them leering and most probably the worse for drink or drugs. West pointed to the skinny, big-eyed girl on the right.

'See this one here?'

With a click on her mouse she enlarged the girl's face, moving it to the right of the screen. Then, on the left, she brought up one of the e-fit images from the clay heads.

'She does look very like our girl.'

West highlighted the e-fit and dragged it across to superimpose it over the face on the snapshot. It was only a rough fit, but they could all see West's point: the same high forehead, the same deep-set eyes.

'What did you say her name was?' asked Walker.

'Ingrid Kestler.'

'Well, let's go and talk to her friend.'

'Bit of a schlep, Gov. She lives in Sweden.'

Walker blinked.

'Sweden?'

He frowned, thinking of the delay, the cost. Then Batchley spoke up.

'Gov, can I make a suggestion?'

'Go ahead.'

'Well, there's this guy in Technical Support who can tell you for sure if she really is our victim.'

'Go on.'

'He can use image enhancement on the photograph to work out the exact dimensions of the skull, and then overlay the photos and see if they match. If they do—bingo! There's your girl.'

Walker, despite himself, was impressed. He said,

117

'Not just a pretty face, are you?'

He looked round.

'Right, let's get on to Batchley's technical chappie. If we do have a match then we need to get this Swedish lady over here.'

Satchell brightened.

'Let's hope she's related to the blonde one from Abba . . . those tight white trousers . . .'

Without meaning to, he had spoken out loud.

'Act your age, Dave,' said someone.

Satchell laughed.

'Abba? That *is* my age—when I was ten. And if I'm not much mistaken, this Greta's a proper Dancing Queen.'

Collins did not join in the repartee. He was still staring intently at the scan.

'Gov?' he called.

Walker turned back to the computer. Collins tapped the screen.

'Is that who I think it is?'

Walker leaned forward and squinted.

'Who?'

'Him!'

Collins was indicating a dishevelled and moustached young man immediately behind the putative figure of Ingrid Kestler. His head was only half in the light.

'Hold on,' said Collins, dragging a box around the face and clicking to enlarge it. The result was badly out of focus but the features could be seen. Walker took a step backwards and looked again.

'It's Richards!' he exclaimed. 'Graham Richards. And he's a lying bastard.'

*　　　*　　　*

118

A search on the Interpol database quickly brought results. Ingrid Kestler was a young German woman, reported missing by her parents near Hamburg in 1981. She had been last heard of in London but the British police, believing she had left the country, had returned the file to Germany. A boyfriend in Berlin was questioned but he knew nothing. Other lines of inquiry led nowhere. The file on her disappearance had remained open in Hamburg ever since.

Meanwhile, working on the Bertrum photograph, Tech Support tested the hypothesis that Ingrid was the second Hallerton Road victim. Analysis of her head provided a range of key dimensions to her skull, which were then compared with the actual skull dug up on 25 September.

'And?' asked Walker, on the phone to the computer technician. The man had been astonishingly efficient, performing the analysis within an hour of receiving the photograph.

'They're a very close match. Virtually identical, actually.'

'But not *actually* identical?'

'Well, there's a built-in margin of uncertainty, of course. Our projected skull dimensions are unlikely to be accurate to the nearest minute fraction of a millimetre. But the correlation between our estimate and the true measurements of the skull from Hallerton Road is so close that we can say we're better than 99.9 per cent certain.'

'And you could swear to that in court?'

'Yes. In my opinion these are either the same woman or identical twins.'

It was enough for Walker. Ingrid Kestler didn't

have a twin.

Half an hour later he was on the phone to Sweden.

'Miss Bertrum,' he said, after introducing himself.

'It's *Mrs* Bertrum, actually.'

'Ah! Mrs Bertrum. Well, I believe you saw a report of our appeal for information about some bodies found at Hallerton Road in north-west London. And the picture of one of our model heads reminded you of a friend, Ingrid Kestler. Is that right?'

'Yes. It was scary. It looked so like her.'

'And the photograph you sent us. Where was it taken?'

She hesitated, then said, 'Look, this is rather sensitive and I really don't want to talk about it on the phone. But the day after tomorrow, by chance, I'm going to be in London. Business. Would you care for me to drop in and see you?'

He raised a clenched fist and shook it in delight.

'On Wednesday? Oh, yes. That would be very good. But look, before you hang up . . . if you could just tell me the name of the club, I'd be very grateful.'

'The Rhinestone. Soho. That's all I can say now. But I'll see you on Wednesday. Bye.'

She hung up.

CHAPTER 12

TUESDAY, 10 OCTOBER

At her work station in the Incident Room, Lisa West put down the phone and scribbled a few details on a memo pad. She ripped the page and swivelled her chair towards Dave Satchell, who was sitting behind her. Having been on the phone all morning to various parts of Europe, he was now waiting for a contact with Interpol in Bonn to call him back. But it was twelve fifteen and he was beginning to suspect the German police had all gone to lunch.

'Dave?' said West.

'Yeah?'

'You know we're trying to trace the owner of the Rhinestone Club?'

'Yes,' said Satchell. 'What have you got?'

'No luck on the owner but I've tracked down one of the dancers for you, via Equity. She's called Tammy Delaney.'

She fluttered the paper with the details.

'Want me to follow it up?'

'No,' he said.

He leapt to his feet and took West's handwritten notes.

'All exotica is mine.'

'I thought you might say that.'

He read the details of where to find Ms Delaney. He read them again.

'Zippo's Circus?' he asked incredulously.

121

Zippo's had recently pitched its big top on Clapham Common for a short season of performances during the school half-term. A large ring of support caravans surrounded the site. Satchell had not been to the circus for years and it felt good to be walking through the showground, with evidence all around of the old circus traditions. Acrobats had put mats out on the grass and were practising handstands and running somersaults. A strong man in a leopardskin leotard and nailed boots strolled across his path. A group of primary school children were being given a masterclass in juggling. Satchell strolled on looking for someone to ask. Two long-legged female performers were coming towards him, dressed in slinky costumes, with huge plumes on their heads and rubber boots on their feet. It wasn't until they came within a few yards that he realized they were identical twins. He asked after Tammy Delaney.

'Wardrobe trailer,' said one.

'At the far end,' said the other.

'By the big top,' said the first.

It was a large trailer stuffed with rail upon rail of costumes: silks, sequins, feathers and masks, and baggy trousers a-plenty. There was a pervasive aroma of the strongest cheap perfume. He paused at the foot of the steps and looked in. A woman of around fifty, wearing a silk kimono and plenty of make-up, was re-hanging an armful of harlequin suits.

'Tammy Delaney?' he called up.

'Uh-huh.'

'Could I have a word?'

Tammy took a look at him. She did not smile.

'If you've got muck on your shoes, leave them outside.'

Satchell checked his shoes for mud and climbed up the steps. He showed his ID.

'DS David Satchell, Metropolitan Police. My shoes are clean, I promise.'

Tammy's face fell when she saw the warrant card.

'Ah, shit. What's that slob done now? We're divorced. I don't know where he is or what he's doing.'

'No,' said Satchell. 'It's you I need to talk to.'

'Oh yes? About what?'

Tammy turned towards him and rested a hand on her hip with perfect grace. Satchell had a weakness for a certain type of older woman, specifically blondes like Tammy. He could easily see what hot stuff she must have been onstage, in her prime.

'Well, you used to work at a club in Soho, the Rhinestone? Back in the late seventies, early eighties?'

Tammy was cagey.

'What about it?'

'Could you just have a look at this? It's a photograph of some of the girls.'

Tammy slipped a pair of glasses onto her nose and examined the photo that Satchell brought to her. It was Greta Bertrum's snapshot taken at the club. Tammy shook her head.

'I'm not on this. I did work there but this must have been taken either before or after my time.'

She pointed to the topless dancers in the foreground.

123

'I don't know either of these girls. I was a solo artist. A contortionist. Had to give it up eight years ago when I had a hip replacement.'

Satchell pointed to Ingrid.

'So you never knew *this* girl? Her name was Ingrid Kestler.'

Tammy took the photograph and studied it beneath the electric light. She again shook her head, this time even more decisively.

'No. Like I said, I don't recognize any of them.'

Satchell did not think she was lying. He moved on to the next topic.

'Do you know the name Graham Richards?'

'No, I don't think so.'

'We think he could have been a customer at the club.'

She reflected.

'Graham Richards . . . No. Now *this* guy here. He was one regular I do remember.'

'Which one?'

Satchell leaned over to look and was startled. She was pointing at the shadowy figure he had already decided was Richards.

'A real charmer, him,' she stated. 'Went through the girls like a dose of salts.'

Satchell tapped the face of the man who might be Richards.

'*This* one?'

'Yes, him. Used to be an older guy with him sometimes. Pair of them were at it . . . bondage! Never tried it on with me. I stayed well clear!'

Satchell arched his brows innocently.

'Why was that?'

Tammy's mouth formed an 'O' in mock surprise at Satchell's question.

124

'Oi, cheeky! I was into a lot of things but not that
. . . Anyway, I heard that he could get a bit rough,
you know, slapped the girls around. Used to do a
lot of . . .'

She put her fingers under her nostrils and made
an exaggerated sniff.

'It made him nuts, of course. It does that to
some people, makes them paranoid.'

'So he'd get high then knock the girls around?'

'So I heard.'

'What about the older guy?'

'I don't know about him. Just *this* guy. Always
had a bag of Charlie to hand out.'

'So he was dealing drugs?'

'No, no.'

Tammy smiled indulgently, as someone who
knew the way of the world better than any young
Detective Sergeant.

'He traded it to get laid. I never touch the stuff
myself.'

'So . . . sorry to ask you again. But when exactly
did you work at the Rhinestone?'

Tammy tried to remember.

'I was there for a year or so, must have been . . .
Oh God! When was the royal wedding?'

' '81?'

'Right. I was there for that.'

Satchell gently took back the photo and tucked it
into his pocket.

'Well, thanks very much for your help.'

She followed him to the door and saw him down
to the ground.

'It just goes to show, doesn't it? Hips might have
needed replacing but the old brain cells are still
working.'

It was odd. Most people when questioned by Satchell wanted to know what it was all about, but not Tammy. She seemed completely detached from it all. Was it Valium? Vodka?

'You want a ticket for the show?' she offered. 'We could have a few drinks after.'

Vodka, then. But Satchell hesitated. Tammy must have been quite something at one time. Then he pulled himself together and said, 'Thanks, but really I've got to get back.'

'I used to top the bill at the Rhinestone, you know.'

Satchell smiled encouragingly, then turned and left.

CHAPTER 13

WEDNESDAY, 11 OCTOBER

Walker sat in his office in the corner of the Incident Room with his hands resting on an unopened document file. He rubbed his face. Lynn had been on the phone the previous evening, giving him a good half an hour's earbashing, mostly about cheques she wanted him to write. She was being as stubborn as a mule about the divorce. She kept badgering him to attend meetings with her solicitors present, though Walker said over and over he wanted to work it all out informally.

'Surely we can sort it, just between the two of us. Hey, Lynn?'

'None of that "Hey Lynn" stuff, Mike. I'm not going to let you just career off with your girlfriend and leave me and the kids high and dry. We won't be ripped off.'

But he didn't want to think about his ex-wife. He wanted to re-enter the world of sanity represented by yesterday's reports. With a sigh he opened the file and scanned Satchell's note about his interview with Tammy Delaney.

It had certainly thrown up a number of possibilities. That Graham Richards had been into sadistic sex, fuelled by drugs. That he was in cahoots with Philip Norton, the 'older man'. That together they had picked up the girls in the Rhinestone Club, lured them to Hallerton Road with the promise of drugs, then raped and killed them. Based on what they knew, and on Tammy

Delaney's evidence, it was possible to believe that this was indeed the story. But Walker, he didn't think it quite added up—at least, not yet.

Tammy's story would need corroboration. She had been unable to confirm the man's name and they were a long way from proving that the man in the picture was indeed Graham Richards. Walker had automatically branded Richards a liar when spotting his resemblance to the moustached man at the Rhinestone. Otherwise the similarity would have to be a coincidence, and he always acted on the assumption, as had been drummed into him years ago at Hendon Police College, that in a murder inquiry there were no coincidences. And yet, and yet . . . Walker had been inclined to believe the essence of Richards's story when he and Satchell had visited the man's home—the belt that went missing, his surprise on learning that under the patio he had helped lay were two graves. And Richards had behaved impressively when he'd come in to look over the heads. If he *were* a liar, he was a bloody good one.

Walker's ruminations were interrupted by Satchell, who entered in a tearing hurry.

'Gov, she's here.'

Satchell was looking flushed and out of breath.

'What are you in such a dither for?' asked Walker.

'She's, well . . . she's . . . in Interview Room 3.'

'Who is?'

'Greta. Our Swedish woman.'

*   *   *

The unattainable Greta Bertrum approached a

128

good deal nearer to Satchell's ideal of a sexy older woman than the needy and vulnerable Tammy Delaney. Both women were blonde and of roughly the same age, but life, chance and the ageing process had been far kinder to Greta. Her long hair, which she wore swept up under pins at the back of her head, was groomed until it shone. She wore designer jewellery, top-of-the-range perfume and an expensive-looking silk suit, its colour a rich pink, the hem of its skirt ending just above the knees. Her legs were still those of a dancer, slim and long, and so was her elegant neck. She showed plenty of cleavage but, in her, even this seemed a mark of class, rather than brass.

Walker introduced himself and his Detective Sergeant, towards whom Greta smiled graciously, inclining her head.

'We met downstairs.'

In manners she was up there with the Queen of Sweden. Satchell took a seat at the table opposite Greta and opened his notebook. He looked mesmerized. Walker paced around the room.

'Well, our Technical Support team have analysed the photograph you sent us,' he told her. 'I'm afraid it would appear that your friend is indeed our second victim. I'm sorry.'

Greta shook her head sadly.

'I knew it was her. It was only by chance that I noticed the newspaper. My husband had been over here on business and brought it back with him. The story hasn't been news in Sweden.'

'How well did you know Ingrid?'

'Not very well. We worked together for a few months when I was living here.'

'And when was that?'

129

'Oh, it must have been . . . 1982, '83.'

'And you haven't seen Ingrid since?'

'No. I moved back to Sweden soon after.'

'You said you worked together, where was this?'

'At the Rhinestone. The club in the photograph.'

Satchell opened a file and produced the photograph, which he laid on the table between them. She reached towards it with slim fingers and touched the figure of the girl on Ingrid's right.

'That's me.'

Satchell raised his eyebrows.

'So you were both . . .'

She looked at him and acknowledged his unfinished question with a slow blink of her long-lashed eyes.

'Exotic dancers, yes.'

Satchell's eyes strayed lingeringly from her face to her cleavage before returning to his open notebook.

'What was Ingrid like?' asked Walker.

'She was very outgoing, and friendly. She hadn't been in London very long. She was from Germany.'

'Do you know where she stayed?'

'I have no idea. We just worked together.'

'So you wouldn't know about boyfriends?'

Greta smiled.

'I never met him, but I knew she had one.'

'Do you remember his name?'

Greta thought hard. Eventually she shook her head.

'No. Sorry. In fact the only reason I remember her talking about him was because he'd got her pregnant and then disappeared. She was so preoccupied and upset about being pregnant . . . kept changing her mind about what to do. One

130

minute she wanted to keep it, the next she was worried about having to stop working.'

Walker stopped pacing and looked at her.

'I thought you said you didn't know her very well. Why would she give you such personal information?'

Greta's tone, previously soft and melancholy, suddenly hardened.

'If you strip down naked next to someone every night, you soon get to know all their intimate details, but that doesn't mean we were close friends.'

Walker and Satchell both nodded. Satchell found himself imagining Greta Bertrum naked. Walker moved on to another topic.

'Do you know if Ingrid worked as a prostitute?'

Greta didn't much like the question and she answered it starchily.

'I have no idea. As I said, we were *not* close friends.'

'Is there anyone else we could talk to who knew her better?'

Greta shrugged.

'The other girls in the club . . . the owner, I guess . . . but I haven't kept in touch with any of them and I think the Rhinestone has closed down now.'

'Did you ever hear Ingrid mention a man called Graham Richards?'

He watched her. The eyes did not flicker. He went on.

'Dark, good-looking guy, moustache, in his mid-twenties at that time, lived in North London.'

'No.'

'How about a Philip Norton? Older man.'

She smiled, as if she wished she knew the name.

'No, sorry.'

'Kathleen or Dorothy Norton?'

Greta looked around for her bag, hooked her fingers around the shoulder strap and stood up. She was clearly terminating the interview.

'No, I am really sorry. I have told you all I know.'

She looked at her watch. Walker nodded.

'And there's no one else in this photograph you can put a name to? Anyone in the background?'

'No.'

'OK. Well, thank you for coming in. Will you be available for further questioning, should we need that?'

Her tone suggested this was not an enticing prospect, but she said, 'I'm in town for another couple of days. At the Ritz.'

Jesus! Walker thought. He said, 'Right! Thanks again.'

Satchell eagerly took responsibility for seeing Greta Bertrum out, leaving Walker alone. He lit a cigarette.

'Gov?'

It was Lisa West at the door.

'I've got the latest from Interpol and—'

Walker interrupted her flow, jerking his thumb in the direction Greta had taken with Satchell.

'We're not coughing up for her stay at the Ritz, are we?'

West laughed.

'No, don't panic, she even paid her own airfare. She was over on business, remember? And look, we're getting a lot of data in for Ingrid Kestler from the Interpol missing persons' list.'

As she proffered the file, Satchell came back, his face alight.

132

'Oh boy, I'd like to see her do an exotic dance.'

Walker stubbed out his cigarette.

'Huh. I bet she offered a bit more than an exotic dance to her special clients. And the odds are so did Ingrid.'

'You're right,' said West, showing the Interpol file, which Walker took. 'It says there she was a known prostitute, only a tecnager, but seeing high-class clients.'

'What, Greta?' said Satchell quickly.

'No, Ingrid Kestler. Skipped a court appearance in Berlin, came to England . . . 1980.'

Walker was leafing through the file.

'Can we get in touch with her family at all?'

'No. Since they made the original missing person report they've moved. We're still trying to contact them.'

Walker smiled and nodded.

'Nice work, anyway, Linda.'

'It's *Lisa*, Gov. And thank you. By the way, you have another press conference at five, remember?'

Walker jammed the Interpol file under his arm and made for the door.

'Good. We can announce that we're holding a suspect for questioning.'

'Who, Gov?' asked West.

'Yeah, who?' chimed Satchell.

Walker turned to them, framed in the doorway.

'Graham Richards,' he said.

*　　　*　　　*

Satchell and Collins drove out to pick up Richards, and it was a touching scene. His three-year-old daughter, in her toddler's dungarees, her face

133

splotched with jam, was lifted up in the hallway for her daddy's biggest ever hug. Mrs Richards looked on, seeming bemused. Satchell wondered to what extent her husband had put her in the picture.

In the interview room, an hour later, Walker and Collins faced Richards across the table. The suspect, as the whole Incident Room now thought of him, had been sullen. He frowned when they told him the interview would be recorded on video.

'Is that necessary?'

'It's standard procedure,' Walker told him. 'And better for both sides.'

'But I don't get this. All this bloody fuss. I can see it's a big case for you, but I've told you everything I know about Hallerton Road.'

Walker let a beat or two go by before he said quietly, 'We have reason to believe otherwise, Mr Richards.'

'What? What reason?'

Richards did not smoke, which annoyed Walker. He wanted an excuse to smoke himself.

'Did you ever bring any girls back to the house?'

Richards shook his head. He was staring fixedly at the table, refusing to meet Walker's glance.

'No, never.'

'So other than Kathleen and Dorothy Norton, you never saw any women at the house?'

'No.'

'Did you have a girlfriend, then?'

The question startled Richards. He looked up.

'What?'

'Did you have a girlfriend?'

Walker could see Richards calculating, trying to work out where this was leading. Eventually he shook his head again—not as a negative but as if to

134

clear it.

'Er, nothing steady, but yeah, there were a couple of girls I saw.'

'Can you give me their names?'

'What? Are you serious?'

'Yes, Mr Richards, I am very serious.'

Richards shut his eyes for a moment.

'Well, one was called Julia, another was Mary something-or-other. They were sisters, don't remember the surname. And I saw a girl from the chemist . . . God, what was her name?'

He looked at the ceiling, screwing up his eyes. Then he shook his head.

'Sorry, I can't remember.'

'You never kept in touch with them after you left?'

'No. No, I didn't.'

'Why was that?'

'Because they weren't serious. Just a bit of fun.'

'Did you have a sexual relationship with these girls?'

'Yes, but they weren't serious.'

'What about the daughter of number 34?'

Richards looked as if he'd been stung.

'What?'

'Kathleen Norton. She'd be around the same age as you. What about her?'

Richards was shaking his head vehemently.

'No way. No, not her.'

'Not your type?'

'You could say that. Look, I have told you all I know. I swear on my kids' lives, I don't know these women, I never saw them before in my life.'

'OK, did you ever go to a club called the Rhinestone in Soho? Exotic dancers, strippers, that

135

sort of thing?'

'No. Not my scene.'

'Did you ever know a girl called Ingrid Kestler?'

Richards thought for a moment.

'No, I don't think so.'

'Might it help you remember if I tell you she was German? Ingrid Kestler.'

'No, I'm sure I didn't.'

There was a file on the table in front of Collins. Walker reached for it and drew out the enlarged image of the dancing girls. He gave it to Richards and pointed to Ingrid.

'This girl, Ingrid Kestler.'

Richards looked.

'No. I don't know her.'

Walker had a pen in his hand. He reached forward and used the pen to touch the figure of the young man with the moustache.

'Is this you?'

Again Richards was ambushed by the question.

'What?' He looked at the face that Walker was indicating. 'No, that's not me.' As he shook his head once again a drop of sweat landed on the photograph.

'The woman you seem to be observing so intently there is Ingrid Kestler.'

Richards's voice was shaking now.

'I just told you, that's not me. I agree he looks a bit like me, but it's just a coincidence.'

Walker slipped another photograph from the file. It was the skeleton belt.

'You have admitted that this belt belonged to you, is that correct?'

'Yes, I think so. But I told you, I lost it.'

'What if I were to tell you that this belt was

136

found round the *neck* of Ingrid Kestler?'

Richards's discomfort suddenly lurched into nightmare. He gasped.

'What? No, no. It can't be mine, then. No!'

'She was buried in the garden where you were living,' Walker said in a level voice. 'And then, just by chance, you happen to build a patio over the area in which she's buried. Just now you said coincidence. But this seems to be quite a string of coincidences.'

Richards seemed to be deeply shocked. The sweat was now clearly visible, crowding in drops on his brow.

'Oh God, I don't believe this is happening.' He looked from Walker to Collins. 'I want a solicitor,' he said hoarsely.

*   *   *

North sat at home in the flat, working on her laptop. She paused from time to time to take up a bowl by her side and sip a spoonful of soup. She had spent the last two hours attacking the teddy-bear wallpaper in the little room upstairs with a brush and a tin of magnolia paint. Walker, of course, had not got round to getting it started. But now she didn't mind that. She had slapped a first coat on and felt a pleasantly peaceful sense of achievement.

Keys rattled in the front door and at the same moment the phone rang.

'It's all right,' said Walker hurrying in. 'I've got it.'

She watched him as, without removing his coat, he seized the phone.

'Hello. Ah, hi there, Princess.'

This was Amy, Walker's nine-year-old. North had come to detest the adoring look that came over his face whenever he spoke to her.

'You did? Hey, that's fantastic!'

He laughed, a shade conspiratorially.

'Hey, don't be cheeky! OK, put her on.'

He pressed the mute button and his hilarity dissolved to a scowl.

'Her ladyship wants a word—again,' he told North, 'Ah, hi, Lynn. Hold on, I've only just walked in myself and . . . *What?*'

North knew she would not be able to listen to this. She got up and carried the empty soup bowl to the kitchen drainer. Then she hurried back through the lounge, where Walker reached out to touch her as she passed. She sidestepped.

'I'm having a shower,' she said. 'There's some soup in the pan with the lid on, if you don't heat it up put it back in the fridge.'

Twenty-five minutes later, when she wandered down in her bathrobe, Walker was still talking, still pacing up and down, still wearing his raincoat.

'I'm *not* throwing you or the kids out of anywhere, for Christ's sakes, but that house is enormous and so is the mortgage. All I'm suggesting is that we . . . Lynn, Lynn, listen to me.'

North poured a measure of vodka, looked at it against the light, poured some more. Then she added tonic.

'I can't *afford* it, for God's sake! I am not throwing you or the kids out. I am simply saying we sell it and split the profits.'

He held the phone away from his ear and looked at North beseechingly. She could hear the voice of

138

the woman she had never met, shrilling at him in indignation.

'No,' he said after listening to more of her tirade. '*Not* fifty—fifty, I didn't mean that. Of course you'd get more because you've got the kids.'

North sipped her drink and walked up to him.

'Mike, why don't you tell her to give you a break?' she said.

She took another swig. She felt angry now.

'It's after nine. You've been on that phone for half an hour. Better still, put the phone *down* on her. She's nuts! And I'm going nuts listening to you. Let her have the house, I don't care.'

Walker was rubbing his forehead, at a loss for words. He was still looking at North and shrugging.

'Lynn, Lynn . . . Listen, I'm tired and I'm hungry. I'll call you back . . . I said, I'll call you *back*.'

He disconnected the phone.

'You cannot talk sense to her. She will not listen!'

'Tell her to keep the goddamned house,' said North.

'That's not the point. I can't afford to keep it and pay out for our place.'

'Well, I'll pay all our rent if necessary.'

Walker raised his voice.

'Oh no, you won't. She's just blackmailing me.'

'Then do something about it. Go and see her. Just stop with the phone calls every night.'

'Fine,' muttered Walker, removing his raincoat at last. 'I'll go and see her. I'm up to here with this case, but *fine*—I'll go and see her.'

'She is your wife, there's nothing I can do— unless . . .'

And suddenly, without meaning to, she gave

139

voice to an idea that had been germinating in her mind for some time.

'Unless I go and talk to her.'

He reacted immediately.

'You just stay out of this. I'm dealing with it.'

But she wanted to shout 'Why should I?' This wasn't just Mike Walker's problem. It was theirs, because they were supposed to be together. Yet he couldn't see it: was that a male thing?

But she said nothing. If they started shouting at each other now, they might never stop.

CHAPTER 14

THURSDAY, 12 OCTOBER

Before their break-up, Mike and Lynn Walker had lived in north-east London, in a downmarket area whose property had been comparatively cheap. Lynn would have liked to settle somewhere more salubrious—she had often mentioned Muswell Hill and sometimes Greenwich—but with Walker then pulling only an inspector's pay, it would have meant settling for a flat rather than the substantial semi-detached family house he eventually bought. With a 100 per cent mortgage riding on it, the repayments on the house had always been punishing. The upside was that the place had five bedrooms, a garage, a fifty-foot garden and a shed.

After confirming with her boss that it would be all right to take another day's leave—the Chief Super had been indulgent—Pat North went straight from the breakfast table to her car and drove up there. She was sick of Mike's prevarications, and sick of the endless circularity of the phone calls which Lynn, in her role as Wronged Wife, had been making almost nightly in the last few weeks. There had also been that dinner with Batchley, which was still nagging at her. It had been a fun occasion. They had laughed together. There had been nothing more, but she still felt painfully guilty when she thought about how she'd fobbed Mike off with a story about Viv being out, and going to see some old friend of hers from university. Pressure was piling up: guilt, pain, grief, love. Something had

141

to give.

But, locking her car as she stood on the pavement outside Lynn Walker's house, North resolved she would be massively conciliatory.

'Imagine you're talking a suicide down from a tower block roof,' she muttered to herself as, with a deep breath, she walked boldly towards the front door. Inside she could hear the moan of a hoover. She pressed the bell and the hoovering died.

The door was opened by a pert, well-presented woman in her early forties. The fact that Walker's wife still took the trouble to look attractive was, for some reason, a surprise.

'Yes?'

North cleared her throat.

'Are you Lynn Walker?'

'That's right.'

North extended her hand.

'Hello, I'm Pat North.'

Lynn looked momentarily shocked. She stood frozen in the doorway, completely ignoring the offered hand.

'I don't want to talk to you,' she said at last.

She immediately tried to shut the door but North planted her foot in the way.

'I think you should. Let's not play games. We need to talk.'

Lynn stopped pushing on the door and gave North a new, longer and more appraising look. Behind her eyes an idea seemed to be dawning. She swung the door wide enough for North to pass through.

'OK. Come in. But as far as I'm concerned there's nothing to talk about.'

North stepped across the threshold and into the

hall, which smelt of polish.

'So, *you're* his girlfriend,' Lynn said coldly, looking her unexpected visitor up and down. 'I did wonder what you'd look like. I asked the kids, but they just said you were tall.'

'Well, I suppose I am,' was the best answer North could come up with.

Lynn turned and led the way into the lounge.

'Taller than Mike,' she said over her shoulder. 'But then that's not too hard.'

The lounge was in every sense a family room, with plastic storage boxes for toys stacked in the corner and video games lined up on a shelf. Yet it was all kept scrupulously tidy. As Walker had once told North, Lynn was one of those wives too house-proud to go out to work. Quickly Lynn stooped to pick up a small car from the hearthrug and threw it into one of the toy boxes.

'Violet—his mother—said she'd met you. I speak to her often, on the phone. She does so like to keep up with the news of her grandchildren. We have long chats.'

It was not hard to imagine what, latterly, the two would have had to discuss so lengthily. But North had not come out here to discuss Violet Walker, a woman she preferred if possible not to think about. The one time they'd met, she had treated North with such unconcealed contempt that communication had been impossible.

'Lynn,' she said, 'can we cut the small talk? I came to see whether we could come to some kind of amicable solution.'

Lynn smiled bleakly.

'Sure. Tell Mike to give me this house and everything's amicable.'

143

'But he can't afford it.'

'That isn't my problem. This is his children's home, my home. I love this house.'

North gestured at the walls, the high ceiling.

'But it's enormous for just the three of you, and it needs such a lot of maintenance.'

'How would he know? He doesn't live here, remember?'

'He knows because he pays the bills.'

Lynn's face was set hard.

'They're his kids, and before you came along it wasn't a problem paying for the house.'

North shook her head intensely.

'Something has to give, Lynn. We have to at least discuss it.'

But Lynn was marching towards the hall.

'Come with me,' she said peremptorily. 'I want to show you something.'

She led the way upstairs and into a brightly coloured room—clearly the children's. Instead of the teddy bears that North had so recently expunged from the walls of the little room at the flat, here were robots and rockets. A large table with a model train layout dominated the centre of the room. In one corner stood a plywood Wendy house.

'Mike built that for Amy,' said Lynn. 'And the big train set was more his than Richard's. He spent hours up here when he came home from work.'

Opposite the Wendy house, against the wall, was a wooden framework supporting shelves stacked with toys and games. Lynn also pointed this out.

'He even started building a big storage cupboard for their toys. Never got to finish that, though.'

Looking about her, at this world of Walker's she

144

had previously only hazily imagined, North suddenly felt assaulted by grief, like a blow to the chest. Her own dead baby could have had all this, or something like it, she thought. Instead the baby was—. North immediately suppressed the train of thought and took a deep breath. She forced herself back to the reason she was here.

'Lynn, I really want you to know that, when I started seeing Mike, he had already moved out.'

'But with *you* around, he never got the space we separated for. He was going to come back.'

Lynn's eyes challenged her visitor to contradict this but North was overwhelmed with a new thought. It was the only possible explanation for Lynn's unyielding obstinacy.

'You still love him, don't you?' she said.

Lynn's tone did not soften.

'He's my husband, the father of my children.'

She made a sweeping gesture taking in the room, the toys and all of the father's love that they exemplified. Suddenly she was spitting out words in a torrent.

'You are breaking up my family. They ask after him every day. It's not fair to them. They miss him so much. *I* miss him. I want him home. This is where he belongs. This is our house, our family, *our* life.'

*   *   *

Afterwards, driving her car mechanically back towards central London, North realized who back there had been more like the suicide on a ledge. She was shaking. After ten minutes she pulled up and rang Sylvia Newberg on her mobile. Sylvia had good news for her. There had been a cancellation and she could see North in an hour.

When she got there, North sat in the same chair as she had occupied before. Sylvia sat opposite.

'I don't know what's the matter with me. I feel like I'm on the verge of tears all the time.'

She had made two resolutions coming through the door, one of which was not to talk about Lynn, whom she probably now hated as much as she'd ever hated anyone. Instead she had talked about that unbidden throb of grief she felt when standing in Mike Walker's children's room. She leaned forward, resting her arms on her knees, and looked hard at Sylvia.

'What should I do?'

That was her other resolution: to make the Newberg woman give an opinion. North did not like doing all the talking.

The pause that followed seemed to last a week. Sylvia simply sat and looked expectantly at North, who felt hot, confused and tearful. North found she was holding her breath and she let it out with a sigh. But still the psychotherapist did not speak. At last it was North who broke the silence.

'I really don't feel I have anything else to say today. There's no point in me being here.'

At this, Sylvia relented.

'You should grieve for your daughter,' she said simply and gently.

North nodded.

'I know, I know, but I'm not very good at expressing my emotions.'

The paper tissues were again on the table between them. One of them protruded invitingly from the box and she reached swiftly and snatched at it.

'Mike's the same.'

She sniffed and dabbed her eyes with the tissue. God, what must she look like?

'We talk about our work, sure, but never about me, never about what's happened to us, never about the . . .'

She dipped her head, as if trying to evade the word. She couldn't.

'About the baby. Anyway, he just can't talk to me, and I can't talk to him. I wouldn't know where to start.'

'Telling him how you feel about the baby would be a good start.'

'I think I'd have to pay him forty pounds an hour if I wanted him to listen to that.'

Sylvia smiled and nodded her head, acknowledging the joke. North went on,

'It's so unfair that it had to happen. And it happened to me, not to Mike, to *me* . . . They told me it was a little girl, asked if I wanted to hold her. I wish I hadn't—'

She wiped her nose with the ball of tissue but already her eyes were filling with more tears.

'I wish I hadn't said no. I wish I had held her. But I didn't. God forgive me, I *didn't*.'

Sylvia's last words were that North must find a way of speaking with Mike about the baby, and sooner rather than later—that same evening if possible. Back in her car North decided to make it even sooner. This was too important to wait.

She called the Incident Room. Surely Mike would be able to break off for a couple of hours. They could go to a pub somewhere, or a café. Suddenly the urge to unburden herself, not to

147

Sylvia Newberg but to a man she loved and who said he loved her, had become irresistible.

'Incident Room?' said a voice.

'Chief Superintendent Walker, please.'

'He's out, I'm afraid.'

'Can you tell me where I can reach him, please? It's personal. It's his—. I mean, it's Pat North. I need to speak to him very urgently.'

'Just a moment.'

After a pause the voice came back.

'He's gone to 34 Hallerton Road. He should have his mobile with him.'

'Yes, of course, thank you.'

Feverishly she dialled Walker's mobile but got only the voicemail message.

'The person you are calling is unavailable . . .'

'Like hell you are, Mike Walker,' she said grimly. 'Just for once you'll have to be available.'

She jammed the car into gear and accelerated away.

*   *   *

After three weeks of police operations, the Hallerton Road house had become like a gigantic decayed tooth being slowly drilled out. The roof and external walls continued to stand but, as the search continued, the internal structure was being steadily ripped away wall by wall and floor by floor.

Under Batchley's direction, the team had finished in the cellar, moved up into the roof cavity and begun working their way steadily downwards through the house. The upper rooms, once occupied by the Nortons' paying guests, had already gone. Using scaffolding to brace the

148

building, the flues had been unbricked, the stairs uncased and the floorboards levered up with crowbars. Now they were beginning on the first-floor rooms and it was under the boards in one of these that they came on something that had warranted an urgent call to Walker at the Incident Room.

'Do nothing till I get there,' he told Batchley and snapped his fingers at Satchell. 'Hallerton Road. They've found something.'

'So? What is it?' grunted Walker as he zipped himself into his white paper suit at Hallerton Road.

'We haven't got it out yet,' Batchley told him. 'It's in a bedroom, under the floorboards.'

Walker sensed the tension at the site. Virtually all work had stopped. Everyone was quiet, awaiting developments.

He crept cautiously up the denuded stairs and into the rear bedroom, where he found two SOCOs kneeling by a hole in the floor. Masked and wearing rubber gloves, they were picking small lumps of grey plaster from the hole and placing them in an evidence bag. Seeing Walker, the SOCOs stood up and made room. Walker bent and peered down. A dirt-encrusted cardboard box was lodged tightly between the joists. He could just make out a label on the lid. It read 24 DE LUXE CHRISTMAS CRACKERS.

'Can you get the lid off?'

Gingerly the lid was lifted, revealing something bundled in an old towel. Walker got down on his knees, lifted the box from the hole and stood, cradling it in his left arm to allow him a free hand to lift the towel. As, very carefully, he did so there was a commotion on the stairs and a familiar voice

149

calling his name.

*   *   *

North had driven straight up to the officer who stood at the gate and flashed her warrant card.

'Chief Superintendent Walker. Is he here? I need to speak to him.'

The PC stood in front of the car holding up his hand.

'Sorry, ma'am. There's no entry here.'

But North was already out of the car and striding towards the shell of the house.

'I need to speak to him. It's most urgent.'

'Ma'am!' called the constable. 'Please come back. You can't park here.'

It was too late. She was already inside and clumping up the stairs. She could hear there were people up there.

At the top she looked around, breathing heavily. The space gaped upwards as high as the roof slates. To her right was an empty room, still more or less intact, to her left, a smaller room with several white-suited SOCOs crowded in the doorway. She shouldered past them and saw Walker standing, with his back turned, in the centre of the ruined room. He seemed to be looking intently at something in his arms.

'Mike!' she called out. 'Look, I'm sorry for barging in like this. But I've really got to talk to you—'

Walker swung round. It took him a moment to register her presence, and then he roared.

'Pat! What the fuck's going on? Get *out* of here.'

One or two officers put up their arms as if to

150

ward her off but she paid no attention as she advanced towards Walker.

'No I won't, Mike. We have to talk. I can't take this any more.'

Walker turned away, as if trying to hide the box in his arms.

'Satch! Take her downstairs. Do it NOW!'

Satchell stepped forward to take North's arm, but she sidestepped and took another step closer to Walker. Then as she reached his side she looked at what he was trying to hide from her. Her hand went to her mouth.

'Oh my God!'

It was the tiny blackened skeleton of what at first sight looked like a monkey. But then as Walker tried fumblingly to rearrange the concealing towel, a tiny plastic object rolled out from the folds and bounced to the floor. She looked down and saw some kind of rattle. Aghast she looked back at the bundle. Topping the skull was a knitted bonnet with a pink ribbon bow at the crown. A cellular woollen blanket hemmed in satin wrapped it. She knew then it was no monkey. Her mouth fell open. Her face creased with pain.

'Jesus! It's a baby . . . a baby!'

Walker at last succeeded in pulling the blanket across to hide the tiny grinning mouth, the nose and eye sockets, from her view.

'Satch, I *said* get her out of here.'

She was already backing away. Her lips were quivering. She bumped into a SOCO, who stepped aside. She took a last, wild look around the room, then plunged out and down the stairs with Satchell and Batchley in pursuit.

'Pat,' shouted Satchell.

151

But she was faster than the two men. She quit the house, scattering gravel beneath her feet as she raced towards the car, which still obstructed the gate. Satchell and Batchley stopped at the door and watched as she plunged into the driver's seat, fired the engine and revved it ferociously. They exchanged a glance and Satchell murmured, 'Jesus! What was *that* about?'

By the time Walker had handed the precious new evidence to one of the SOCOs and thundered down in the wake of North, she had already turned the car around.

'Pat. Wait!'

But he could only watch as she drove off through the gate on screeching tyres. Looking after her he thought of what she had seen, of what he had discovered.

'I was holding it,' he whispered to himself, shaking his head slowly. 'I was holding it in my *arms*.'

A quarter of a mile away, North had turned into a quiet residential street and parked. She rested her head on the steering wheel, making no attempt to control her convulsive sobs.

*   *   *

By nightfall North had gained some kind of perspective. It had been completely out of order barging in on Walker like that and, of course, she had paid a ghastly price. But for him to be actually holding the skeleton of a baby at the moment she arrived was . . . well, it was the most horrible coincidence imaginable, yet it had happened.

When Walker at last came home, after a day

152

lengthened by the extraordinary new discovery at Hallerton Road, she was ready to face him, to explain.

'I went to see Lynn,' she told him.

Walker swung round in disbelief.

'What? You did what?'

'That's why I needed to talk to you so urgently. You see I thought I could talk her round, make her see it your way, but . . .'

Walker shut his eyes wearily.

'I appreciate the thought but I really don't need you fighting my battles for me.'

His tone made her angry again.

'Don't you? Well, in that case maybe you should make the time to fight them yourself. She still loves you. She wants you back.'

Without warning he took her in his arms and hugged her, then still holding her shoulders, looked into her eyes.

'Pat, I love *you*. I am not going back to her.'

'Well then, go and see her. Make her understand. Stop bottling out.'

Walker nodded.

'I will. I'll go and see her.'

'When?'

It was a challenge. He sighed.

'Stop putting pressure on me. I've got enough to deal with as it is.'

'*When?*'

'I'll go after work tomorrow, OK? I'll sort this out, I promise you.'

Gently she removed his hands from her shoulders. Her face wore a sceptical look. Time would tell.

CHAPTER 15

FRIDAY, 13 OCTOBER

Walker knew as soon as he woke up what kind of a hellish day he faced—the press again, the extra sorting out needed at Hallerton Road, the forensics, the pathologist. Not least, he had to interview Kathleen Norton and he fancied that would be a gruelling encounter. He also had to work out how the discovery of a baby under the floorboards affected his case against Richards. Could he have had anything to do with it? It was possible.

And then there was his wife. As he saw it, he didn't have any choice now. North had backed him so completely into a corner that he would *have* to go out and see Lynn. Before he left for the Incident Room, he made the call. In North's hearing, he asked her if he could drop in around seven thirty. Lynn had not been exactly friendly, but she was always extra difficult in the early morning. No, she told him sarcastically, she had no hot date tonight. So, yes, he could come round. Walker hung up and left for the mortuary, where Foster's examination of the baby was due to begin at eight thirty.

*　　　*　　　*

The examination was over by a quarter past nine. Satchell and Walker waited as the distinguished pathologist pulled off his rubber gloves and removed his mask.

154

'It's a female foetus,' the pathologist told them. 'About eight months. I can't, at this stage, give any details of the cause of death or when it was buried.'

'But Forensics can test the DNA?'

Foster nodded.

'Yes, but they can't determine the paternity from the bone DNA, only the maternity.'

'But there were stains on the towel the baby was wrapped in.'

'Yes, if there's foetal blood, they should be able to obtain the full DNA profile from that—the father as well as the mother.'

*   *   *

After yesterday, North couldn't face a return to work. She sat instead in Sylvia's armchair. It was becoming a habit.

She told all about the events that had followed their session yesterday.

'I just couldn't get a grip on myself. My partner's a detective, you see, and I went round to see him . . .'

She rubbed her temples with her fingertips

'Oh God . . . this is all confidential, right? I mean, it's an ongoing case. I shouldn't talk about it.'

Sylvia smiled.

'Don't worry. It won't go any further.'

'Well, I'm sure you've heard about it: the skeletons found in a garden in North London? I went round to the scene because they'd told me he was there. Anyway, when I arrived, they'd just found something . . .'

'Go on.'

'It was all laid out on an old towel. It was a . . . a

155

baby. A dead baby. God knows how long it had lain there. It was a skeleton basically. Anyway, I could hardly look at it.'

'It upset you?'

'Yes, of course it did. Because I lost mine . . .'

North was looking intensely at a randomly chosen point on the carpet. She was kneading her hands together.

'I had it all ready. The nursery was decorated; cot, mobiles and everything was fine. But of course it wasn't . . .'

She looked at the psychotherapist desperately but Sylvia maintained her usual silence.

'Well, I can't bear the pain and the emptiness,' cried North, the words coming in a rush now. 'It's just there and I can't get rid of it. I've never been afraid of anything before in my life, but now I'm so afraid. I'm afraid I'll never have a baby. I'm afraid that I can't love Mike. I blame myself. I blame Mike for not being there, blame him for what happened. I just want it all to go away. I can't eat, I can't sleep, I can't function.'

*   *   *

Kathleen Norton was brought in by DC West exactly at the appointed time. She wore the same green mac, the same type of floral dress underneath, and seemed not in the slightest put out by today's summons to assist the police.

'I can't stay for long,' she said lightly, as if paying a social call. 'My mother can't cope on her own. I've had to get someone in to do the lunches.'

'We'll be as quick as we can, Kathleen,' Walker assured her.

156

Kathleen sat down heavily at the table. West sat too, but Walker remained standing, so that he could pace around the room at will. By the door stood a uniformed woman constable.

'Can you verify something for me on this diagram of number 34 Hallerton Road?' began Walker.

He placed before Kathleen a plan of the first floor of the house and pointed to one of the rooms.

'This room marked with a cross . . . What room was it?'

Kathleen looked.

'That was my bedroom.'

'Well, we have made a very tragic discovery in that room.'

He let the information sink in but Kathleen seemed to make nothing of it. Walker went on.

'We found the remains of a baby.'

He scrutinized her. She had not given so much as a twitch.

'Can you tell me anything about this?'

There was no answer.

'We need to know, Kathleen, how the body of a baby came to be buried under the floorboards in your bedroom.'

Kathleen looked blankly at the plan of her old home. Walker waited five seconds, then five more, then took up his thread again.

'We are presently testing a bloodstained towel which was wrapped around the remains, and from this blood we will be able to extract DNA. Do you understand what that means?'

Kathleen snapped her head up. She did not like being treated as an ignorant person.

'Of course I do,' she said sharply. 'I was a nurse,

157

wasn't I?'

Walker did a double-take.

'You *what?*'

He had read her file, every word, just an hour ago. There was nothing about her having been a nurse. He turned towards West, frowning, thinking, *How the hell did the team miss that?* But the DC took it as a cue to come in on the questioning.

'Would you be prepared to give us a DNA sample to eliminate you from our inquiries?' she asked gently.

Kathleen shook her head sadly.

'I don't need to,' she said. 'I know whose baby it is. It's *my* baby. Mine—and Graham Richards's.'

*   *   *

In the adjoining Interview Room, Satchell and Collins had been talking to Richards himself, with a smartly dressed young solicitor, Amy Birchill, sitting beside him. Ms Birchill was taking notes on a legal pad.

Satchell had wasted no time on small talk. Ten minutes earlier he and Walker had roughed out a line of questioning and he launched straight into it.

'Tell us about your relationship with Kathleen Norton, Mr Richards,' he invited.

Richards no longer cut the confident figure of a few days ago. He was shaken and nervous, mumbling his replies.

'Relationship? I never had a relationship with her. This is unbelievable. I contacted you to start off with, you know.'

'You must have known her, though, Mr Richards. You lived in the same house for nearly a

158

year.'

Richards leaned forward. He was sweating profusely.

'Look, if she's been saying things about me . . . Well, she's completely off the wall, you know.'

'Why do you say that?' asked Collins.

'Whatever she says about me is all lies. What has she told you? What has she been saying?'

'Why don't you give us your version?'

Richards flicked a glance at his lawyer. She leaned sideways and whispered, 'Graham, you can ask to take a break if you wish. Do you want to take a break?'

He shook his head.

'No, no I don't.'

'Just say it as it happened.'

Richards nodded.

'All right,' he said, raising his voice a fraction. 'This is God's honest truth. Maybe I should have brought it up before, but . . . well, I didn't because it . . . didn't seem relevant.'

He took a drink of water, swallowing audibly. The plastic cup had left a ring of water on the table and with infinite care he replaced it on that exact spot before continuing.

'For the first few weeks I was there, I got along quite well with Kathleen. I felt sorry for her actually, she didn't seem to have any friends. But then I started to get a little wary, thought she might fancy me, you know. She followed me around like a puppy dog, always making me tea and snacks and bringing them to my room.'

He took another drink, and went through the same routine of replacing the cup.

'One night I'd had too much to drink. I came

back, crashed out, and the next thing I knew she was climbing into bed with me.'

'So you had sex with her?'

This was Satchell.

'She said I did.'

'Well? Did you or didn't you?'

Richards shrugged.

'I couldn't remember if I had or not. But the next morning she was all flushed and giggling. So I told her there wouldn't be a repeat performance. It was just a one-night stand. It was nothing more.'

'What did she say to that?

Richards shifted uneasily in his seat.

'What could she say? I wanted to make sure there would be no more visits, so I put a lock on my door.'

'How did she react to that?'

'I think she tried to get in, found it was locked and from then on she avoided me. She'd rush into her room as soon as she saw me. That's all it was, I *swear* to you: a one-night stand.'

*   *   *

Walker was still seething over the business of Kathleen's having been a nurse. He couldn't see all the implications yet, but such an elementary mistake was inexcusable. He looked up at the woman sitting opposite him and somehow guessed what she was going to say next about her pregnancy, good Catholic girl that she was. And it came out just as he had expected.

'He was drunk, he came into my room, and . . . he raped me.'

West frowned sympathetically.

160

'Why didn't you tell us this before?'

'It's not something you *talk* about. It was terrible.'

'When did it happen?'

Kathleen closed her eyes.

'Saturday the 11th of September 1982,' she recited, then opened her eyes again. 'I couldn't tell anyone, my mother or my father. Especially Dad, as he got on so well with Graham.'

She sat up a little and blew her nose.

'I suggested he leave, but Dad needed his help with the renovations.'

'This is a very serious allegation, Kathleen,' West warned.

Kathleen bristled.

'It's *not* an allegation, it's the truth. Graham Richards raped me and if you want to know whether I'm telling the truth, then get him to give you *his* DNA.'

Walker stared at her for a few moments then said, 'Would you excuse me for a few moments, Kathleen?'

He spoke for the benefit of the tape. 'Interview suspended at eleven forty-three. Detective Superintendent Walker now leaving the room.'

The room in which Satchell was talking to Richards was just up the corridor. Walker strode to the door and rapped loudly.

'Satch! Out here!'

Half a minute later, Satchell came out, jerking his thumb back towards the door.

'He's just admitted having a sexual relationship with Kathleen Norton.'

The satisfied look on the Detective Sergeant's face soon disappeared when he saw the fury on

161

Walker's.

'I have just discovered,' Walker said grimly, 'that Kathleen Norton was a nurse . . . and I had to wait for *her* to tell me. How on earth did you miss that? We've got computers coming out of every orifice, technology that could beam me up to bloody Mars, and yet none of you knew she used to be a nurse! I'd say this puts a very different slant on the case, wouldn't you?'

This is what he had been thinking while Kathleen was bitterly denouncing Graham Richards as a rapist. A nurse might have had contact with a pregnant girl such as Ingrid Kestler. She might have had access to deadly drugs.

Satchell was too slow picking up the thought. Walker thrust his face close to Satchell's.

'It puts her right in the frame, doesn't it?'

Satchell shrugged.

'I'm sorry. She never mentioned it in her interview. Did she qualify? I mean, if she didn't, then—'

Again Walker interrupted.

'I want all her records.'

He began counting the other things he wanted on his fingers.

'I want to know everything about her. I want you to get Batchley out of his mud hole, bring him back here and see if he can do any better. Because sure as shit he can't do any worse.'

Satchell blinked. *Christ*, he thought, if Walker was bringing Batchley back into the fold, he must be serious about nailing Kathleen Norton.

'What do you want me to do with Richards?'

'Right now, I want a DNA swab from him. I want a solicitor for Kathleen and I want *you*'— he jabbed a finger at Collins, who had followed Satchell out—'to go and talk to her mother, find out what she knew about this goddamned baby.'

'Gov?'

Collins was puzzled. Walker sighed and cast his eyes up to the ceiling in exaggerated fashion.

'She admits the baby was hers,' he hissed. 'She claims the father was Richards. She says he went into her room and raped her. See what Dorothy Richards has to say about all that, will you?'

*　　　*　　　*

'Rape?' cried Richards, when Satchell laid before him what Kathleen had been saying in the next room. There was suddenly a new panic in his voice, and he looked from Satchell to the DC who was sitting in for Collins, shaking his head jerkily.

'I never raped her. I had sex with her, once, just once. But I told you, I'd had too much to drink. She came into my room, not the other way round. She was after me. I couldn't stand her following me around, pestering me.'

'So,' went on Satchell judiciously, 'you had sexual relations with her just the one time?'

'Yes.'

'Did she ever say anything to you about being pregnant?'

*　　　*　　　*

Kathleen had told the police that the solicitors Clarence Clough had represented her family in small items of legal work in the past and that she had always found them satisfactory. They were

163

contacted and one of the partners, Derek Waugh, though he knew nothing of the Norton family's connection with his firm, elected to take the case on himself. He arrived within the hour, spent thirty minutes closeted with his client and now sat beside her in front of Walker and West.

Lisa West began by asking why Kathleen did not tell Graham Richards that she was pregnant.

'I didn't want anything to do with him, I couldn't tell him about the baby. I just wanted to forget about him and look forward to having my child.'

'So you were going to keep the baby?'

Kathleen was emphatic.

'*Yes!* Of course.'

'Did you ever consider an abortion?' Walker put in.

Kathleen looked shocked. She shook her head but seemed temporarily unable to speak.

'Kathleen,' murmured Waugh. 'Do you need to take a break?'

She did not reply.

'Kathleen?' he prompted. 'A break?'

Kathleen shook her head.

'No, I want the truth to come out about him, and about what happened. I wanted my baby. I wanted my baby, and . . . I was all alone, you see. I was all alone and when my waters broke I knew it was too early. I went down to the cellar and . . .'

She was on her feet now, her face tight with remembered pain, her hands clamped on her belly.

'I knew by the way the contractions were coming, hardly a minute between them . . .'

The solicitor put a restraining hand on her arm.

'Sit down, Kathleen.'

Kathleen ignored him. She was back in that

164

cellar of seventeen years ago, reliving the whole horror.

'She didn't move. She didn't cry. She was just still and lifeless in my arms.'

Kathleen started to convulse, her words coming thick and indistinct between heaving intakes of breath.

'I tried to make her breathe, I *tried*! But there was nothing . . . there was nothing . . . I could do. Oh God! Oh God!'

'Here, sip this, Kathleen,' said Waugh, offering more water. 'Just try and stay calm.'

Kathleen jammed the cup to her lips and sucked in the water. Walker waited for her convulsions to subside before asking, 'Kathleen, if you wanted the baby that badly, why didn't you go to hospital when your waters broke?'

With an effort of will, she steadied herself.

'There wasn't time. The only one I could have made it to was St Jude's but I couldn't have gone there.'

'Why not?'

Kathleen looked at him as if he were stupid.

'Because I worked there and none of my colleagues knew I was pregnant.'

'So, who else knew about this?'

'No one. Everyone just thought I was putting on weight.'

'What did you do once you realized the baby was dead?' asked West.

'I went upstairs, back to my bedroom. I wrapped her in a towel and I . . . hid the body. I put her under the floorboards and pulled my bed over her.'

Kathleen fetched a deep, shuddering breath.

'I didn't know what else to do.'

165

'Did you ever tell Graham Richards about this?'

'No.'

'So he didn't know the child had been born,' asked Walker, 'or that it was his?'

'No, I went straight back to work. I told no one. No one at all.'

*   *   *

Dorothy Norton was particular about her flowers, which she always took in fresh from the local florist. Dorothy would never consider buying supermarket flowers. She thought it important to have one arrangement in each of the reception rooms and she regarded arranging the blooms as one of her finest abilities.

Doug Collins found her putting carnations in a vase. She selected each stem and inspected it critically before trimming it off with a pair of scissors. After a few pleasantries, Collins put it to her that her daughter had been pregnant in 1983, and that Kathleen had admitted as much. Dorothy clicked her tongue and shook her head.

'No, no, no!'

She snipped an inch off the bottom of a carnation stem.

'I don't know why she is saying these things. Kathleen is a good Catholic girl.'

Collins spoke quietly.

'We have found the remains of a baby, Mrs Norton, and Kathleen has admitted to hiding it.'

Dorothy's voice became shrill and her hand shook as she tried to poke the flower into the already overstuffed vase.

'I don't know why she is admitting this at all. It's

166

not true.'

'So you didn't know anything about your daughter's pregnancy?'

Dorothy grabbed a handful of fern and looked for a place in which to ram it. She gave up and turned to Collins. Her lip was quivering.

'This is all very distressing for me. My daughter's got to come home. The grocery shop won't deliver the order for this week. And now *this*.'

Dorothy took a tissue from her sleeve and dabbed at her eyes.

'Do you recall any boyfriends, or relationships Kathleen might have had at that time?' asked Collins.

'You've seen my daughter . . . well, she's a very good and caring woman but, she's never really expressed an interest in . . . that sort of thing. The idea she could have been pregnant, well, it's ludicrous.'

She adjusted the position of the flower arrangement, picked up the old newspaper in which she had collected the offcuts and unused fern and made a ball of it. She walked with it towards the door. Collins made after her.

Dorothy started to leave the room.

'So why do you think she has told us this?'

Dorothy stopped and turned to him.

'I have no idea. She's upset and confused. She doesn't know what she's saying. Maybe she's covering for someone else.'

'Any idea who that might be?'

Dorothy gave him something like a smile as she shook her head.

'None whatsoever, I'm afraid. Ask her.'

In the hall, Collins made his excuses.

'Thank you very much for your help, Mrs Norton. I'll let myself out.'

But he turned before he opened the door.

'Oh! Just one more thing, Mrs Norton. You wouldn't happen to have a photograph of Kathleen in her nurse's uniform?'

*   *   *

Batchley had been delighted to hand over site management at Hallerton Road to another DI. To be back bathing in the sunshine of Walker's favour was a relief. So was not having to breathe plaster dust all day. His aim now was to avoid fouling up in Walker's eyes.

Batchley's first task was a doddle: to go down to St Jude's, the hospital where Kathleen Norton had been working at the time of her pregnancy. His contact was the small, twinkly Sister Osbourne from County Limerick, whom he found bustling around the geriatric ward.

'As you know, I'm trying to trace anyone who knew a nurse who worked here about seventeen years ago.'

'Yes,' said Sister Osbourne cheerfully. 'Kathleen Norton, right? Well, your luck's in, she started here at the same time as me, so fire away with your questions. But I can't be long, I've got bed baths to get on with.'

They were standing beside the nursing station. She tapped the shoulder of a passing nurse.

'Would you take over on Mr Hughes?' she asked her, then turned back to Batchley and led him into a small and empty waiting room. 'I've left the poor man half naked.'

Batchley took three e-fit photographs out of his pocket.

'Did you ever see Kathleen Norton with any of these three women?'

He spread the photographs like a hand of cards and then gave them to her. Sister Osbourne looked carefully at each one in turn.

'She really didn't socialize much at work, and, no, I'm sorry, I don't recognize these at all. Too young for this ward.'

She pointed to the photograph of the topless Ingrid Kestler.

'And not nurses, as far as I can tell.'

A sudden image of topless nurses appeared before Batchley's mind. He wiped the involuntary smile from his face and went on.

'Can you tell me what you know about Kathleen herself?'

'Well, she was nice enough. We got on well, but she was quite a private person. I always felt that she never let anyone get too close.'

'Did she have a boyfriend, perhaps? Someone who might have got to know her a little better.'

'Well, yes, she did have a boyfriend for a little while, a cleaner here . . . Ed, Eric or . . . something like that, but don't ask me his surname. I do remember one thing that happened. It surprised everybody, her being like she was, you know, so strait-laced. They got caught having nookie in one of the offices. They were both given serious warnings. About the only action this place has ever seen, if you want to know. She was a very good nurse, though, Kathleen, very caring.'

'Do you remember Kathleen being pregnant?'

This question greatly surprised Sister Osbourne.

'Pregnant? Lord, no I don't. Was the cleaner the father?'

Batchley shook his head hurriedly.

'No, no, we don't think so. And did Kathleen only work here? Did she ever have any dealings with the maternity department, for example?'

'Well, if she was pregnant she probably had herself checked out. But she wouldn't have anything to do with them through her work here. This is the geriatric ward. We've never had a pregnant eighty-year-old yet. Mind you, some of them are very sprightly and get up to all sorts. Anyway, look, I'll show you . . . The maternity clinic is over the way, through those double doors at the far end.'

Batchley held out his hand.

'Well, thank you very much for your time.'

They shook.

'It's been my pleasure, Mr Batchley. I'll ask around about that cleaner. Edgar, was it? Personnel will have his name anyway.'

* * *

At the Incident Room, West came to the open door of the SIO's office and rapped. Walker sat with his feet on the desk reading a file with intense concentration. He looked up.

'Yes?'

'Gov, you have Richards for another hour, unless we go for an extension.'

Walker looked at his watch and sprang from his chair. He grabbed his raincoat, pulled it on and swept past her into the central area of the Incident Room. A patently worried Satchell came up to him.

170

He had just heard that Kathleen was being released.

'Aren't you going to arrest her for concealing the birth of a child?'

Walker shook his head.

'No. We need to wait for the DNA results to confirm whether she's telling the truth. The baby could still be Ingrid Kestler's.'

'Why would she lie?'

Walker shook his head mysteriously.

'Who knows what goes on in a woman's mind where a baby's concerned? No, we let them both go, Kathleen *and* Richards, until we can confirm the baby's parentage.'

'What about the fingerprint on the belt?' Satchell wanted to know.

Walker tapped the pocket that contained his mobile phone.

'I've just spoken to the fingerprint officer. The foreign print on the buckle is Kathleen's.'

Satchell's face showed frank amazement.

'And you're still going to let her go?'

Walker jutted out his chin. He was annoyed that Satchell could question his judgement in front of other members of the team.

'Yes,' he said airily. 'We need to get a bigger picture. Who knows what else we've missed? Anyway, I've got to go. I'll see you all tomorrow.'

He had got halfway through the door when he turned and pointed at Satchell.

'And before you take those two nice people back to their nice homes, I want you to get a complete CV from both of them. Everything they've done, everywhere they've lived, all their boyfriends and girlfriends. Got it?'

*   *   *

He played with the kids while Lynn made supper: chicken breasts cooked in a tomato sauce, followed by wine and cheese. Walker knew why she'd done the chicken dish. Years ago he'd told her it was the recipe of hers he enjoyed the most. It was obvious that Lynn's attitude had turned about since their conversation this morning. She was making quite an effort.

And the chicken still tasted good.

With Richard and Amy in bed, the children became the topic of conversation between the estranged Walkers. School grades, reports, meet-the-teachers evenings, friends, an upcoming birthday: these were subjects that both of them were reliably interested in. Once or twice Walker tried to steer the conversation around to the divorce settlement but she refused to be drawn, turning back to Amy's new project on Florence Nightingale and Richard's difficulties with his spelling.

It was growing late. Lynn asked Walker if he'd mind fixing a framed picture that had fallen off the wall. This was a blown-up snapshot of the family at some open-air attraction. Dutifully he'd hammered in a new picture hook, though this was something he knew Lynn herself to be perfectly capable of. When he had done, he looked at the photo.

'Hey! This is nice, who took this?'

'You did. Don't you remember? That time we went to that theme park, and on the water chute you said it was safer sitting at the back because you only got wet if you sat in the front, and'—she was

172

giggling now—'it came over the sides and you got soaked.'

In a rush, as sudden as when it had happened, his soaking came back to Walker and he laughed with her.

'That's right! It never even touched the people in front, but *whoosh*, it went all over me.'

'And your baseball cap was floating in the water.'

Their laughter died down as Lynn poured the wine.

'We had some good laughs, didn't we?' she said quietly. 'They loved having you here tonight.'

Walker shook his head.

'Lynn, don't.'

But she was determined to continue.

'Do you *know* what you're throwing away, Mike? I mean, Pat seems nice enough, but we're your *family*.'

Walker sighed. He was not up for this. He sneaked a look at the wall clock and stood up.

'Listen, it's late. It's been a long day. Can we talk about this tomorrow? I've told the kids I'll pick them up at lunchtime.'

He went to the hall and grabbed his coat. Getting to the door before him, she opened it and stood waiting for his departure.

'When exactly are we going to talk if you're out with the kids all day?'

'Well, I . . .' A thought occurred to him. 'Why don't you come with us? It'd be good for them to have both of us together.'

'*That's* very brave of you.'

Lynn looked hard at him as he stepped outside.

'You sure we can spend a day together and remain civilized?'

173

He turned to her.

'We've managed this evening, haven't we?'

Walker heard the door close behind him as he reached the gate. He turned once more and looked up at the house where he had lived for a decade of his life, where his children still lived. He felt caught between the two women, and their two kinds of loving, and he felt, for a moment, bitterly lonely.

CHAPTER 16

SATURDAY, 14 OCTOBER

It was hardly light and Walker was in the kitchen, gulping down a cup of coffee, when a bleary-eyed North drifted down the stairs. She was wrapped up in a bathrobe.

'Mike, what on earth are you doing up at this time on a Saturday?'

Walker bit deeply into a piece of buttered toast, chewed for a moment and swallowed.

'We had some big developments at work yesterday. But I can't break my promise to take the kids out later. So I'm going to have to go into the office now.'

'But it's half past six! What time did you get in last night anyway?'

'About midnight, but we're all getting in early. No weekend break.'

He tapped his chest in mock self-importance.

'I'm a cruel taskmaster.'

'Did you sort things out with Lynn?'

Walker had been dreading this question. He sighed over the last dregs of his coffee.

'Yes, kind of. I'd have talked it over with you when I got in but you were flat out. Listen, I really have to dash, sweetheart. Can I put you in the picture tonight?'

He put his cup in the sink and went for his coat, pecking her on the cheek as he passed. Before she could protest, he had disappeared through the front door.

The baby skeleton under the floorboards at 34 Hallerton Road had been accounted for, at least to Walker's satisfaction. The question that now occupied him was how it related, if at all, to the three adult bodies found at the same address. If Graham Richards was indeed the young man in the back of the photograph from the Rhinestone Club, then he must be the link. After all, Kathleen had accused him of rape. But she might have had her own demons prompting her to say this. And, if Richards was a sexual psychopath, why hadn't he murdered Kathleen while he was about it?

It was this aspect that troubled Walker at the morning briefing. He could not convince himself that Richards was a sadistic killer.

'If he is, what's he been up to during the intervening seventeen years?' he asked.

'He stopped,' suggested Satchell. 'Settled down.'

Walker shook his head.

'No. Serial killers rarely stop. If Richards did kill Ingrid Kestler, Kerry Willis and the other poor girl, I'm fairly certain he would have killed again, or at least tried to. So this morning, let's have a detailed trawl through all unsolved murders and rapes of females since 1983, to see if we can correlate them in any way with Richards's own movements.'

Four hours later Satchell was still hard at work on HOLMES, the police national computer database. He looked up from his screen and saw the SIO sitting in his office, talking agitatedly on the phone. Walker finished the call, checked his watch and swore loudly.

'Satch, I've got to go,' he said, coming out with a bunch of emails. 'I promised Lynn and the kids I'd take them out. Can you cover for me until I get back? Batchley's playing in some bloody rugby match.'

Satchell glanced despairingly at the mound of papers on his desk, which Walker now added to with those in his hand. He sighed and waved Walker away.

'No problem. You go.'

Walker tapped the Detective Sergeant's arm.

'Thanks, Satch, I appreciate it.'

*   *   *

On the way back to his old house to collect the children, Walker bought a kite. It would give them all something to do when he took Richard and Amy to the park, as he almost invariably did on these occasions. In the end Lynn came too, after they'd booked four seats for a new Disney picture that was showing in the late afternoon at Leicester Square.

The kite-flying delighted Walker. It took some time to get back to the level of skill he'd developed during a single fortnight as an eight-year-old, standing on the banks of the River Clyde. His dad had given him a kite that Christmas and, during the rest of those school holidays, the two of them had taken it out daily to fly over the river. His father showed the boy how to manipulate the two strings and make the kite twist and turn, soar and dive giddily, like an airborne puppet. But three weeks later, as January turned to February, his dad had walked out on him and his mum. Walker had put the kite away then. He never flew it again.

But now he was getting back his old skill. Neither Lynn, Amy nor Richard had proved promising, or even enthusiastic, apprentice kite-flyers. They sat huddled disconsolately on a park bench guarding his coat while he displayed his own mastery of the air, making the kite skitter about the sky madly.

'Will you just look at that?' he called back to them. 'That's class, that is. Real class.'

From inside his coat pocket, on the bench beside Richard, his mobile phone bleeped. He did not hear it. Nor did he see Richard's hand slip into the pocket and, on his mother's instructions, switch the mobile off. Lynn was determined that work was not going to disrupt their afternoon together—their first as a family since Walker had moved out.

*   *   *

Dinnertime had come round again at the Norton Retirement Home and Kathleen was back in her routine. She had been let go by the police, pending further inquiries. Mr Waugh had told her they would almost certainly be forwarding the papers in the case to the Crown Prosecution Service, which might decide to prosecute her for concealing the birth of her child. This was a serious offence but, bearing in mind Kathleen's otherwise good character and the long lapse of time, he doubted she would go to prison. But this seemed cold comfort. The prospect of legal proceedings was a horrifying one to Kathleen: the intrusiveness and exposure would be sheer purgatory.

She laid out the residents' plates, each with a

178

portion of sliced ham, in a row on the kitchen table. Picking up a bowl she started spooning out cold potato and beetroot salad. Suddenly waves of shuddering possessed her and she began to hurl the food onto the plates, until one portion missed its mark and slopped onto her shoe. Kathleen snapped then. She kicked her shoe off and hurled the bowl at the wall. It shattered, the potato mixture exploding across shelves and worktops. She looked at the plates on the table, lined up so complacently, and shouted at them in an inarticulate howl of rage. Then she swiped them savagely to the floor with her arm.

The noise brought her mother to the door.

'What's happened? What have you done?'

Kathleen had covered her face with her hands, pressing it as if trying desperately to hold it in place.

'Nothing,' she mumbled. 'I'll clear it up. Just leave me alone.'

Dorothy stepped into the kitchen and felt her foot slip momentarily. She looked down to discover she was standing on a slice of ham.

'Are you having one of your migraines again, Kathleen?'

'Just leave me alone, Mother,' Kathleen shouted, taking her hands down. 'Get out, and leave me *alone.*'

Dorothy sniffed and walked out, after scraping the piece of ham from her sole. Kathleen was breathing heavily. She leaned back against the counter and felt a KitKat beneath her left hand. She ripped off the wrapper and consumed the chocolate in one bite.

During their dinner at the Café Casablanca, North had casually mentioned to Batchley that she'd never seen a rugby match.

'You can come down on Saturday, if you like,' he offered. 'I'm doing my stuff against a bunch of hairy-toed blokes from the Essex force.'

She already had a session with Sylvia, but the attraction of meeting Batchley, while Mike was with his children, was strong.

'I'll try and make it. I've got an appointment that I can't break. But I'll come down as soon as I've finished.'

He gave her directions and she drove there straight from the psychotherapist's. But she found the players emerging from the clubhouse in their flannels and blazers, with wet hair and ruddy faces. The match was over.

'You missed a good match,' crowed Batchley. 'We won.'

They touched cheeks.

'Well done,' she said. 'Where do you want to celebrate?'

Batchley knew he was due at the Incident Room.

'Well, I haven't got too long . . .'

North insisted.

'Your choice. It's my treat.'

'Why?'

'Just a thank-you.'

'Well, in that case, vintage champagne at the Ritz it is.'

'Nice try.' She laughed, moving towards her car and opening the driver's door. 'Come on, get in.'

They went to a pub and she bought Batchley a

pie and chips. He ate hungrily while she picked at a salad.

'Listen,' he said, growing serious as he pronged a chip and wiped up the last of his food with it. 'About the other day at the murder site. I wasn't going to bring it up but I was worried about you.'

He really was an extraordinarily nice man. She found she smiled more with him than with anyone.

'Yeah. Thanks for hustling me out of there. It was embarrassing. I just lost it for a moment.'

Batchley patted her hand.

'Hey, you don't have to explain, but I just didn't want you to think I was ignoring what happened. You were pretty upset.'

'I know. But I'm fine now, really.'

'So you don't want to talk about it?'

'Not really. Do you mind?'

'Of course not. So, how are things generally?'

'Fine. Mike's off seeing his kids this afternoon.'

Batchley raised his eyebrows.

'Oh really? I thought he would be in work after all the shit that went down yesterday.'

'What happened yesterday?'

'Didn't he tell you? Kathleen Norton claimed that Graham Richards raped her, and that the baby was theirs. Then we discovered that she'd worked as a nurse, at which point Mike went ballistic!'

'I'm not surprised. Nursing's a pretty big lead to have missed. Does that get you any closer to finding a link between the victims?'

'No. Not really. Kerry Willis was a teenage runaway, a heroin user. Ingrid Kestler was a pregnant German dancer. And we've got next to nothing on the third.'

'*Pregnant?* One of your victims was pregnant?'

181

'According to our witness, but we've no idea who by or whether she even had the baby for that matter.'

North rapped the table with her fingertips. She was suddenly interested.

'But that's the link. There seem to be a lot of babies involved in this case so what about antenatal clinics? Have you checked them out?'

'No, not yet.'

'But you just said Kathleen Norton was a nurse?'

'Yes,' said Batchley. 'But on the geriatric ward.'

'It would be worth checking to see if your pregnant victim visited that hospital, though.'

Batchley considered for a moment.

'Yes,' he said slowly. 'And maybe the other one as well.'

*   *   *

'How was the rugger match?' asked Lisa West as Batchley strolled into the Incident Room half an hour later.

'We won.'

He looked around. The place seemed unusually quiet, even for a Saturday afternoon.

'Where's everyone else?'

'Doug's out chasing up phone calls, Satchell's around somewhere and God knows where the Gov is. He disappeared this morning and hasn't returned yet.'

'So it's just the skeleton staff, then.'

She closed her eyes in protest at the joke. Meanwhile Batchley had crossed to the information board and was looking at a schedule of tasks facing the team over the weekend. One of

182

them said *Hospital Records—DI Batchley*. It was a reference to the records of Nurse Kathleen Norton, which he had been working on yesterday. But now he was thinking of other types of record. He tapped the list.

'I think our next move should be to check out local maternity-clinic records. Starting with St Jude's Hospital.'

'That the Gov's idea?'

'No,' said Batchley. 'But I don't reckon he's going to object, seeing as he brought me back specifically to check out Kathleen Norton's nursing connection.'

West was shaking her head.

'Kathleen's a sad case. But a killer? And what about Graham Richards?'

Batchley's gaze drifted across the information board. It fell on the photograph of Kestler and Bertrum at the Rhinestone Club.

'If that's him in the photograph, we need to know why he lied.'

'Yes,' said West simply. 'And it was his belt.'

*   *   *

After leaving Batchley, North found herself drawn irresistibly to the shops of Covent Garden, thinking of a new pair of shoes perhaps, or a bag. On her way across Leicester Square she started to walk into a cinema to check out the times of a film she wanted to see. But then there was a voice she knew calling out, 'Richard!'

She looked and saw the Walker family at the head of the queue. She moved quickly on to avoid being seen, and did not turn back until she had

183

covered a safe distance. When she did she saw Walker and Lynn, with Amy and Richard in tow, entering the cinema. There was something so convincingly real about the family image that, just as she had when she'd stood in Richard and Amy's room, she shuddered.

CHAPTER 17

MONDAY, 16 OCTOBER

Doug Collins had had Saturday and Sunday off and Lisa West was bringing him up to speed on the weekend's results. The research into Graham Richards's movements had been disappointing. So far they had been unable to put him close to any unsolved murder committed since 1983.

'It was a long job,' West told him. She nodded towards Walker who was on a call in his office.

'Would have been a sight quicker if skivers like you and Walker had been there to help.'

'Hey, shut about me. It's not every day one of my brothers gets married.'

She laughed.

'Well, I don't think Walker was at a wedding.'

'You mean he didn't turn up at all?'

'Just a few hours in the morning. I was here until six o'clock. He gets us in at seven thirty then pisses off before lunch. Then his mobile was switched off. God knows what he was doing.'

The man himself emerged from his office.

'That was Forensics,' he said to the room in general. 'Dr Smith's got the DNA results. The baby was Kathleen Norton's and guess what—the father was Graham Richards.'

Batchley whistled. Satchell said incredulously, 'Bloody hell, you mean he actually slept with her?'

'And why shouldn't he?' asked West tartly.

'Oh come on,' said Satchell, 'you've seen her.'

'What? She can't have sex because she's not

185

beautiful, is that it?'

Satchell shook his head.

'No, no. But you must admit she's pretty weird.'

'God, with chauvinist pigs like you on the case, the poor woman doesn't stand a chance.'

'So are we going to arrest them both?' Collins wanted to know.

'Not yet,' said Walker. 'Kathleen has already admitted the baby was hers. Richards has already said he slept with her once. There's no reason he'd know he got her pregnant. We need more evidence.'

'Let's see what we get from St Jude's,' suggested Batchley. 'I've got them checking maternity records to see if any of our girls paid them a visit. We also have the name of a hospital cleaner who had a relationship with Kathleen Norton when she worked at St Jude's, a Mr . . .'

He clicked his fingers, his memory chasing up the name. Satchell got there before him.

'Edward Colly,' he said. 'I'm already trying to trace him.'

Walker rubbed his hands together and looked around.

'My, my,' he said. 'We are on the ball, aren't we? Come on, Batchley, let's go and pay a visit to St Jude's.'

*　　　*　　　*

The white-coated administrative assistant of the St Jude's obstetric and maternity service was called Tara Gray. She led Walker and Batchley into a strip-lit basement with rows of steel shelf-stacks stuffed with files and records.

186

'Everything's computerized now,' she was explaining. 'But we keep hard copies and, of course, we need to hang onto the old pre-computer records. Some of this stuff is ancient archaeology.'

'So 1983's no problem?' asked Walker, scanning the file labels. He saw one shelf label which read ST JUDE'S OBSTETRICAL CONFERENCE: 1967 and, a little further on, EVIDENCE TO THE BLAKENHAM INQUIRY 1943—whatever that was.

'Oh, no. But that's the miscellaneous historical section you're looking at. Clinical records are along here. We have them subdivided into various categories such as antenatal clinics, postnatal clinics, labour ward records, the Prem Baby unit . . .'

'What's a "Prem Baby" when it's at home?' asked Batchley.

'It's not at home,' she told him with a tinkle of laughter. 'It's here, and in intensive care, because it's been born early. It's a premature baby.'

Like a tiny stab, the thought of his own premature baby pricked Walker. *Somewhere here amongst all this paperwork could be her records*, he thought, until he remembered it was the wrong hospital, the wrong district. Then he remembered Kathleen and her own dead baby. There would be no record of that one here either. Indeed, there would be no trace, in any archive, of that little one's brief and secret existence. Except, of course, now, in the police records.

Tara Gray drew them further into the archive room and consulted a handwritten list.

'I'm afraid there is no record of any of your names coming here in the normal course of antenatal check-ups,' she told them. 'But pregnant young girls do come in for other reasons too, so I

187

took the liberty of going through the termination of pregnancy files as well.'

She pulled down a thick file which she carried over to a small table and began leafing through the records.

'They weren't on the computer, so I checked back to the early 1980s—and you're in luck.'

Walker and Batchley exchanged glances.

'Go on,' said Walker.

'I found records of both Ingrid Kestler and Kerry Willis visiting the clinic here.'

'What for?' asked Walker. 'Abortions?'

Tara nodded.

'Yes, but neither of them had one. They were both over the legal term. In other words, they'd left it too late. Here you are.'

She pulled out a printed form with figures and remarks entered by hand. Walker studied it, with Batchley peering over his shoulder. The form was headed SUMMARY PATIENT ASSESSMENT. The name at the top read KERRY WILLIS and the procedure for which she was being considered was *termination of pregnancy*.

'Does that mean they might eventually have had the babies here?' asked Batchley.

She shook her head.

'It might, but it didn't. I've looked. They definitely didn't give birth in St Jude's, neither of them.'

Walker scanned the uppermost record in Kerry Willis's file. At the bottom of the page the consultant had checked a box labelled *Not accepted for termination*. He turned the page and found the patient's medical notes. Abbreviations were scattered throughout: FHH, LMP, NAD, with ticks or dates scrawled next to them. Results of an amniocentesis test for foetal abnormality were given. On another page was what appeared to be a psychological assessment of the patient.

'That should make interesting reading,' observed Batchley.

Walker merely grunted.

'Can I have copies of these records, please?' asked Walker. 'And also whatever you have on Ingrid Kestler?'

Tara Gray nodded.

'Yes, that should be no problem. There are a couple of forms you have to sign to do with confidentiality. But come back up to my office and I'll get started on the photocopying.'

Before they left, Walker thanked Tara Gray fulsomely.

'That was a good turn you did us,' he told her, 'checking for those names in the termination files. I will be sending officers down to carry out a general search of all the files on terminations. For now we'll concentrate on the years 1982—4. Would you mind letting your director know about this? Tell him I'd be pleased to talk him through it if he wishes.'

'Well, Mr Walker, I can't see any problem. I'm sure your officers are all extremely well behaved.'

On the way out, Batchley was jubilant.

'Pat was right, Gov. She told me pregnancy was our link.'

Walker did not much like being reminded of Batchley's friendship with his girlfriend.

'But we've gone a step further now,' he said. 'It's not just pregnancy that links our two victims. The point is that they were both refused abortions.'

Batchley grunted.

'And what's the betting that—'

'That our third wee girl was in the same fix. And, if she was, her name's got to be somewhere in those files.'

CHAPTER 18

TUESDAY, 17 OCTOBER

The search of St Jude's records had taken all afternoon and much of the night. The data gathered about pregnant girls who had been refused abortions at the hospital was still being analysed and Walker, impatient for action, was pacing about the Incident Room.

'Gov,' called Satchell from his workstation, beckoning to Walker. 'I've found the boyfriend.'

He tapped a command on his keyboard and across the room the big network printer chattered. Satchell left his chair to rip the printout, which he handed to Walker with a flourish.

'I present Edward Colly, window cleaner!'

Walker skim-read the printout and called to Collins.

'Hey, Doug, I need you.'

*   *   *

After inquiries at his home, a flat on a large estate in Willesden, they found Colly's van parked close by, outside a semi-detached house. Halfway up his ladder, Colly, a small, spare man of fifty-plus, was giving all his attention to the house's windows. Collins hailed him.

'Mr Colly?'

The window cleaner's leather squeaked across the glass.

'I'm fully booked today,' he told them, scarcely

looking down from his perch.

Collins held his warrant card high.

'Can you come off the ladder a minute? We just need to ask you some questions.'

The ladder wobbled as Colly looked aside and realized he was confronting the police. He stopped polishing.

'Police?' he said nervously. 'Oh, OK. Be right with you.'

When he reached the ground he seemed glad to have done so safely. He breathed heavily.

'What's this about?'

'Some missing women,' Walker told him, 'seventeen, eighteen years ago. Here.'

He handed Colly the snapshot of Kathleen Norton as a nurse. She posed in the open air, smiling proudly.

'Oh God, what happened to her?' asked Colly. 'Yes, I knew her. Kathleen. Kathleen Norton. Up at St Jude's when I worked there. Has she disappeared?'

Without comment, Walker took back the photograph and handed him three more. One was a detail of Greta Bertrum's photograph showing Ingrid's face in close-up. The second and third were the computer e-fits of Kerry and the other victim. As Colly studied them with care, Satchell noticed his hand was trembling.

'No,' Colly said at last. 'I don't know any of them.'

Suddenly realization came to him. He put his fingers to his lower lip.

'Oh God Almighty, I read about these women . . . the skeletons, yeah? It's been in all the papers, this.'

192

'Did you ever see Miss Norton with any of these women at the hospital?'

Colly shook his head anxiously.

'No, I don't think I did. Holy shit! I got nothing to do with this.'

'Were you aware that Kathleen Norton was pregnant seventeen years ago?'

'Bloody hell, no.'

He looked panic-stricken.

'It's not mine! She wouldn't let me touch her. What's she said?'

'She hasn't said anything Mr Colly. The baby isn't yours.'

Colly visibly relaxed.

'Well, that's a relief! I thought she was saying . . . Well, I didn't know what she could have said, but she screamed blue murder at the time.'

'About what?'

'About me making a pass at her.'

He paused for a moment in recollection.

'She slapped me when I tried to kiss her, told me she'd scream rape. But I didn't mean to scare her.'

'What did you want?'

'Well, that's obvious.'

Walker came back at him hard.

'Not to *me* it's not. What did you want?'

Colly shrugged.

'Well, sex of course. I thought she was up for it.'

'What gave you that impression?'

'She had this habit of following me everywhere when I was doing my rounds.'

'Cleaning?'

'Yeah. I'd, like, tease her a bit.'

'What about?'

'Oh God, I don't know . . . about her size, I

193

guess. Me being so skinny, her so big. Made me laugh. Then I gave her a kiss, nothing heavy, just a kiss. But she went all coy and in the next office we came to she says she'll wait for me there later. So I whip round cleaning like a mad thing, but when I get back, she's changed her mind, apparently. Just told me to get out.'

'Why was that, do you think?'

'I don't know. Looked like she was doing some work. She was in the filing cabinet. I went to give her a bit of a grope and then Sister Lewis barged in and caught us.'

'And this was the geriatric ward?'

'No.'

He screwed up his face trying to remember, then shook his head.

'Sister Lewis was maternity, I think. I won't get in trouble, will I?'

'No, you're not in trouble, Mr Colly,' Walker assured him. 'Thank you very much. We'll be in touch. You've been very helpful.'

*   *   *

By midday the Incident Room had come up with a provisional list of girls whose names had cropped up in the St Jude's files and who had fitted the same criteria as Kerry and Ingrid seventeen years ago. Meanwhile, Walker had returned from Willesden.

'Begin with those giving addresses closest to Hallerton Road,' he ordered. 'They're all to be interviewed, everyone you can find. We're specifically looking for connections with our Kathleen. The information I've just got from

194

Edward Colly circumstantially supports Graham Richards's story, at least to the extent that Kathleen warned Colly off by threatening to cry rape. I'm more and more certain she's the key to all this. I don't know how. I don't know why. I just know.'

Satchell was working his way through phone numbers given to the hospital by girls on the list. He had no joy until he came to Hannah Palmer, who had cited an address at 45 Leabery Avenue. It was within half a mile of Hallerton Road and the phone line was still connected.

'I'm Edith Palmer, that's her mother,' said a stiff, elderly voice when Satchell got through and asked for Hannah. 'But I don't see her. Not at all. She went and married a man I can't abide. Who's calling, anyway?'

Mrs Palmer was startled, and then put out, when Satchell told her. But she grudgingly provided him with her daughter's phone number.

'I only have it for emergencies,' she said crossly. 'I don't know if it works. Her married name's Day.'

When Satchell called the number, he was informed in a light, cheerful, female voice: 'If you have a message for Hannah or Steven, please leave it after the beep.'

He checked the address—a Berkshire village close to the M4—and decided to drive out there and get Hannah Day's story. He took Lisa West. An hour later, they were ringing the Days' doorbell to no discernible effect.

'No one at home,' Satchell said. 'I left a message for her to wait in.'

It was a 1930s, brick-built house with bay windows on either side of the door. West was peering through the leaded panes into what appeared to be a sitting room.

'No. No signs of life.'

She stood back and looked up. A hint of smoke smudged the air around the chimney. 'But they've not gone on holiday.'

Satchell walked to the side of the house and peered up the path to the rear garden. As he did so a small car pulled into the short driveway behind him. He swung round. It was driven by a fair-haired woman, with a man beside her. The back seat was heaped with supermarket shopping.

'Mrs Day?' he said as she got out.

'Yes?'

He showed his ID.

'I'm Detective Sergeant Satchell and this is Detective Constable West from the Metropolitan Police.'

He was interrupted by a mobile phone chirping. The Day woman rummaged in her bag.

'Hold on a second,' she said, putting it to her ear.

'Hello. Yes? Ben?'

By now the man had also emerged from the car.

'Is it about our kids?' he asked the two police officers warily. 'Has something happened?'

'No,' said Satchell. 'We're from London. It's a personal matter actually, concerning Mrs Day.'

Mrs Day passed the phone to her husband.

'You talk to him. I *told* him to take his football boots.'

Steven Day cast his eyes towards the sky.

'They were outside his bedroom door, in his kitbag.'

He took the phone.

196

'Ben, if you've left them behind it's your fault. No, I can't bring them to school ...'

'So how can I help you?' his wife was asking Satchell.

'Is there somewhere private we can talk, Mrs Day?'

She frowned.

'Whatever it is, I'd like my husband with me.'

They filed into the house, with Satchell and West both lending a hand by carrying a bulging shopping bag each into the kitchen.

'So?' she said enquiringly.

'We're working on a murder inquiry,' Satchell explained. 'And I'm hoping you may be able to help us.'

Hannah looked at him dumbstruck. Steven Day, who was unpacking shopping, swung round in disbelief.

'Help you with a *murder* inquiry?' he said.

'Yes. You may have seen it on the news. The house in Kilburn, where the skeletons were discovered.'

'Yes, yes. I've seen it,' he said. 'It's been all over the TV.'

'But how can *I* help you?' his wife asked. She was pulling distractedly at strands of her hair.

Satchell cleared his throat and looked between Steven and Hannah Day. He had a bad feeling about this.

'Well, it's rather sensitive, Mrs Day. Do you mind if we sit down?'

Satchell indicated the small kitchen table and chairs.

'Oh sorry, yes,' she said. 'Go ahead.'

All except Steven Day sat.

'We understand that in July 1983 you visited the termination clinic at St Jude's hospital, North London. Is that correct?'

Her eyes dilated in shock.

'No,' she said, her voice wavering. 'You must have mistaken me for someone else.'

'You were formerly Hannah Palmer?'

She flicked a glance at her husband.

'Yes,' she admitted. 'But there must be another Hannah Palmer. You must have it mixed up. Sorry.'

She was lying, of course. And, from the way she kept looking at Steven Day, it was obvious that he was the problem.

'Well, I'm sorry to have troubled you.'

Satchell looked at West and signalled with his eyes towards the door. He nodded at Hannah.

'Perhaps you can show us to the door. Thank you, Mr Day.'

At the door, Satchell spoke to her in a low voice.

'Mrs Day. I can understand that this is very personal, but hospital records show that a woman called Hannah Palmer of 45 Leabery Avenue did visit the termination clinic. Are you saying you never lived at that address?'

Mrs Day closed her eyes and there was a long pause.

'My husband doesn't know,' she said at last. 'I didn't go through with it. I had the baby adopted. Is this about him?'

'No, no. Look, do you think we can have a chat without your husband being present?'

She looked back up the hall and beckoned them to follow her.

'Come into the sitting room.'

They could hear Steven clattering around in the

kitchen, still stashing the shopping. Hannah Day explained the circumstances of her attendance at St Jude's.

'My mother didn't know I was pregnant. I kept quiet about it for weeks, just pretending it wasn't happening. But then I came to my senses. I realized I couldn't hide it much longer so I went to the hospital to ask about a termination. I was seventeen. They said they probably could have done it if I'd come in sooner but now I was too far gone.'

'Can you remember that day at all well?' asked West.

'Yes, I remember it all right because I was in such a state. The doctor was a really nice woman, really sympathetic. But she just said it was illegal to do a termination when you're as far gone as I was. So I wandered out of her office and had a good cry. I couldn't think straight.'

'After seeing the doctor, did you have any contact with anyone else from the hospital?'

'Well, yes, strange you should ask, but I did. Not officially, though.'

She took a deep breath.

'As I said, when I came out I was pretty upset. I sat outside on the hospital steps, crying. And yes, I remember, there was this nurse . . .'

'Outside the hospital?'

'Yes. She came up and asked if I was all right. She was ever so nice, very comforting, and I ended up telling her what had gone on. She said she might be able to help me.'

Satchell was aware that the noise from the kitchen had stopped and that Steven Day was standing in the hall, listening to his wife's words.

Hannah also knew he was there, but this time he did not inhibit her.

'Did she say in what way she could help you?'

'She said she knew someone that could do an abortion, even though I was so far gone. She said it would cost a lot of money, two hundred pounds, I think. I said I didn't have the money, but then she said it didn't matter. It was really odd. One minute she was asking me for money, and then the next it didn't seem to matter. It made me suspicious.'

'Did she say where you would have to go?'

'I don't think so. I can't really remember, but I think it was a private arrangement.'

Satchell leaned forward.

'Can you remember what this nurse looked like?'

'Kind of. She was quite big, strong; she gripped my hand so tightly it scared me.'

'So would you recognize her again?'

'Yes. Yes, I think I would.'

'Even though you met her only once?'

Steven Day had stepped into the room by now. He stood, a mute witness, by the door.

'Well,' said Hannah, looking at him, 'I was in a kind of heightened state of awareness. The whole day had been ghastly, but it wasn't one I was likely to forget.'

'And why did you not go ahead with this nurse's suggestion? The illegal abortion.'

'Well, as I said, I was put off by her odd behaviour. I couldn't work out her motivation—whether it was money or just doing good, helping desperate people. In the end I began to suspect that she herself might be the abortionist, though she'd never actually said this. But if she was—and

200

she'd told me she was still only a student nurse—I knew I wouldn't have confidence in her. There was something off-putting about her manner. So I said I'd contact her if I decided to go ahead and just disappeared. In the end, I braved my mother, had the baby and gave it up for adoption.'

She looked up at her husband, her china-blue eyes appealing for his understanding.

'It was the right thing, I'm sure,' she said. 'It was the right thing to do.'

CHAPTER 19

TUESDAY, 17 OCTOBER, NIGHT

North found herself on Batchley's doorstep at nine in the evening, ringing his bell. This time she had had no need to lie to Walker about where she was going. Walker had not yet returned home. If he had come in at a reasonable time, or even phoned, she might have suggested they go and see that film she had been wanting to see in Leicester Square. She was certainly tired of sitting around in the flat alone. But there had been neither sign nor signal from Walker and she was damned if she was going to play the needy victim by phoning him.

Coming out to see Batchley had not been a spur-of-the-moment thing. She had brooded on it for an hour before picking up her keys and leaving the house. She liked Batchley. He was kind, considerate and understanding—everything a self-respecting woman ought to love in a man, and everything Walker was not. At the moment she did not think she loved Walker. Knowing there were men like Batchley around put Walker in a different light and she suddenly saw a bridge in front of her, one that she might cross. On the other side lay a new life with Batchley and—perhaps—some kind of happiness.

Batchley came to the door in tracksuit bottoms and a slightly ragged T-shirt. His feet were bare.

'Hi,' she said, suddenly wishing she had called him first. 'I hope you don't mind me turning up on your doorstep, Jeff.'

Batchley's face had that look of benign bemusement which she had found so attractive in the past.

'Course not,' he said. 'Come on in.'

She sat on his big sofa, looking around his living room. The place hadn't changed that much since she'd last been here, though the pot plants looked as if they were getting more attention these days. As Batchley brought in two mugs of coffee and handed one to her she said, 'Is this a bad time?'

Batchley smiled that sweet smile of his and sat next to her.

'No, it's not. So, how are things?'

North was looking into her coffee, watching a bubble going round on its surface. She took a deep breath.

'Good, really. I've been sorting stuff out in my head.'

'Hey!'

He put his hand reassuringly on her shoulder.

'I did mean what I said, Pat. I'm always here if you need me.'

She caught his hand and touched it with her cheek.

'I know, and I appreciate it. The thing is . . . I don't think it's going to work out between me and Mike.'

She sipped her coffee and looked at him. His eyes had opened wide in surprise.

'I'm sorry. Sorry to hear that.'

'I sort of knew it was coming. And with you being . . . well, meeting up with you again helped me come to a decision, you see?'

Batchley's face lost its startled look. Now he seemed puzzled. He took a swift gulp from his own coffee and put it down on the low table in front of them.

'Look,' he said slowly, picking his words with care. 'I did mean what I said about being a friend for you. But, well, I don't want you to take it the wrong way.'

'What do you mean?'

'Well, I am just what I said. A friend. Mike is my boss.'

Batchley looked steadily at her and North suddenly felt the sting of acute embarrassment.

'I mean,' he continued, 'I do respect him, in a strange kind of way.'

She was about to interrupt him, stop him at all costs. This, she suddenly realized, had already gone too far. Batchley was making excuses, but it was she who ought to leave. Just then, the bedroom door opened and a young woman drifted out yawning. She was wearing a man's shirt, clearly one of Batchley's, and little or nothing else. She stopped short when she realized Batchley had company.

'Oh, hi! I'm sorry, I didn't know anyone was here,' she said.

Batchley jumped up and put his arm around the girl's shoulders. With a pang of envy, North saw not only that she was the right side of thirty, but she was astonishingly beautiful.

'Justine, this is Pat North. Justine's just got off a long-haul flight,' he added by way of explanation. 'You want a glass of water, Jus?'

Justine yawned again.

'Oh yes please.'

He tripped off to the kitchen. Justine smiled pleasantly at North. She clearly did not see the other woman as any kind of threat.

204

'I have to drink gallons,' she said. 'Otherwise I get dehydrated.'

'Oh? Where have you been?' North asked in an attempt at a light, conversational tone.

'Hong Kong. It's such a long flight.'

Batchley returned with Justine's water. She took it and kissed him swiftly on the mouth.

'Nice to meet you,' she said to North, nodding once, before padding back into the bedroom and closing the door behind her.

Back at the flat's front door, North felt forlorn and foolish.

'Jeff, I'm really sorry,' she said. 'I got it all confused, and you're right, it's no good going back.'

He kissed her cheek.

'You'll work it out, I'm sure of it. You're strong.'

She left him, wondering if he was right. She wondered too if Walker would be waiting for her, and what she would tell him.

*   *   *

In the event he wasn't. And when he did come in, what she said was just conventional.

'You're late. Where've you been?'

Walker breathed out beerily.

'Just having a drink with Satch. What about you? Been out tonight?'

She looked at him, feeling a certain defiance. He could go out drinking with his muckers, while she . . .

'Yeah. Only been back ten minutes or so, actually.'

'I suppose you were with Vivien, like you said you were the other night.'

He put a kind of deadly emphasis on the word

205

'night'. She jumped. So he *knew* she had lied about that evening? It was the first time he'd said anything about it. Vivien had called her, of course, to tell her that Walker knew North had not been with her. But Walker had never openly challenged North's story about the university friend. But now she knew he had been nurturing dark suspicions all along.

'What's been going on these past few weeks?' he asked. 'I don't like being lied to.'

'If you really want to know,' she said, braving his mood, 'I've been seeing a shrink.'

He was suddenly angry, bitter.

'Oh *that's* what he is now, is he? Interesting sideline for Batchley. *Amazing* you can find the time to talk to him and not me.'

She could not speak. He actually knew about Batchley. Guilt, regret, shame—whatever it was—temporarily paralysed her speech centres.

'Why did you lie to me, Pat? I know you've been talking to Batchley. Why can't you talk to me?'

North swallowed hard. He had only mentioned *talking* to Batchley. That didn't sound as bad as it could have been. If he'd imagined she was sleeping with him, what then? Well, she wasn't and he hadn't. Her ability to speak returned.

'Because you never want to listen. Yes, it's true, I *have* been talking to Jeff. He's been a good friend. But when I said I'd been to a shrink, I meant it.'

'You really have?'

'Yes.'

'Why didn't you tell me?'

'Because I knew how you'd react.'

He thought about North with this unnamed, unknown psychotherapist. He said, 'What do you

206

talk about? Do you talk about us?'

She sighed sardonically.

'What do you think?'

'So what does this therapist think, then? Does he think we have a future?'

'*She* doesn't make rash judgements. And I reckon you'd benefit from seeing her as well.'

'Why on earth do I need to see a shrink?'

'Because you have some serious thinking to do and I think she can help. I saw you with Lynn and the kids going into the cinema on Saturday.'

'You *what*? How?'

Now it was Walker's turn to be startled. He'd never said anything about Lynn having been part of the expedition. But North steadied him by holding up her hand, palm outwards.

'Now steady on. Before your paranoia kicks in, I wasn't following you. I was checking out the times for a film I thought we could see.'

'Pat—'

'No! Just let me finish. I felt like I was intruding on your life, on what it could be, I mean, with your wife, your kids. You looked like a family, and one that I have nothing to do with. And I . . . I so wanted a family with you.'

'Hey!'

He crossed to North and, taking her by the shoulders, turned her round to face him.

'I *want* to make it work.'

Her eyes were glistening.

'It's not that easy. I really think we need help. Please, Mike, come and see Sylvia with me.'

He embraced her.

'But how can a total stranger help?'

North drew back and lightly touched his face.

'Because she is just that, a total stranger. I don't even particularly like her. But she's good at her job.'

As she and Walker got ready for bed, both of them knew tonight had been the closest they had come to a real conversation for many days, even weeks. But they also knew what a long way they still had to go. Unfinished business had been piling up around their relationship like street garbage. As Walker brushed his teeth, with his usual savage energy, he made up his mind.

'All right,' he said, coming back into the bedroom. She was lying curled under the quilt, reading a magazine. 'All right. I'll come and see this Sylvia of yours.'

'No strings?' she asked.

'Just one. I refuse to lay down on any bloody couch.'

CHAPTER 20

WEDNESDAY, 18 OCTOBER

Walker had been jubilant when, around mid-afternoon on Tuesday, Satchell had briefed him about Hannah Day's evidence.

'That sounds like our Kathleen, all right. Well done, Satch.'

He rubbed his hands together, savouring the moment.

'What are you going to do?' Satchell asked.

'If the identification stands up tomorrow, I'm going to have her for murder.'

Satchell was a step or two behind his boss.

'Eh? What do you reckon happened, then?'

Walker stared into the middle distance and thought for a moment. The story, as he conceived it, was a simple one.

'Kathleen was an abortionist, working out of Hallerton Road. But she was fatally incompetent, more or less a butcher, and, when her "patients" died, which happened to our knowledge three times, she simply buried them in the garden or the coal chute.'

Satchell frowned.

'But she strangled one of them!'

'OK. Maybe that particular one was so horrified by Kathleen's crude methods that she threatened to expose her. So Kathleen killed her.'

'With Graham Richards's belt?'

Walker nodded.

'Exactly. Maybe it was her way of exacting

209

revenge on him for turning his back on her.'

Satchell considered this, but was unconvinced.

'She's got to have been phenomenally lucky to get away with it at the time. All three girls were untraceable. So what happened next? She just stopped doing it?'

Walker nodded.

'Yes. The death of her father may have had something to do with that. Or perhaps she saw the error of her ways. Her conscience bit her. There seems to have been plenty of religion floating around that house.'

Satchell still did not like it.

'OK, but how does all this connect to her own pregnancy?'

'It gave her the idea,' said Walker simply. 'Her miscarriage, I mean. It made her realize she could do this.'

'But that would mean she did it as a business. She told Hannah Day that the money wasn't important.'

'You mark my words, Satch,' Walker told him, shaking his finger. 'Maybe I haven't got all the details right. But she did it.'

*   *   *

Requiring Mrs Day's identification to be confirmed, Walker asked Collins to organize a photographic identity parade, a simple procedure which could be done in the Days' own home. Snapshots of five anonymous nurses were ordered up from the technical department, to place alongside the one of Kathleen that Collins had secured on Friday from Dorothy Norton. After an infuriating delay the five photographs were forthcoming and Collins made the journey to Berkshire.

Hannah Day, when she saw the six images laid out on her kitchen table, was in no doubt.

'That's her. Yes, that is definitely the woman outside the hospital,' she told Collins, tapping Kathleen Norton's face. 'The one who approached me that day and offered me an illegal termination.'

Back at the Incident Room, Walker had been waiting. As soon as Collins called in with his result, a call for back-up was made to the Richmond Police. He then sent Satchell and West speeding down to the Norton Retirement Home with an arrest warrant. It was Kathleen herself who opened the door to them.

'Kathleen Norton?' asked Satchell, though he knew perfectly well who she was.

Kathleen glowered at him.

'What do you want now? Why can't you leave me alone?'

But Satchell, closely followed by West, stepped smartly across the threshold, forcing Kathleen to move aside. There was no chit-chat.

'I am arresting you on suspicion of the murders of Ingrid Kestler, Kerry Willis and a third, as yet unidentified, girl. You do not have to say anything, but it may harm your defence—'

'Go away! GET AWAY FROM ME!' Kathleen screamed, putting her hands up as if to ward him off.

As Satchell recited her rights, Kathleen backed away towards the stairs. Behind her four wizened figures, one of them pushing another in a wheelchair, shuffled into view at the door of the

211

Daytime Lounge, their eyes darting with lively interest from Satchell to Kathleen. By the time Mrs Norton pushed through them to see what the commotion was about, Kathleen was screeching hysterically.

'Get AWAY from me. Mummy! Don't let them TAKE me, Mummy! Mummy!'

But Dorothy Norton stood immobile. She held her face averted from her daughter's, her hands gripped together in a tight clasp beside her stomach, as her daughter was handcuffed and taken away.

*　　　　*　　　　*

'Get your laughing gear round that.'

Satchell slid a pint towards Walker as, several hours later, they stood at the bar of a pub near the Incident Room.

The day had been tense and seemingly endless, as they always were when a prime suspect in a big case is identified and collared. Walker did not want Kathleen getting bail and had a long meeting with the Crown Prosecution Service, in order to be ready for the Norton lawyer Derek Waugh's predictable application for an immediate bail hearing. The request was granted and Waugh told the magistrate that his client denied all charges, that the Retirement Home couldn't function without her and that she was unlikely under the circumstances to abscond. The CPS argued, on the other hand, that this was a case of enormous public interest and that pending psychiatric assessments it was impossible to predict what Ms Norton might do. She might harm herself and may be in a

212

position to destroy important evidence.

These were tense moments but the decision had gone Walker's way and his suspect was at last parked safely in overnight custody.

'Well, at least now she's been charged you can breathe a little easier.'

'Me?' challenged Walker, taking a long pull on his pint. 'What's that supposed to mean? We all can.'

Satchell put his own pint down on the bar deliberately and turned to Walker. He was looking serious.

'Gov, I'm not being funny, but I think you should have charged Richards too. I mean, there's still a lot of evidence against him. Why not charge them both and let them fight it out in court? Least we've covered ourselves then.'

Walker lit a cigarette. He squinted through the smoke.

'You may be happy just covering yourself, but I want to get it right.'

'You're not on about the nursing thing again?'

'I'm sure he didn't do it. I mean, coming forward and admitting ownership of the murder weapon is hardly deflecting suspicion from himself.'

'Come on! Criminals are always putting themselves in the frame for stuff they actually did.'

'Yeah, but usually by pointing to someone else.'

Satchell held up a hand with fingers spread. He counted them out as he spoke.

'Fact, he helped lay the patio. Fact, his belt was round the neck of one of the victims. Fact, he lived in the house during the time we think they died.'

Walker stubbornly shook his head.

'I still think he's innocent. If I'm wrong, it's my

head for the chop, not yours.'

'You said it,' commented Satchell, taking another swallow of beer.

'Tenner says I'm right,' challenged Walker.

Satchell put down his glass and held out his hand for a shake.

'You're on.'

An hour or so later Walker and Satchell were still in the pub and the worse for several more pints of bitter, washed down in Walker's case with whisky chasers. Satchell knew the signs. When the boss was like this it usually ended with something getting broken.

'You know, I sometimes wonder whether I've done the right thing, Satch.'

'No backing out now,' Satchell replied. 'The bet stands. Ten quid.'

'No, not that . . . Pat and I are hardly speaking, and when we do it's only to argue.'

'That's women for you.'

'Yes, I know. But it's more than that. Ever since Pat lost the baby she . . . she was too focused on her bloody promotion, couldn't slow down, and wasn't looking after herself properly.'

'What happened to the days when women were at home and looked after the house, husband and kids, eh? Now they want to do it all.'

'At least Lynn's a good mother. You know sometimes I wonder if I could go back and live there, for the sake of the kids. Here's my family, they still need me, rely on me. Pat doesn't need me for anything any more. I mean, at first she didn't even want to keep the baby, I was the one who persuaded her. Now the baby's gone, she blames me for everything that's happened! She's just not

214

the same person.'

'I know, mate, I know.'

'She's also been seeing Batchley as well.'

Satchell, who had been growing bored with the conversation, was suddenly interested again.

'No! Are you serious?'

Walker was serious.

'Seems she'll talk to him, but she won't talk to me.'

'You don't think they're—? No! No way.'

'Why not? They did before I came along, remember?'

Satchell didn't like what he was hearing. With this going on, the Hallerton Road team would be torn apart.

'Well, you'd better confront him, Mike. Sort this out.'

Walker stared into his beer for a moment longer, then picked it up and drained it.

'Too right I'm going to sort him out. Where does the prick live? Do you know?'

Satchell raised his hands in warning.

'Oi, Mike, when I said sort it out, I didn't mean, you know, take him on. He's a big bloke.'

But Walker was already on his way.

'The bigger they are, the harder they fall,' he said over his shoulder.

*   *   *

Walker got Batchley's address from the Incident Room, caught a taxi and twenty minutes later Batchley opened the door to his swaying and truculent boss.

'I only got one thing to say to you,' snarled

Walker, pushing an index finger into Batchley's chest. The big man backed a few paces into his hallway. 'You're having a scene with Pat. Well, go right ahead, because even if I'm through with her, I'm not through with you.'

Almost tripping forward, Walker took a swing at Batchley, who snapped back his chin, and the punch connected only with air.

'Hey, don't go jumping to conclusions, Mike. Don't do this. Don't make a fool of yourself. You've been drinking.'

This incensed Walker even more. He gathered himself and threw another punch, which glanced off Batchley's shoulder.

'Hey!' warned Batchley. 'Back off, don't make me do something I'll regret. I mean it.'

But Walker was not backing off. He was beckoning with both sets of fingers.

'Come on, come on, you big lout. Try and get one in. Come on. Try and land one on me!'

Batchley's mouth distorted in a fit of rage. All the sallies, slights and put-downs which Walker had been aiming his way from the start of the investigation suddenly welled up in him. He bunched his sizeable fist and drove an explosive left hook into Walker's bony face. Walker toppled backwards, bounced off the wall and slumped down. He sat there dazed, clutching his cheek as the pain seeped into it.

Just then a blurry vision appeared to him: two naked legs, a nightshirt, big blue eyes, a mop of blonde hair.

'What's going on, Jeff?'

It was a girl. Batchley took her hand and spoke through set teeth.

'Mike, this is my girlfriend Justine.'

They both looked down at the man in the dark coat who lay sprawled and defeated on the floor, massaging his face. Dark blood had begun to flow from his nose.

'This is Mike Walker,' Batchley said to Justine, gesturing. 'My boss.'

Walker lay there puzzled, looking at the two of them. He pushed himself up and stood unsteadily, keeping a precautionary hand on the wall. Very slowly, comprehension dawned on him. Batchley was holding hands with the girl. Batchley was *with* the girl. Batchley was innocent. He aimed a smile, twisted from pain and embarrassment, at Justine.

'Nice to meet you,' was all he could think of to say.

*   *   *

In her comfortless cell, Kathleen did little. She did not ask for reading matter or writing tools. She did not want to phone or be phoned. Apart from lying on her bed staring at the ceiling, she desired only to eat and to sleep.

She tussled with herself. She shrank from stooping to ask for help. She had always made a point of self-reliance, that was her way. But, at last, in the middle of the night, she pressed the call buzzer and waited anxiously for the night-shift officer to respond. Finally the flap in the door was lifted and she saw a pair of eyes peering through.

'What do you want, Kathleen?'

'I can't sleep.'

'But you were given something earlier.'

'Well, it didn't work.'

217

'I always count sheep.'

The officer's voice was kindly, verging on jocularity. Kathleen nodded her head sadly.

'Yes, but you haven't been accused of murder.'

'Would you like a hot drink?'

'Yes please. I need to get some sleep. I'm meeting my barrister tomorrow and I need to make a good impression.'

'I'll get you some hot milk.'

The flap rattled again and Kathleen started to her feet, calling out.

'And a chocolate biscuit?'

The officer heard her.

'I'll see what I can do,' she trilled.

Kathleen sat down again, exhaling in relief.

'Thank you,' she said.

CHAPTER 21

FRIDAY, 20 OCTOBER

The criminal bar may be a haven for eccentrics and would-be actors but, even by that standard, Rupert Halliday QC was a flamboyant figure. As one who spent his infrequent holidays fishing for salmon on the best Scottish rivers, he possessed the same intuitive feel for the mood and expectations of a jury as he did for the fish he lured. If it advanced his cause, he was capable of extraordinary histrionics in court, but he could also deploy charm, wit and bluff common sense to considerable effect. Amongst the elite criminal advocates in London, he was Derek Waugh's favourite, which is why he briefed him to lead for the defence in the case of Kathleen Norton.

At about midday, Waugh arrived at Halliday's chambers in the Middle Temple, carrying a fat legal briefcase. A conference room had been reserved for the meeting, its imposing mahogany table stacked with the case files, platters of sandwiches and a selection of soft drinks in cans.

'Sit yourself down, Derek,' said Halliday, pulling out a leather-upholstered chair. 'I thought we should have a quick chat and a bite before going off to meet Miss Norton. You know Lawrence Camplin, I take it?'

He indicated his junior, who was tapping a laptop computer. Camplin and the solicitor acknowledged each other by nodding their heads. With a sweep of his arm, Halliday indicated the food and drink.

'Help yourself—the more serious the case the better the sandwiches the clerks provide—triple murders rate the full monty of chicken salad and cheese and pickle.'

Waugh beamed. He rarely wasted a chance to fuel up his considerable bulk.

'Thank you, Rupert. I'll remember to brief Tudor Chambers for all serial-killer cases in the future.'

He popped open a fizzy drink and reached for the sandwiches. Halliday held out his hand for a sheet of paper from Camplin. It contained his junior's summary assessment of the charges and evidence. Halliday had already taken a look at the brief overnight and was pleased to see that Camplin had not spotted anything he himself had missed.

'OK. What have we got here? Three murder counts . . . victims found buried on the defendant's property . . . one apparently strangled with a belt. Plus a stillborn baby found under the bedroom floorboards.'

He rubbed the musketeer beard that he had recently been cultivating on his chin.

'The medical evidence, at least, tells us that the baby was not murdered. But the Crown have, somewhat ungenerously in my view, put a count on the indictment of "concealment of birth, contrary to section 60 of the Offences Against the Person Act 1861".'

Waugh chewed for a moment and swallowed.

'Well, Kathleen admitted the offence of concealing the baby in interview,' he observed.

'Yes, she did.'

As Halliday knew perfectly well, under ideal circumstances the details of an admitted offence by the defendant could be excluded from the evidence on other charges, which she may deny. This would be good for her because the jury would not hear them and form a prejudice against her as someone of bad character. But there were problems.

'The trouble is,' the QC went on, 'even if she pleads guilty to that count, the Crown will still call the evidence. They'll get it in as similar fact.'

Waugh's mouth had taken another sizeable half-moon out of a cheese sandwich. Temporarily gagged, he nodded.

'Oh right,' he said, swallowing at last. 'The fact that we hide one dead body under the floorboards is circumstantial evidence that we had something to do with the other three dead bodies found interred or entombed in the same property.'

'Quite. Of course, we'll try to get it excluded, but I don't imagine we'll succeed.'

They spent the next twenty minutes going over Kathleen's statement before repacking their papers and moving off down the stairs.

'In isolation, the three murders might be a classic whodunit,' Halliday was saying. 'I'm afraid the stillborn baby rather complicates the position. I mean, why hide it under the floorboards, rather than burying it in woods in the countryside somewhere? Or even leaving it in someone's dustbin or in a skip? Why hang onto it so you're reminded of its presence every time you go into the room? A touch macabre, isn't it?'

They reached the open air where Halliday breathed in deeply and set off through the Temple precincts at a fast walk. The autumnal air was

221

spiced with the smoke of incinerated garden leaves.

'From what she's told me,' said Waugh, walking hard to keep up with the brisk figure of the barrister, 'she was distraught when she lost the baby. It's understandable, she must have been in a pretty troubled state of mind.'

With Halliday walking strongly in the lead, they went through the security barrier that marked the confines of the Temple.

'Troubled enough, the Crown will no doubt maintain,' said the QC, 'to go looking in hospital records for girls who didn't want to keep their babies and were looking for abortions? Troubled enough, perhaps, to offer them after-term abortions and then do them in, eh? Troubled enough then to bury them close to her own baby so as to teach them some sort of symbolic lesson? An imaginative psychiatrist would have a field day with that one.'

'So what are you saying?' asked Waugh. 'Kathleen Norton's a diminished-responsibility case?'

'Well, that's the problem. At the moment, it's an I-haven't-done-anything-except-dispose-of-my-stillborn-baby-under-the-floorboards case.'

'The instructions she's given me are perfectly clear and they are that she was upset about the baby at the time, couldn't tell anyone and didn't know what to do, so she hid the body. Kathleen is adamant that she knows nothing about the other bodies.'

Halliday nodded, thinking deeply without relaxing his pace.

'And that is exactly what she told the police. On the face of it, no responsibility at all for the

222

murders, so no room for diminished responsibility.'

They were on Fleet Street now and Waugh was almost panting. Halliday tapped his foot in exasperation as he waited for Camplin to catch them up under the burden of his files. As he did so, a cab appeared, with a yellow light shining. Imperiously, Halliday flagged it down and climbed in with Waugh. Camplin told the driver they were bound for Highfield Prison.

'It's a straightforward plea of "not guilty",' Halliday was saying as he settled in next to Waugh. 'Mark you, the case against her is by no means overwhelming—in some respects it's really quite thin. I don't want to be sexist here, but burying bodies underneath paving slabs or plastering over coal holes at first blush would appear to be somewhat of a male activity. In these times of equal opportunity, nothing can be taken for granted, but for choice, I'd go for something muscly and grizzled, wielding a spade and a cement mixer.'

Waugh, not known for his sense of humour, saw the funny side of this and sniggered.

'You haven't seen Kathleen yet,' he said. 'That's not a bad description of her.'

'Well, there's no forensic evidence apart from our thumbprint turning up under the buckle of the belt inconveniently found around victim number two's neck. It clearly doesn't help us, but as against that, Graham . . . what's-his-name?'

'Richards,' supplied Camplin, perched uncomfortably on the jump seat.

Halliday inclined his head.

'Yes. Graham Richards has been good enough to step forward and claim the belt was his. In any view, in the light of his undoubted paternity of our

223

stillborn baby, we must have had the trousers off him on at least one occasion, so to speak, so our thumbprint on the buckle of what once held those trousers up may not be entirely fatal to our case.'

Camplin looked seriously at his leader.

'You can do it, you know, without taking your t-trousers off.'

He only had a slight stammer, but it was always exacerbated in the mandarin presence of Halliday. The QC did nothing for his junior's self-esteem by snorting derisively.

'It's comforting to know that we have an expert on the team, Lawrence. But I'd keep your personal reminiscences to yourself, if I were you.'

He looked out of the window.

'Why on earth didn't he go through the park?' he demanded. 'This is going to get us into deep traffic around Piccadilly.'

*   *   *

Arriving at last at Highfield, they announced themselves as the legal representatives of Prisoner 357B Norton and submitted to security checks. In the legal visits suite, they sat awaiting their client.

'We'd better ask her about her medical history,' Halliday pointed out. 'Although I don't suppose for a moment that she has one, at least not in retrievable form. More importantly, I think, do we get a psychiatrist to see her now? On the face of our instructions, there are no mental or medical issues in this case, and all a psychiatrist will be able to tell us is that women who give birth to stillborn babies and hide them under floorboards would probably thereafter suffer from a degree of depression. As against that, Kathleen appears to have survived the intervening years without too much trouble.'

'You know that the main objection to her having bail was that she might harm herself?' Waugh mentioned. 'She was behaving pretty erratically at the police station.'

Halliday thought for a moment, his fingertips pressed together.

'Well, I think we should ask her if she wants to see someone, but I'm not sure I'd encourage her to at this stage.'

'Yes,' said Waugh, 'I agree. We could be opening up Pandora's box, contents unknown.'

'Lawrence, could you see about a cup of tea? And for you, Derek?'

Waugh asked for coffee and Camplin was at the door when Halliday had an afterthought.

'Oh, and find out who's prosecuting, will you?'

Camplin wondered how Halliday thought he could obtain this detail from the hot drinks machine. But, in any case, he didn't need to.

'I already have,' he said. 'It's Willis Fletcher.'

'Ah!'

With Camplin out of the room, Halliday turned back to Waugh.

'Tell me, does Kathleen herself have any theories as to how the three bodies ended up where they did?'

'She's not really given to the theoretical is our Kathleen.'

'Well, she's clearly going to have to think about how those skeletons got there. Corpses, unlike mushrooms, don't just grow in dark places. They have to be planted.'

He looked at his watch as Camplin returned with two cups.

'On that light philosophical note I wonder if Miss Norton has escaped her captors. It's almost two thirty.'

Camplin frowned.

'Surely, Rupert, that's not really a ph-philosophical note. It's more of an agricultural note, or possibly even a horticultural one.'

Halliday closed his eyes for a moment.

'Lawrence, as they say in the world of mushrooms, *button* it.'

At this moment the door opened and Kathleen entered with her escort. Waugh rose.

'Kathleen,' he said. 'This is Mr Halliday who will be acting for your defence in court. And this is junior counsel, Mr Camplin.'

She shook hands with Halliday and Camplin as Waugh drew out a chair for her. She sat, placed her hands on the table and smiled pleasantly. She decided to treat these gentlemen as she treated the select residents. She must charm them.

*　　　*　　　*

What hurt Walker was not his nose or bruised cheek, but the sense that he had lost control and allowed private animosity to spill over into a professional relationship. This morning he had taken three Alka-Seltzers, followed by two decisive actions. First he phoned Batchley and apologized as profusely as he knew how. Batchley reassured him that he bore no hard feelings and was prepared to forget last night's altercation, if Walker would. They both knew this was in the best interests of everybody. Clearly the fact that Batchley had dumped a senior officer on the seat of his pants—whatever the provocation—would not look good on his CV. But, equally, if Walker's drunken antics became known to his superiors, they must have a serious, perhaps terminal, effect on his career in the SCG. They also both knew that, morally, Walker was much more in the wrong than Batchley. He had, in fact, been completely out of order and rarely felt so chastened.

His second decision was the direct result of this lurking guilt: he phoned Sylvia Newberg and made an appointment for himself and North.

Now he sat beside her in Sylvia's consulting room. They had been there just a few minutes, but the atmosphere was already tense.

'We want to try to sort things out,' North was saying. 'But he's still finding it difficult to talk to me.'

Walker grunted. Beforehand he had wanted to be reasonable, but everything about this situation was alien to him. If not exactly washing your dirty underwear in public, it was tantamount to asking a total stranger to help you sort out the socks from the smalls. Now, hearing what he interpreted as a sally from North, he bridled.

'Pass the buck, why don't you.' He spoke morosely to Sylvia. 'As you can see I'm blamed for bloody everything.'

'Oh come on!' cried North. 'That's not fair. Look, I know this isn't easy for you—I mean, it's taken me long enough to get you here, but being here isn't enough. You have to make an effort. We need to talk about the baby. You can't even mention it. In your eyes it's happened and it's over.

But I can't forget that easily.'

Walker nodded.

'Yes, but it's something that happened. You lost the baby. We just have to learn to deal with it.'

'Actually, Mike,' interposed Sylvia, 'it's your loss too, you lost a daughter. Perhaps we should spend some time talking about how you feel.'

Walker sat forward.

'My feelings? You want my feelings? OK.' He turned to North. 'Since you and I have been seeing each other it's changed my relationship with my kids and my family.'

North closed her eyes.

'Oh God! So you blame me for that, do you?'

Again Sylvia intervened.

'Pat, let him speak.'

'Look,' Walker went on, 'you wanted me to talk so why don't you try to listen to me for a change? I'm not close to them any more. I don't see them as much as I'd like and, if you must know, I feel caught between you and Lynn. You both demand too much of my time, my energy. Frankly, you and Lynn have become the same nagging person—'

'Oh, thank you very much for comparing me to your psychotic wife.'

'I'm trying to tell you how I feel. It's always pressure, pressure, pressure. The baby was a chance for us to start a family together. A new life. It was everything I wanted. I wanted a baby with the woman I love, but that's gone now. It's over. You think I didn't want that baby as much as you? *I* wanted it . . .' He found he was shaking. He tried to control it. 'I wanted it more than anything, Pat. I did want to have a proper family, a baby, with you.' He turned to Sylvia. He thought at any moment he

228

might start crying. 'I'm sorry. I'm sorry. This is so embarrassing.'

North was touched. She reached for his hand, but he withdrew it. He was breathing heavily.

'That's OK, let it go,' Sylvia told him. 'It's OK.'

All three sat for a moment in silence. North and the therapist looked at Walker. He looked at the floor.

'This was our baby,' North broke in. 'And it's not about trying to be strong and blocking it out any more.'

'I'm not blocking anything out. But please try to see it my way.' He appealed again to Sylvia. 'So, come on then, what can we possibly do now? That's why we're here, isn't it? What next? Because *I* don't know what to do!'

'You've made a great sacrifice coming here today, Mike,' she said calmly. 'And Pat, I think you should see this as Mike's expression of his love for you.'

'It's true,' Walker added. 'I wouldn't have come if I didn't want to give it a real go, to try to make it work. I just don't know how to . . . say things.'

North found she was smiling and, suddenly, full of love.

'I know,' she said. 'I know you don't.'

*   *   *

'Do you have that photograph of the belt to hand?' asked Halliday, snapping his fingers at Camplin.

Kathleen had been trying their patience, refusing to discuss the case against her, as if to do so were the same as confessing her guilt. Camplin opened an album and leafed through it. They all

229

caught a glimpse of images of the three victims as he turned the pages. Then he came to two prints of the belt, one of which was a close-up of the buckle. Halliday turned the album and showed it to Kathleen.

'Do you remember Graham Richards wearing a belt like this one?'

She shook her head firmly.

'No. I've been asked this before.'

Halliday pointed to her hand.

'Show me your right thumb.'

She did so. He grasped it and turned it so that the ball of the thumb was uppermost.

'That thumb, Kathleen, came into contact with this buckle at some stage.'

'How do you know? You were there, were you?'

Halliday took a breath and continued.

'Let's just think about this. As you already know, this print on the back of the buckle is your thumbprint. So you must have handled it at some stage . . . Take your time. We know it's Graham Richards's belt. Now, how would your print get onto his belt, eh?'

But Kathleen's face was set.

'I don't know. Ask him.'

'I'm sure I will, if I get the chance. But I wouldn't mind having the answer from you first.'

Kathleen's eyes suddenly filled with tears. She averted her face.

'He raped me. You know that, don't you?'

'Do you think he may have been wearing that belt when he raped you?' put in Waugh. 'It's quite distinctive, isn't it?'

'How do you expect me to remember what he was wearing?' she said scornfully. 'He raped me and you are asking me all these stupid questions!'

'Kathleen,' said Halliday persistently. 'You're going to have to deal with this in court, so you may as well start thinking about it now. I know it's difficult for you.'

Kathleen took a tissue from a box thoughtfully provided by the solicitor and blew her nose delicately. She composed herself.

'Well, Mr Halliday, it may have been that, but I just can't remember.'

A thought came to her.

'Oh, unless I picked it up when I cleaned his room.'

The idea developed. She warmed to it.

'I probably rolled the belt up and put it away in a drawer.'

Halliday beamed.

'Good! You see? That's excellent. From what you've just said the Crown will be able to establish through your evidence that, at the very least, you had access to that belt. You see, *they'll* be suggesting that you took it, perhaps from his room, and then used it to strangle . . . er . . .'

He looked to Camplin, who began to supply the name.

'Ingrid K-K-K . . .'

'Kestler,' completed Waugh.

Kathleen looked at her three visitors in turn. She looked shocked by the suspicion Halliday had just voiced.

'I don't care what they say. I never even met that poor girl.'

She flipped her hand at the album of photographic evidence, pushing it away. The album slid off the table, taking with it a half-full polystyrene coffee cup. The hot contents spilled onto Halliday's lap.

Halliday leapt to his feet with a yelp.

'Oh I am so sorry,' cried Kathleen. 'Here, do you want my tissue? Did it get on your trousers?'

But Camplin had already whipped out a tissue from the box on the table and Halliday was using it to dab ineffectually at his pinstripe trousers. When he had done his best to minimize the damage, he returned to his seat.

'Never mind, never mind,' said Halliday testily. 'Accidents happen.'

'Yes they do,' said Kathleen. She pointed at Halliday's midriff. 'And if I'd helped you take your trousers off, my thumbprint could have been on *your* belt.'

She favoured him with a light, quick smile. Halliday looked sharply at her then realized he had been bested. He laughed.

'Too true, Kathleen.'

Waugh was looking through a file of prosecution statements.

'Now what about this Edward Colly chap,' he asked 'and what he says about you looking at patient records? You understand the problem here, don't you?'

Kathleen did not much like Waugh's patronizing tone.

'No,' she said shortly. 'What problem? I wanted to find out what I should do with my own pregnancy, because I was dealing with it all on my own.'

'But you were a nurse, weren't you?' said Halliday.

'Only part-time and on the geriatric ward. I

didn't know anything about the maternity side and that was all I was doing, checking up things for myself.'

Waugh leaned forward and turned back the album pages to the images of Ingrid Kestler and Kerry Willis.

'But you see,' he said, 'the problem for us is that in amongst those records would have been the details of the two girls who ended up under the patio at Hallerton Road.'

'I didn't know that.'

Waugh looked at Halliday, who was smoothing his beard thoughtfully.

'So Mr Colly has got it right?' he mused. 'You were looking at medical files late one night and—'

'Mr Colly was only interested in one thing. How would he know what I was doing?'

'Well now, they do have another troublesome witness. What about Hannah Day?'

'Who's she?'

'Mrs Day says she met you outside the maternity unit,' Waugh said. 'And that you discussed abortions with her.'

Kathleen was shaking her head piteously.

'I don't understand. Why would a complete stranger make up lies about me? All I've done from the start is tell the truth.'

CHAPTER 22

TUESDAY, 5 DECEMBER

In the following weeks Dorothy Norton was forced into a new, lonely and thoroughly unwelcome way of life. She felt anguished and bitter at what she had lost and blamed it all on her wayward daughter. This resentment was partly why she stayed so long away from Highfield Prison, but there was another reason. She had an idea, mostly drawn from her girlhood reading, that prisons were dank, grey fortresses of flagstoned cells with iron doors and high, barred windows. They were patrolled by grim-faced warders jangling their keys on large steel rings in an atmosphere ringing with the rhythmical drumming of cheap cutlery on metal plates and the ululations of insane prisoners howling for freedom. The prospect of walking through this living purgatory was a torture to her.

But, when desperation and loneliness finally drove Dorothy to visit Kathleen in the modern Remand Wing at Highfield, she was pleasantly surprised. The visiting room, she found, was like a cross between a doctor's waiting room and a station buffet. There were upholstered easy chairs grouped around low tables on which tea, coffee and biscuits were laid. She did not eat but sipped her tea and watched as Kathleen worked her way through a plateful of chocolate digestives.

'How are my wrinklies doing without me?' Kathleen asked at last, wiping chocolate from her lips with a paper napkin. Her tone was a touch complacent, her mother thought. She gave Kathleen the facts.

'In the end the social services found places for all four of them, and they've arranged meals to be delivered for me. Nice woman, the social worker, very pleasant. She gave me a buzzer connected to the telephone and if I fall or anything I just press it. But I'm still on my own. How long will you have to stay here, Kathleen?'

'How should I know?' said Kathleen gloomily.

'But this is all so terrible.'

Kathleen looked sardonically at her mother.

'Well, you seem to be doing all right. Everyone running around after you, but then that's nothing new, is it?'

Dorothy, choosing to ignore this barbed remark, said plaintively, 'I'm worried sick about this whole dreadful situation.'

'All you're worried about is yourself. That's all you've ever cared about.'

Dorothy's lips trembled at her daughter's unkindness.

'That's not true, Kathleen. Now just you stop this. Have you any idea what I'm going through?'

'You never cared what *I* was being put through,' snorted Kathleen. 'You still don't.'

Dorothy was on the edge of tears now.

'I *did* care. I've always cared for you, Kathleen.'

Kathleen smiled slyly.

'But you cared a lot more for Daddy, didn't you? And he got away with murder, didn't he?'

Dorothy crossed herself reflexively.

'May God forgive you for saying such a thing. Your father had nothing to do with those girls.'

'I wasn't speaking literally, Mother. I meant the

235

way he treated me, the way you both *abused* me.'

Dorothy opened her eyes wide.

'Abused you? How can you say such a thing? Why are you telling such terrible lies?'

Kathleen felt she had her mother on the run now. She pressed home her attack.

'But they're not lies and you know it. If what my father did to me was ever to become public—'

'STOP IT!'

The words had come out louder than Dorothy intended. Heads around the room turned and Dorothy was suddenly aware of how very public their situation was.

'I won't listen to you,' she said more quietly.

'If you want me to continue keeping my mouth shut, then I hope you do listen. I'm only protecting you, Mother.'

'You know I only want the best for you, dear,' protested Dorothy, thoroughly frightened now. 'That's all I've ever wanted.'

Kathleen laughed.

'You don't have to pretend, not now, Mother. I know I was never what you wanted. You fed me packets of crisps and bags of sweets to keep me quiet, but you never loved me.'

Kathleen raised her arm, in a signal to the officer standing at the end of the room that she wanted to return to her cell.

'So,' she said in a sweet-sounding voice, with just an edge of menace to it, 'you say one word against me and I'll make you *so* ashamed about what went on.'

Dorothy started, if not actually to cry, then to simper tearfully.

'I'm so sorry,' she sniffled. 'I'm so sorry. I let you

236

down. I did . . .'

Kathleen stroked Dorothy's hand.

'I forgive you, Mummy. I forgive you.'

She leaned across the table and with both hands drew her mother's wrinkled, sagging face towards hers. She kissed her on the lips and stood up. On the table between them was a box of chocolates, brought to her by the visitor. Kathleen snatched the gift up, tucked it under her arm and walked away.

*   *   *

'Willis! I heard you were in court today.'

Rupert Halliday sprinted to intercept Willis Fletcher just as he was pushing through the main door of one of the Crown Court buildings that ring London. They had both arrived for work—on separate cases—and with the Norton trial due to open in a few days in Kingston Crown Court, Halliday was anxious to have a word in advance. With relatively few witnesses, the Crown Prosecution Service had not found it a complicated case to prepare and was bringing it to trial in unusually short order.

The two men strode through the hall together, Fletcher smiling happily. He enjoyed his work.

'Yes, I'm here, for my sins,' he said. 'Court five. And to which court are you giving your weighty presence?'

Halliday wagged a finger.

'Actually, Willis, I've lost a considerable amount of weight recently. I am calorie-conscious now.'

Fletcher pointed to Halliday's still fairly novel beard.

'And are the chin whiskers part of the new

237

image?'

Halliday looked at Fletcher's more bushy facial growth.

'No, no,' he said. 'I just didn't want to be upstaged . . . I hear you're against me over Kathleen Norton at Kingston next week, is that right?'

'Ah yes, Ms Norton. No Wedding and Four Funerals. Let me guess: you want to know if I'll accept manslaughter?'

Halliday let Fletcher's supposition hang, neither confirming nor denying it.

'The short answer, I'm afraid, is no,' Fletcher continued. 'On current information, we say that she's bad and not mad.'

'Well, may I politely suggest you reconsider, Willis? If your side's version of events is anything like the truth, it *is* rather barking behaviour, by any standards.'

They had reached the robing room now. The two QCs hung up their coats and began to fix their white neck bands. Then Fletcher crossed to the mirror and dragged a comb through his thick, wavy hair.

'Well, we have no indication of any history of mental illness,' he said, 'either at the time of the killings or since, and there was nothing said to the officers in interview to suggest any past or present mental aberration. Funnily enough, I listened to her interview tapes last night at home for exactly that reason, and she sounded pretty well *lucid* to me. I'm sorry I can't be more helpful to you on this.'

He was putting on his gown while Halliday inspected some sandwiches next to the coffee

238

machine. He lifted the bread on one or two to check the fillings and, spying one with ham, he picked it up, removed the meat and ate it, dropping the bread neatly into a bin.

'No, no,' he said, feeding his arms into his gown. 'As a matter of fact that's very helpful. But you're jumping the gun a bit. In fact, pleading to manslaughter wasn't really what I wanted to discuss, although it does help me to know your views. That said, from my all too brief acquaintance with her, she does strike me as, how can I put it, possibly a couple of volumes short of a full set of law reports?'

Fletcher was standing in front of the full-length mirror, straightening his wig.

'Oh, I wouldn't hold that against her,' he said drily. 'There's hardly a complete set of law reports to be found anywhere in the Temple. But, if manslaughter wasn't on your mind, what was?'

'Well, I'm more concerned at the moment about this concealing-the-birth count. She'll plead guilty to that, which may come as no great surprise to you. What I'm really concerned about is not to have the evidence relating to that count in front of the jury: it's pretty prejudicial stuff, and really doesn't prove anything in the murder case, as I see it.'

Halliday reached for his wig.

'If you think about it, the prejudice that would create in the jury's minds would be utterly overwhelming.'

Fletcher had finished with his own wig. He grabbed an armful of briefs and other papers to take with him into court.

'You know, I'm not sure about that. I mean, any

239

prejudice might actually work in your favour and not against you. The jury might feel dreadfully sorry for her. But I'm afraid you'll have to raise this one with the trial judge, if you want it excluded.'

Halliday was now standing at the mirror where he crowned himself with his wig. He was humming quietly, as if nothing mattered very much either way.

'Well,' said Fletcher with continued good humour. 'I must get into court. See you next week at Kingston.'

Halliday was staring at his reflection in the long mirror. He sucked in his stomach and turned to view himself sideways.

'Looking forward to it, old boy,' he called towards the door, but it was already swinging shut behind the hurrying prosecutor.

*   *   *

It was almost seven weeks since North and Walker had made that first appointment with Sylvia. They had been back twice more and were due again this week. The psychotherapist thought they were 'progressing nicely', which sounded to North like a school report. But it was true that she was more relaxed, and more human, now that a line of communication had been opened with Walker. And so was he.

With Kathleen Norton in custody and awaiting trial, the inquiry had settled into a less pressurized routine. Walker regularly got home for supper and they had caught that film North had wanted to see at Leicester Square. But today he did something quite unexpected by turning up at her office in the

240

Yard for a surprise visit.

'Hello!' she exclaimed, finishing the call she was on. 'What are you doing here?'

Walker had been seeing the Commander and, with the meeting finished, had a free lunchhour.

'Thought I'd come and take you out for lunch.'

Just a few minutes earlier she had committed herself to a short working lunch with an Oxford University criminologist, who was due to speak to a seminar she was organizing. After that she had a two o'clock meeting.

'Oh, why didn't you call?'

'I wanted to surprise you. Look if you're busy it's not a problem.'

'I'm really sorry, but . . . Any other day would have been great, it's just I'm up to my eyes. I'm really sorry.'

He smiled, accepting the situation without question.

'No, no, it's my fault,' he said. 'I should have called. It's no problem, I'll see you later.'

He pecked her on the cheek and left. North closed her eyes and cursed, because it would have been nice to go with him. But for all that, she thought, the signs were positive. A few weeks ago there would have been a flash of anger in Walker's eyes and a churlish parting shot. Instead he had been easy about the failure of his idea. The three words 'it's my fault' were not often heard on Walker's lips.

*   *   *

The Incident Room was still up and running, with the team cross-checking statements, following up

241

additional leads and preparing paperwork for the use of the Crown Prosecution Service and Willis Fletcher. The third victim had still not been positively identified from a number of possible candidates and it now seemed possible they might never know her name.

Doug Collins and Lisa West packed up the clay heads, ready to go to court. Fletcher had decided the jury would like them, and anything that beguiled a jury was in his book worthwhile. Besides, an old case like this, involving skeletons dug out of the ground, risked becoming mouldy and impersonal. The presence of these exhibits would freshen up the victims and make them real. They already had that effect on Collins, who was easing number three into a box.

'Sad, isn't it?' he mused. 'She's somebody's daughter. It's bloody tragic.'

His train of thought was interrupted by Batchley's voice, coming in from the corridor.

'Look, just LEAVE it, Satch!'

The big Detective Inspector swept into the Incident Room, followed by the unrepentant figure of Satchell.

'Look,' Satchell was saying, 'Richards lied in interview. He should have been charged.'

'But he wasn't. Even if he did rough up a few hookers, it doesn't prove anything. Walker made the decision not to charge Richards and we have to stand by him.'

'Oh yes?' challenged West. 'If they're hookers, it's OK to smack them around, is it?'

Batchley turned to her with a hurt expression.

'I didn't mean that, and you know it. I'm just saying that if the Gov's made a decision not to

242

charge Richards then we should stand by that decision and not go behind his back.'

'I'm not going behind anyone's back,' Satchell said. 'But I have every right to question any decision that's made, and that's all I'm doing. If Richards is our killer, he should be in court on trial with Kathleen Norton.'

'You think Walker's letting him off the hook, then?'

Satchell nodded.

'Too right I do—in a way.'

'What way?' asked West.

Satchell delved into the box and grasped the second head, shrouded in its bubble wrap.

'Graham Richards was into bondage,' he said, feeling for a safe grip on the head. 'And his goddamned belt was round her neck. Oops!'

Satchell had yanked the head out but, underestimating its weight, almost let it slip from his fingers. Batchley called out a warning and grabbed at the head but Satchell had it safe in his arms by now, and was virtually cradling it. He gently patted it on the crown.

'Sorry, sweetheart,' he said to the head and then took up the argument again. 'Walker's not infallible, you know. Nobody is. And I think he's wrong about Graham Richards.'

Collins shook his head.

'We don't know for sure that Richards was ever at the club. Nothing we have places him there except that photograph, and the image was too fuzzy for the lab to match it with Richards's own head. No one we've found who worked at the club could positively identify him.'

'Not even your friend the contortionist,' put in

243

Batchley. 'Just because you've got a tenner on with Walker that Richards is in the frame—'

'No,' corrected Satchell. 'I've got the tenner on *because* I'm sure he's the one who should be standing trial.'

He looked down at the head in his arms, its large blue eyes staring straight upwards.

'I think Richards raped and killed all three girls, buried two of them under the patio which *he* helped to lay, and put a third into the coal chute. Anyone else want to bet?'

CHAPTER 23

MONDAY, 11 DECEMBER, MORNING

The opening of the trial of Kathleen Norton for the triple murder in 1983 of Kerry Willis, Ingrid Kestler and another, unknown, young woman attracted considerable media interest. Reporters, photographers and TV crews were camped at the bottom of the courthouse steps while, kept at a further distance by police, were members of the public, many of whom had been turned away from the oversubscribed queue for the public gallery. The cameras filmed the arrival of the principal witnesses—the pathologist John Foster, Dorothy Norton, Graham Richards with his solicitor and Mrs Day with her husband. Then attention switched to the barristers in the case. Halliday and Camplin were followed closely by Fletcher, accompanied by his junior Harold Burgess, and at this point one of the sharper of the court reporters noticed that Willis Fletcher QC had shaved off his famous beard.

Nor did this escape the newly bearded Rupert Halliday, when he spotted Fletcher inside the courts. Halliday laughed at the sight, though at a deeper level he was slightly miffed.

'Well, well, I see you've had a close encounter with your razor for the first time in living memory. I hardly recognized you, Willis.'

Fletcher massaged his clean-shaven chin.

'Smooth as silk, eh?'

Halliday scratched his own beard and arched his

eyebrows.

'Winfield will probably see this as a conspiracy to confuse one of Her Majesty's judges.'

'Confuse Winfield?' queried Fletcher. 'Perish the thought of that!'

By turning up late, Detective Superintendent Walker and Detective Sergeant Satchell had attracted less attention. They slipped into their seats in the police section of the court as the jury was being sworn in. Then, from the Bench, Mr Justice Geoffrey Winfield began reminding them of their responsibilities.

'Members of the jury, I should tell you at once that you may find some of the necessary details in this case distressing: it is inevitable that, as judges of the facts (for that is what you are), you will have to consider the whens, the hows and the whys of these deaths. You will no doubt find your task the easier if you approach the material placed before you in this courtroom as dispassionately as possible. Try to leave emotion behind when you come into court, so that you can try the case in accordance with the oaths you have just taken. Yes, Mr Fletcher.'

'May it please Your Lordship.'

Fletcher stood, cleared his throat and, as tradition dictates, introduced himself, his junior and the defence barristers, each by name, to the jury.

In his opening address he described the history of the house under the occupancy of the Nortons, and its decline into decrepitude after they left. He succinctly narrated the events at Hallerton Road in the previous September, when the remains of an adult female had been uncovered by demolition

246

workers, to be followed by the three other skeletons found by police. He told how the identities of two of the victims had been discovered and linked to a hospital where Kathleen Norton had been working part-time. Finally he stated that, in the view of the prosecution, Kathleen Norton had approached the pregnant women and offered them illegal terminations, an offer that was nothing but a lure to lead them to their deaths.

'And why did she do it? She did it, as the Crown will demonstrate, because she was bent on a twisted kind of revenge.'

Fletcher paused dramatically, to emphasize that motivation remained the most profound question in any murder case. The answer he gave was not quite as Walker had once inferred. He did not suggest that Kathleen had ever operated as an abortionist for, if she had, there was not a shred of evidence for it.

'Revenge,' he went on, 'for the death of her own baby, bent on punishing these women who had actually asked for terminations, when she herself had suffered a grievous and involuntary abortion. In the violent deaths of these unfortunate young women, she sought a spiteful and murderous redress for her own loss.'

Fletcher then turned to the first of his witnesses.

In a case which had begun with the discovery of three anonymous seventeen-year-old skeletons, it was appropriate that the court should first hear the forensic evidence of pathologist Dr Foster and Dr Malik. This was straightforward enough and gave the defence little leeway in its cross-examination. But the scientific evidence was followed by that of Hannah Day, whom Halliday considered was the first weak link in the prosecution case. Fletcher had kept his questions to her simple, and her answers were assured. She told of the approach by Nurse Norton and how Hannah had backed off when the nurse's inconsistent manner unnerved her. But, when Halliday rose and fixed her with his most sceptical stare, Hannah began to feel flustered and uncomfortable. Up in the gallery, Steven was sitting. She glanced at him and he flashed her his secret, just-between-us smile that she loved so much. She needed the courage because Halliday's questions were as severe as they were unexpected.

'Mrs Day,' he boomed. 'You told us earlier that you went through with the birth of your own child. Did that take place at St Jude's hospital?'

'Yes, that's right.'

'What about the obstetrician? What was he like?'

Hannah frowned.

'I'm sorry?'

'Was it a he, or a she?'

'It was a man.'

'Tall? Short? Thin? Fat? I know it's difficult after all these years, but do your best for us.'

Hannah was nonplussed. She couldn't remember. Halliday pressed on.

'What about the midwife who attended you? What did she look like?'

Hannah shrugged helplessly.

'I really can't remember.'

Walker and Satchell exchanged anxious looks. Their witness was not holding up too well. Walker glanced at Kathleen, sitting listlessly in the dock. He noticed for the first time that she was wearing lipstick, which he'd never known her do before. It

248

gave her an oddly theatrical appearance.

'Do you think it's unreasonable for me to expect you to remember these people after all this time?' asked Halliday.

'Well,' said Hannah. 'It's the better part of twenty years ago.'

Halliday reached for an enlarged photographic print from among his papers. He held it up for Hannah to see.

'All right. If I were to show you a group photo taken of the hospital staff that summer, would you be able to pick them out, do you think?'

'Well, I'd have a pretty good guess, yes.'

'That's very fair of you, Mrs Day.'

Again he paused, as if about to conclude. But he didn't conclude.

'And that's really what you were doing, when that policeman showed you the photos of all those nurses, wasn't it? Just guessing?'

*   *   *

Edward Colly, too, was given an easy, coaxing ride by Fletcher. But, again, it was a different matter when Halliday rose. He continued with the general theme of memory, and in particular with the mnemonic powers of the witness.

'So you have an impressive memory and we can rely on it, can we, Mr Colly? And on you?'

'Of course you can,' said Colly.

'Well now, let me ask you about some events, memorable events, a little closer to the present. Do you remember where you were on 6 December 1990?'

Colly looked confused.

'No.'

'Or 16 May 1991?'

'No, I don't. What's this all about?'

'Well, let me remind you, if you don't recall.'

Halliday selected another piece of paper and ostentatiously referred to it before delivering his *coup de théâtre*.

'You were at the South London Magistrates Court on those dates. Does that ring a bell?'

Colly's visage darkened and he swung towards the judge.

'Is he allowed to do this? It's got nothing to do with this.'

Winfield was writing on his notepad. He stopped and looked down at Colly across the top of his spectacles.

'Answer his questions, Mr Colly, and if he asks you anything he shouldn't, you can leave that to me. Yes, Mr Halliday?'

Colly turned reluctantly back to Halliday, who did not repeat the question but waited patiently for the witness to reply.

'That was all a misunderstanding about some property,' Colly managed at last.

Halliday smiled patronizingly.

'Well, *two* misunderstandings, to be strictly accurate. On those occasions you pleaded guilty to theft, did you not? The theft of patients' property from hospitals at which you were working?'

Colly gripped the edge of the witness stand.

'If you've got all the sodding answers, why are you asking me?'

He checked and took a deep breath. Then he bobbed his head towards the bench, from where Winfield was glaring at him.

'Sorry, My Lord.'

Winfield accepted the apology with a frosty and momentary smile.

'Just help me with this, then,' continued Halliday. 'What was the property? What did it consist of?'

'I haven't got a clue,' Colly said after a moment's thought.

'No,' said Halliday, 'I don't suppose you have. Any more than you have a clue as to what happened on the night you were telling us about seventeen years ago.'

Triumphantly his eyes swept the jury box before settling on Winfield, who laid down his pen and looked with pained disapproval at Fletcher, and then more kindly at Halliday.

'Mr Halliday, it may help you to know this . . .'

He turned to the jury.

'I direct you to wholly disregard this witness's testimony. For my part, I cannot see why he was called in the first place.'

Halliday bowed his appreciation and returned to his seat, giving way once again to Fletcher.

'My Lord, I call Graham Richards.'

The dark, saturnine good looks of the new witness impressed the gallery, whose members craned forward to see him enter the court. A soft murmur rippled round the room, which Winfield quelled with a glare from the Bench. Richards swore the oath and Fletcher began.

'Is your name Graham Richards?'

'Yes, it is.'

Walker turned his head again to look at Kathleen. She was playing with her hair, her face immobile except for a tightening of the mouth. But her heaving shoulders told him she was breathing

251

deeply.

Richards's evidence for the prosecution was given in a clear enough manner, though the witness's underlying nervousness was already apparent and, by the time defence counsel rose to cross-examine, a sheen of sweat was forming on his upper lip. Halliday began by handing Richards the photograph of Ingrid Kestler and Greta Bertrum, topless in the Rhinestone Club. He informed the judge and jury of the number of the photograph in their albums of photographic evidence. There was a pause as they all found the relevant page, and Halliday cleared his throat.

'Do you recognize any of the girls in the photograph, Mr Richards?'

'No, I don't.'

'You see, the one on the left—with her pink bikini bottom still on—is Ingrid Kestler. You're sure you have never seen her before?'

'I've just told you. No.'

Richards began to put the photograph down but Halliday stopped him.

'We've not quite finished with the photograph, Mr Richards . . . Have a look at the man sitting at the first table there. That's not you, by any chance, is it?'

Richards shook his head.

'No, it doesn't even look like me. I've been through this.'

'The police thought it was you in the photo, did they not?'

'Mr Halliday,' said the judge sternly, 'this witness cannot answer for what the police may or may not have thought.'

Halliday bowed.

'My Lord, of course.'

He turned back to Richards.

'You were shown this photo by the police some months ago, during the inquiry, weren't you?'

'Yes I was, but that doesn't mean . . .'

Suddenly the witness looked as if he feared a trap and was trying to bluster his way out of it.

'I mean, all this . . . it doesn't make sense. You'll be suggesting that I killed the girl next.'

Halliday smiled seraphically.

'Not without My Lord first giving you a warning, I won't.'

He sat expectantly and Winfield obliged.

'Yes, Mr Richards,' he said firmly. 'I must tell you that if, whilst you are in the witness box, you are asked if you have committed a criminal offence, you do have the right not to answer that question if you do not wish to do so. Just indicate to me if you don't wish to answer. Of course, if you *want* to answer, you are at liberty to do so, but you are not obliged to. Do you understand?'

Richards bobbed his head in acknowledgement.

'I understand.'

At which, Halliday bounced back to his feet.

'Thank you, My Lord. Well, did you?'

'Did I what?'

'Did you meet Ingrid Kestler at some strip club, and on a later occasion, for whatever reason you may have had, wrap your belt around her neck and throttle her until she was dead and then bury her under the patio you were building at number 34 Hallerton Road?'

'No, I did not.'

There was another fleeting buzz of conversation around the court.

'Thank you, Mr Richards. Just put the photograph to one side, please. Now, you helped to build the patio, did you not?'

'Yes, with Philip.'

'With Philip. That's Philip Norton? What happened? Did one of you do the digging whilst the other laid the paving? Who did what?'

'We both worked on it, but I did the bulk of the heavy work.'

'Laying a patio is nearly all heavy work, I should imagine. There must have been quite a bit of digging to do, I imagine.'

'Well, yes, to get it level.'

'And you both got stuck in, did you?'

'Yes, I suppose so.'

'Do you see yourself as being quite handy with a spade?'

'Sorry. I don't understand.'

'Experienced. Are you experienced with a spade?'

'Well, yes. I mean I've been around enough building sites in my time.'

'So then you can help us with this, perhaps. How long might it take a man to dig a hole, say, two metres long, half a metre wide and a metre deep?'

'Well, it depends what you're digging.'

'London clay, Mr Richards, London clay.'

'Well, it would be difficult. Clay's hard work.'

'And two holes, I take it, would take twice as long?'

Richards was still at sea.

'I don't follow.'

'You didn't dig two such holes yourself, did you?'

'No, no . . . No, I didn't.'

'Well, do you remember seeing anyone else

254

doing that sort of digging?'

Richards's mouth tightened.

'No!'

'Philip Norton, perhaps? Though by all accounts he wasn't in the best of health with his heart, was he?'

Richards relaxed slightly.

'No, that's right, he wasn't.'

'Kathleen Norton, then? Hardly a woman's job. Have you ever seen her with a spade?'

Walker was having trouble understanding why this felt so bad. But, put the way Halliday was putting it, the case against Graham Richards was far more compelling than he had appreciated.

'No, I haven't,' the witness replied, sounding faintly disorientated again.

'So, if two such holes were dug in the back garden of number 34, they were dug without your knowledge?'

'Of course.'

'And you don't recall seeing two areas of recently disturbed ground? At around the time your *belt* went missing?'

'No.'

'And so you can't help us as to how two young girls were both murdered, one with your belt wrapped around her neck . . .'

Halliday demonstrated by placing his hands around his own neck and squeezing.

'And how both then turned up underneath the paving stones that you put in place?'

'No. No, I can't.'

Halliday took a sip of water before resuming.

'I take it you didn't do any DIY in the area of the coal chute in the cellar? Because a body of a

255

young girl was found in there too.'

Suddenly Richards's face creased in anger. He knew quite well that Halliday was deliberately goading him, but he could not help himself.

'How many times do I have to TELL you? I know nothing about any of this.'

Halliday aired his disbelief with an expressive sigh.

'Let me ask you about something else, then. Were you Kathleen Norton's lover?'

'No, I wasn't.'

'But you did have sex with her once, didn't you?'

'Yes, well, I think I must have done but, as I told the police, I don't remember much about it.'

'You'd describe it as something of a one-night stand, would you?'

'I wouldn't describe it as anything. I remember nothing about it.'

'You had sex with her without her consent, did you not?'

Richards looked in panic towards Winfield, who leaned forward in reassurance.

'Once again, Mr Richards, you do not need to answer that question if you do not wish to do so.'

Richards smiled his thanks and ran his tongue over his dry lips. Halliday took a pace towards him.

'Well? Did you *rape* Kathleen Norton?'

In a fit of fury, Richards slapped the witness stand with the flat of his hand.

'NO! NO, I DID NOT! I wasn't even attracted to her. I ended up having to lock my bedroom door at night to keep her out.'

Halliday's smile purported understanding.

'Well, we are at least agreed on this, Mr Richards: you slept with Kathleen at least once, because you fathered her child?'

Richards was ashamed of his previous outburst. He dropped his head.

'That's what the tests showed,' he mumbled. 'So I guess I must have done, but like I said, I don't remember much about that night. I was very drunk.'

In the public gallery, the colour had drained from a thunderstruck Mrs Norton's face. She sat, muttering silently to herself, shaking her head.

'Yes,' agreed Halliday enthusiastically. 'The DNA tests conducted earlier this year showed that you were undoubtedly the father of the baby found under the floorboards at 34 Hallerton Road . . .'

With a small, just audible cry, Dorothy stood up and began shuffling and pushing past the knees of those sitting in her row.

'I take it you knew nothing about that as well— or did you?' asked Halliday.

'No, no, of course I didn't. What do you think I am?'

'That's not for *me* to say,' Halliday said archly. He bowed briefly. 'Thank you, Mr Richards. That is all.'

As Halliday sat, the courtroom doors could be heard squeaking as they closed behind the accused's mother. Winfield raised his voice before Fletcher had a chance to call his next witness.

'We'll take a twenty-minute break and sit again at twelve fifteen.'

The judge rose, bowed to the court and headed for his chambers.

*   *   *

257

Walker and Satchell joined members of the public spilling out of the court and into the wide, vaulted corridor. Some headed for the toilets, others for the fresh air and a smoke. Walker would have liked a smoke but he had noticed Dorothy Norton's hurried exit from the courtroom and when he saw her amidst the throng, apparently looking anxiously for someone, he went up to her. She looked deeply relieved when she saw him.

'Mr Walker!' she exclaimed. 'Thank goodness you're still here. I wonder if we could have a word.'

He found a vacant wooden bench opposite the courtroom and sat her down.

'You look troubled, Mrs Norton. Is there anything I can do?'

In a few words she summarized what Kathleen had told her about the pregnancy, and the baby's father.

'And God help me, Mr Walker, I thought it might be true. Or at any rate that people would believe it was true, with all this talk of paedophiles and abuse and what-not in the papers all the time. But now—well—it can't be true, can it? She's a wicked girl, a *wicked* girl. Oh, how I would like to *do* something—'

'Oh, but you can, Mrs Norton,' said Walker in the most reassuring voice he was capable of. 'You *can* do something.'

Fletcher, when he heard the news, took the necessary steps. The judge had to be informed and also the defence counsel. Halliday did not take the information well. He cursed and almost threw his wig to the floor.

'I'd better go and see Kathleen,' he said to Camplin. It was a task for which he had little relish.

258

For the duration of the recess, Kathleen had been taken down to the holding cells below the court. She was sitting calmly, content to do nothing but stare at the wall. But as Halliday walked in, she turned her head.

'Why haven't we gone back in? The judge said twenty minutes.'

'Well,' said Halliday, 'there has been a rather unfortunate development. It's with regard to your mother.'

Kathleen caught her breath.

'She's not had a stroke, has she?'

'No, no. She is making a statement to the police and it looks as if they're going to want to call her as a prosecution witness, so—'

'She's senile, you can't believe a word she says! If you want the truth of it my mother has always hated me.'

'Kathleen if you could just listen—'

'Whatever she says will be lies. If you're here because you think you can make me change my plea, then you've got another think coming. You are supposed to be defending me! I am not guilty and you won't make me say I am!'

Halliday held up his hand.

'I have no intention of telling you to change your plea and I will defend you in the very best way I can, Miss Norton. That is my job. I am looking out for you and you have my assurance of that.'

'Well, you'd better do your job, Mr Halliday, because nobody else is looking out for me. Even when I was a little girl, no one cared what

259

happened to me, not even my father.'

She returned her gaze to the wall.

'He bought me one of those Russian dolls once, said it reminded him of me. Do you want to know why? They don't talk, they don't cry, they don't do *anything*. I unscrewed the top and there was another identical round wooden doll inside, and another, and another, all with the same painted, expressionless faces. All they did was get smaller and smaller until the last one was the size of my thumb.'

'Kathleen!' Halliday spoke kindly. 'I have every intention of defending you to the best of my ability, whatever your mother has to say about you.'

'She never wanted to know who I was. You know, Mr Halliday, there aren't only seven sins.'

She hesitated, thinking it through.

'Yes?' prompted Halliday.

'Yes. The eighth sin is the mother who does not love her daughter because she is not in her image. If you unscrew my head, there is the same painful Kathleen inside, and another one the same inside that. It's layer upon layer of pain. Please don't let her hurt me any more. Please!'

Halliday would admit to being touched, even a little shaken. It cannot be said that, until now, the case had struck him as anything other than an intellectual exercise, a challenge to see if he could best Willis Fletcher. But suddenly he saw Kathleen as a vulnerable human being, who needed help. Fat, graceless, perhaps cunning . . . but a human being, like himself. He reached out his hand and gently touched her on the shoulder.

'I'll see you in there,' he said, almost in a whisper.

CHAPTER 24

MONDAY, 11 DECEMBER, AFTERNOON

At a few minutes after two o'clock, Dorothy Norton stood glacially in the witness box, the pallor of her face accentuated by her black dress. She clasped her hands tightly together and stared straight ahead. She would not look in the direction of the dock and Kathleen.

It had been necessary to inform the judge of Mrs Norton's unexpected decision to give evidence for the prosecution. She did not appear in the list of prosecution witnesses, disclosed several weeks ago to the defence. But when Winfield discussed the development in his chambers with Halliday, he said that he saw no reason why it should unfairly prejudice Halliday's case. He would, after all, have the chance to cross-examine her and Winfield had promised to give him time to prepare.

'Two o'clock all right?' he said.

Halliday had agreed.

'Mrs Norton,' Fletcher now began, 'you lived, I think, at number 34 Hallerton Road, Kilburn, from May 1976 to September 1984?'

'Yes.'

'Towards the end of 1982, your daughter, Kathleen, fell pregnant. Were you aware of this?'

'Yes.'

'How did you learn of the pregnancy?'

Dorothy's face tightened.

'Well, at first I thought she was just putting on weight but by the end, I knew.'

261

'By the end?'

'Well, just before it was born.'

Kathleen, from the dock, was staring fixedly at her mother, playing all the time with the gold crucifix on its chain around her neck. Fletcher turned a page of his notes.

'The baby was born prematurely, wasn't it?'

'It was stillborn,' Dorothy corrected him.

'Did Kathleen tell you that?'

'She didn't have to. I was there.'

Whispers fluttered through the court. They quickly subsided, in anticipation of the witness's next revelation. In the brief silence that followed, the insistent chink of Kathleen's crucifix could be heard.

Fletcher showed no surprise at the news that Mrs Norton had been complicit in the stillbirth of her grandchild.

'What did Kathleen do with her stillborn baby?' he asked.

Dorothy sighed, not wearily but with remembered impatience.

'I said we should give it a Christian burial but she refused to let me help, said she'd take care of it.'

'Take *care* of it?'

'She told me she'd bury the baby.'

'And where would that be?'

'She didn't say and I didn't ask.'

Kathleen was shaking her head now. She let go of the neck chain and, leaning forward, massaged her face with her fingers and the flat palms of her hands.

'So you personally never knew where the baby was buried?' Fletcher was asking.

262

'Well, a few weeks later I heard a noise down in the cellar, late one night, and when I went down to investigate, I saw Kathleen pushing some kind of putty around the door of the coal chute. I asked her what she was doing and she said that she was burying her baby.'

A new flurry of talk swept through the court. Winfield paused in his note-taking.

'Burying her baby in a coal chute?' he queried.

He looked over his notes, to check that he had written correctly, then at the witness again.

'It doesn't sound like a very Christian ceremony to me.'

Dorothy's face showed no reaction.

'I tried to talk her round, get her to bury it properly, but she wouldn't listen,' she explained.

Winfield picked up his pen and indicated that Fletcher could continue.

'And you say this was a few weeks after she gave birth?' asked the barrister.

'Yes.'

'Did she tell you where the body of the baby had been until this time?'

'No she didn't. I didn't want to think about it.'

'Did you believe her when she said she was hiding the baby in the coal chute?'

'Yes.'

Fletcher refreshed his memory from his sheaf of papers.

'The access door to the chute was plastered over and covered with plasterboard or similar cladding. Who carried out this work?'

'My husband did.'

'Did he know about the baby?'

Dorothy shook her head.

263

'I told him we wanted it for security, that I was worried people could get in from the street.'

'So he didn't know about the baby being buried?'

'No.'

Fletcher smiled and bowed.

'Thank you, Mrs Norton. Would you wait there, please?'

As he rose to take the floor in Fletcher's place, Halliday glanced at his client. In the dock, Kathleen seemed restless, as if simmering with suppressed feelings. But she noticed Halliday's look and answered with a nervous smile. He turned to Dorothy.

'You have testified that you were present at the birth of your daughter's baby. So why didn't you call an ambulance?'

Dorothy shut her eyes, as if visualizing the scene seventeen years ago.

'I wanted to,' she said. 'But she wouldn't let me. She said she was a nurse and she knew what she was doing.'

'I see. Now . . . you told the police in your original statement that you knew nothing of your daughter's pregnancy, didn't you?'

'Yes.'

Dorothy's answer was a whisper, little more than a breath. Her eyes were still shut.

'I'm sorry, Mrs Norton,' called the judge, 'could you please speak up.'

Dorothy opened her eyes and said more clearly, 'Yes.'

'That was a lie, wasn't it?'

The witness was silent.

'You *did* lie, didn't you? Why?'

Dorothy's lower lip quivered.

264

'Because . . . because, I was too ashamed. You see, Kathleen had told me that my husband was the father of her baby.'

The court broke out into whispers again, but they were quelled when Kathleen suddenly leapt to her feet in the dock and pointed dramatically at her mother.

'And *you* believed me!' she shouted, then swung round towards Halliday.

'Ask her *why* she believed me. Ask her!'

'Miss Norton!' growled Winfield. 'If you interrupt these proceedings again, I'll have to have you removed from court. Please remain silent.'

The security guard sitting with Kathleen touched her arm and she allowed herself to be drawn back into the seat, muttering under her breath. Halliday imperturbably returned to the subject of the coal chute. During Mrs Norton's evidence in chief he had spotted a hairline discrepancy and saw a chance to widen it.

'You told my learned friend that you asked your husband to close up access to the chute on the inside because you were worried about security. But the other end of the chute, leading out onto the street, had been securely bricked over since before you moved in, hadn't it?'

'Yes.'

'So would you enlighten me, Mrs Norton? How could you persuade your husband that sealing it off on the *inside* would add significantly to your household's security?'

Dorothy's brain searched for a convincing answer. She knew she had been led towards a trap but she could see no way of avoiding it. Halliday sensed her unease and followed up.

'Protection against burglary was not, in fact, the reason why Mr Norton so carefully closed off access to the coal chute from inside the cellar, now was it? *Was* it, Mrs Norton?'

Dorothy Norton's mouth puckered and tears welled up in her eyes. She stammered.

'Well, you see, I . . . I had to tell him. I told him . . . I told him that I knew, about him and Kathleen and that he was the father of her baby and . . .'

The old woman's face crumpled completely now and she hid it in her hands. The court was hushed, waiting. Suddenly Dorothy dropped her hands and turned, face powder streaked with tears, to face her daughter for the first time.

'You killed him!' she screamed. 'His heart couldn't take the strain. YOU did it! YOUR LIES KILLED HIM! The baby wasn't his at all. It was all lies. But the accusation was too much for him. It was YOUR fault, you wicked, sinful girl.'

In the middle of Dorothy's tirade, Winfield took action, striking his gavel and speaking above the hubbub to the jury.

'Members of the jury, would you be so kind as to go to your room?'

Obediently and as one, the jury rose and began to file out. Winfield went on.

'Mrs Norton, I'm going to rise for a few minutes to allow you to compose yourself before we resume with the jury.'

But by this time the defendant, meeting her mother's ferocious accusing gaze with another just like it, had lunged forward until she was almost hanging over the edge of the dock.

'He *deserved* it after what he did to me!' she shouted. 'You knew what was going on, but you just ignored it. You carried on praying like a good Christian. You bloody hypocrite! You whited sepulchre!'

Winfield rapped with his gavel two, three times.

'Miss Norton, please sit DOWN. I will not tolerate this.'

But Kathleen had only just begun. She swung around and shouted at the jury as they shuffled away, reluctantly now that so much excitement was in the air.

'I'll tell you something,' she shouted. 'You want to know? Those women deserved to die. I was doing God's work.'

She heard the judge's voice vainly calling for her to cease. She turned to him with the full force of her scorn.

'I don't care what you do to me, I DON'T CARE! They deserved to die.'

Winfield looked to her security detail in momentary panic.

'Take her downstairs. I shall rise. I shall rise!'

He stood and bowed hastily, preparing to withdraw. But Kathleen, gripping the bar that circled the edge of the dock, had not finished with him.

'They didn't deserve any pity,' she screamed at him. 'They were all whores, whores.'

The security guards tried to prise her hands from the bar but Kathleen's grip was strong.

'It was God's will that I took their lives. It was punishment!'

She kicked at the guards as they grappled to loose her fingers from the rail.

'Get away from me. Stay away from me!'

By now the judge had scuttled from the Bench

and disappeared from view. Most of the public gallery was standing to get a better view of the uproar. They saw Kathleen being handcuffed and dragged from the dock. Despite the restraints, she was putting up a thrashing resistance, while never for a moment ceasing to rant.

'I loved my baby but they wanted to destroy theirs! I had to do what I did. They had sinned and God wanted me to punish them. God took my daughter to show me the way.'

Then she was sobbing with great heavings of her shoulders and juddering breaths. Her fight had ended as abruptly as it had begun.

'He took her!' she snuffled, her nose running with liquid snot. 'My baby, my baby, MY BABY! He took her! He took her!'

She was led from court.

*　　　*　　　*

On the courthouse steps, Walker lit a cigarette, inhaling deeply. He had a fancy that God, or Fate, or whatever it was, had been with him. Things had been looking bad, with Halliday pulling one stroke after another, lampooning and discrediting his witnesses, while Kathleen's facade of innocence had seemed impossible to crack. But putting Dorothy in the stand had done the necessary. Kathleen had been broached and now she was done.

He felt a slight pressure on his shoulder from behind. Twisting round, he saw Satchell's fingers holding, between them, a folded orange-brown banknote. He took it and unfolded the note to reveal the tousled figure of Charles Dickens printed on it.

'Thanks, Satch,' he said. He trousered the money and drew deeply on his cigarette. It was, all in all, a moment to savour.

CHAPTER 25

MONDAY, 11 DECEMBER, NIGHT

North was busy firming up arrangements for her seminar but she, too, had been caught up in the events of the trial. As she followed the news throughout the day, she felt envious of Walker and remembered the last time she herself had brought a murder case to trial, with all the tension, the will-they-won't-they speculation about the jury, the last-minute shocks and changes of strategy. But about mid-afternoon, in her office at the Yard, came the promise that her wishes would soon be realized. The phone rang. It was the Assistant Commissioner.

'Pat, there's a feeling we need you back on investigatory work. I hope you don't think that would be a backward step.'

'No, no, sir, it wouldn't be taking a step back, far from it. To be honest, I'm fed up with paper-pushing. I want back in on the action.'

'Well, as you know, the whole idea of the fast-track scheme was to locate the type of policework best suited to your undoubted talents. And we think Serious Crimes Group, don't you? Pity to waste all that effort you put into studying crime-scene management.'

Her heart thudded. It was just what she wanted to hear.

'Exactly,' she said. 'It makes sense for me to be the one who puts the theory into practice.'

The AC was a man she liked and respected, a

270

man who appreciated straight talking. She talked straight.

'I don't want to play second fiddle, though, sir. I want to head up murder cases.'

'Yes, I'd say leadership was your thing. We're implementing a few new initiatives and we'd like you to be involved. Shall we get together in a day or two and talk about the details?'

'That would be great,' she said. 'If you let me know when and where I'll make sure I'm free. Thank you, sir. Oh and sir . . . when the time comes, I'd like to pick my own team.'

'Goes without saying,' said the AC.

Later, back in the flat, she had dragged suitcases out from under the bed and started going through her wardrobe and drawers. It was time to de-clutter. She filled two suitcases with clobber for Oxfam, dragged them down the stairs, and was beginning on a third, when she heard Walker slamming in. Seconds later he had sprinted up the stairs, his face aghast.

'Pat! PAT!'

'What?' she said from a kneeling position in front of the open suitcase. 'What is it?'

'The suitcases,' said Walker. 'What are you doing with the suitcases?'

'Well, we're very short of space. I'm getting rid of clothes that I don't need. Are you all right?'

Walker stood for a moment, his mouth open, then collapsed onto the bed. He spread his arms wide.

'You just put the fear of God into me! I thought you were *leaving* me.'

North stood up and planted her hands on her hips.

'Me, leave? Who found this place? Who decorated it? Who chose the carpets? Who fixed the toilet flush? If anyone's departing it'll be you.'

Walker leaned up on his elbow.

'I'm not going anywhere.'

She clicked her fingers.

'Damn! I was going to rent out the spare bedroom to Vivien.'

They laughed and she flopped down beside him.

'Ahhh, you really thought I was leaving? You big softy!'

'No, no, of course not. Look, I've got something for you.'

He was fumbling in his pockets.

'What happened in court?' she asked. 'Did they break early?

Walker grinned happily.

'No, it's all over. Kathleen flipped in court. Last thing I heard she was tearing the holding cell apart. But listen, that's not what I wanted to talk about.'

'Did she kill those women, then?'

Walker nodded, his finger closing on a small box in his trouser pocket.

'Yes. Said she did.'

'Why?'

'She was psychotic. Went nuts after losing her baby. Her mother testified against her, I think that's what pushed her over the edge.'

North shook her head, appalled.

'God. Do you think if her baby had been born . . . I mean, if it had been OK she wouldn't have—'

But Walker put a finger to his lips.

'I don't want to talk about Kathleen Norton. I don't want that horror invading my home.'

He pulled the box out and showed it to her, the

272

gesture of a magician about to perform an illusion.

'Just sit down for a minute. Sit down, come on.'

'What are you up to?'

But she sat on the edge of the bed and Walker went down on his haunches before her.

'Here, this is for you.'

He opened the box to reveal a small, jewelled ring.

'Rose diamonds and two rubies,' he said proudly. 'I designed it myself. Give me your hand. The other one, your engagement finger. You see I love you, I want to marry you. You're the most beautiful and intelligent woman I know.'

She had put out her hand, ring finger extended, and he tried to thread the ring onto it. But it stuck at the knuckle.

'Why won't it go on?' he said, pushing at the ring. 'I made sure . . . I took that ring with the little pearls to get the right size.'

'The one my grandmother left me? From my jewellery box?'

'Exactly. They must have cocked it up at the jeweller's.'

'Oh Mike,' she said, trying not to laugh. 'I don't wear the seed pearl ring. It's too small.'

Walker pushed and pushed again but made no headway past North's knuckle.

'It's not going to.' She laughed. 'But it's a really beautiful ring, and the care you've taken getting it made specially. Well, it's very . . . very touching.'

'What are you laughing about?' he demanded. 'This is a deeply tragic situation.'

He dropped the ring back into its box and held her and they laughed together in a way they had not done for many months.

DAYS LATER

It was a dark, overcast day, towards evening. The dilapidated house loomed above the figure of a woman who appeared like a ghost in front of the door. Dorothy Norton, dressed in her usual black, paused in the shadow and then pushed at the door, which swung open. She stepped hesitantly into what remained of the home she had once known so well.

As she wandered from one gutted room to the next she heard whispers coming out of the gloom.

Mummy, Mummy!

It was God's will that I took their lives. It was punishment!

Don't let them take me! Mummy!

She shivered and crossed herself. Holding onto the wall as best she could, she mounted the ruined staircase, reaching the first landing. Dorothy had to pick her way across the floor, many of whose boards had been ripped up, revealing the laths of the ceiling below.

The room she entered had once been her daughter's. There, towards the far wall, was a particularly jagged hole in the floor. Dorothy forced herself to approach it, to look into it. There was nothing to suggest that for seventeen years this had been a baby's grave, but that did nothing to alleviate the sense of its horror, and her feeling of pity mixed with shame. Into her mind came the words of the judge.

Kathleen Norton, I order you to be detained without limit of time at a secure mental institution . . .

It was God's will, said the whispers gathering

274

around her ears, crowding out the memory of Winfield's sentence. *They were all whores, whores. It was punishment. Mummy! Mummy!*

Dorothy shivered, crossed herself again, and began to pray.